**BARBARA P**

"Able is compro

"They're going deep black to Charlie Mike but we need to get them a new and arrange resup

"When it rains, it p

"What?"

"I got a message from James on the ground in Brazzaville, text-based."

"Why text?"

"He couldn't get a signal out, so he put a communication in the system for the repeater relay. It's twelve minutes old. They were compromised on initial insertion. They think their Congolese police counterpart might have set them up."

Akira Tokaido leaned back in his chair and whistled. "Phoenix under fire, Able on the run—this mission is blown right out of the gate."

DON PENDLETON'S

# STONY

AMERICA'S ULTRA-COVERT INTELLIGENCE AGENCY

# MAN®

# UNCONVENTIONAL
# WARFARE

A GOLD EAGLE BOOK FROM

# W⊕RLDWIDE®

TORONTO • NEW YORK • LONDON
AMSTERDAM • PARIS • SYDNEY • HAMBURG
STOCKHOLM • ATHENS • TOKYO • MILAN
MADRID • WARSAW • BUDAPEST • AUCKLAND

Recycling programs
for this product may
not exist in your area.

First edition August 2011

ISBN-13: 978-0-373-61998-6

UNCONVENTIONAL WARFARE

Special thanks and acknowledgment to
Nathan Meyer for his contribution to this work.

# UNCONVENTIONAL WARFARE

# CHAPTER ONE

*Beijing, People's Republic of China*

The Beijing Inn was a traditional structure nestled just beyond the more Westernized buildings of the international financial district. The architecture of the inn recalled China's glorious past. Consisting of two stories under a peaked tile roof, the inn was divided into rooms of various sizes using internal support posts.

In a small room tucked away from the densely populated restaurant area sat Chao Bao, official of the clandestine Central Control of Information Division of the vast Ministry of State Security.

Bao sipped his tea, face inscrutable and emanating an air of timeless patience. While perhaps cliché to Caucasian sensibilities, his inner calm was authentic. At first glance he presented an unassuming figure. He looked younger than his forty-seven years, stood six inches over five feet and was built in a slight manner. His eyes were dark and unreflective, his hair thinning on top.

He could have been a tailor or perhaps an accountant.

On closer inspection a discerning eye would have noticed his build was not slight, but efficiently lean, supple as a leather whip. His knuckles were misshapen to chunks the size of dice by decades of martial-arts training.

He'd earned a reputation as a brutal interrogator of prisoners and as a virtual ghost on special-operations reconnaissance missions deep in enemy-controlled territory.

He was a practiced killer and as such, he was able to recognize that quality in others of his ilk. Even if he hadn't already been intimately familiar with the personnel file of the man who now joined him in the quiet, shadowed alcove, he would have recognized a kindred spirit.

"*Sifu,*" Xi-Nan acknowledged.

"Valued friend." Bao nodded. He gestured toward the empty padded bench across the low table from him in the private booth.

Despite being dressed in civilian clothes rather than a military uniform, General Xi-Nan was obviously a soldier. Tall for an ethnic Chinese at six feet, the commander of the Fifth Army was a fit man with a rigid posture ten years Chao Bao's junior.

"Forgive my lagging manners," Xi-Nan said. "But let us come to the point."

His apology was perfunctory. He wasn't sorry to drive straight to business without the culturally required period of idle talk. It was, in fact, the way he preferred to execute all his dealings, especially those involving the placid-faced man sitting across from him who seemed content sipping green tea from eggshell-porcelain cups.

Bao absolved him. "I understand your urgency. Please continue."

"There is a complication with our African venture."

"Somalia?"

"No, Congo," Xi-Nan attested.

Bao lifted a single eyebrow and sipped his tea.

"Americans," Xi-Nan further explained. "CIA or their NSA perhaps. They have compromised the periphery of our operation."

"Then they must be stopped from gaining further insight."

"Just so," Xi-Nan agreed. "However I am afraid to use the *Hayabusa* on this. It would leave a paper trail."

*Hayabusa* was the Mandarin word for "Falcon" and was used as the unofficial designation for the Chengdu Military Region Special Forces Unit.

Established in 1992, the unit specialized in target location and interdiction, airborne insertion, sabotage and rapid offensive strikes.

"A paper trail that could lead back to our personal Hong Kong bank accounts," Bao finished the general's thoughts.

"Exactly," Xi-Nan agreed.

"You have a dossier for me?"

The corrupt general immediately slid a flash drive across the smooth teak table to the spymaster, who promptly pocketed the item.

"That is everything we know about the operations the Americans are calling the Niger Station," he said.

Chao Bao smiled as he set down his empty teacup. The smile did not reach his eyes.

"Leave everything to me, old friend," he said.

TWENTY MINUTES LATER Chao Bao arrived on the Beijing waterfront.

He lost himself among the twisting alleys and chaotic heavily populated fish markets until he found a dilapidated warehouse on an unassuming wharf. The building was nondescript and appeared abandoned with piles of rotting fishing nets and soggy old shipping pallets set on the oil-stained concrete loading dock.

Spray painted on the doors were the worn and peeling ideograms representing the Water Dragon Triad.

Bao entered the building and immediately three men armed with Type 64 Chinese submachine guns emerged from shadows. The street soldiers were flat-faced with black eyes that glittered with sinister light.

He countered their advance with a few simple words of identification and was allowed to pass unmolested into the inner sanctum of the triad gangster known only as Illustrious.

Bao stepped across the threshold and the door to the room was slammed shut behind him. The room was ornately furnished and uncomfortably warm, darkened to the point of gloominess.

Three brass braziers smoldered, providing a red-tinged light that served more to throw shadows than to illuminate. On a couch of red silk cushions, his face obscured by a demonic mask of black plaster, reclined Illustrious.

To his left, immobile as a statue, stood a massive bodyguard. Bao had once witnessed the giant execute a disobedient underling with a single well-placed punch to the back of the neck.

Bao stopped, brought his feet together and gave a respectful bow.

"Thank you for granting me an audience," the intelligence officer said.

"How may Illustrious be of service?" the masked figure replied.

The mask was more than a petty affect designed to create an aura of mystery. The Communist Party ran the People's Republic as a totalitarian police state and did not suffer organized crime lightly. There were many in Chao Bao's own agency who would gladly see such a powerful underworld figure dead.

"It seems we have a situation," Bao explained, "in Africa."

"Yes?"

"I'm going to require the use of your Armenian connection."

*Ciudad Juárez, Mexico*

THE JUÁREZ CARTEL had turned the city into a free fire war zone.

In the year leading up to August of 2009 the border city had the highest murder rate in the world. Chaos was rampant in the streets, and the police department was utterly ineffective, or completely corrupted, in the face of drug money and paramilitary criminal violence.

Bodies littered the streets. People were executed, abducted and assaulted on an hourly basis. Sexual predators and serial killers so afflicted the city's female population that Amnesty International had become involved with international relief efforts to save the women.

Federal police and Mexican army troops deployed in huge numbers to the area in an attempt to restore order. The drug cartels responded by fighting an insurgency campaign with weapons every bit as powerful as those wielded by the military.

The U.S. sent money and resources to help combat the problem, but the warfare spilled across the border, causing a dramatic increase in kidnappings and gang violence in El Paso and as far west as Arizona.

The drugs still flowed north. In return, money flowed south. Many analysts claimed American firearms flowed south, as well. While this might have been true to a degree, the cartels combated each other, as well as the police and Mexican army, with military-grade hardware unobtainable by the citizens of the United States.

The wealth to be accrued was so great that corruption

was systemic. It filtered its way up from street cops to judges to army generals and national politicians.

Like a disease passing so quickly it was pandemic, the stain of drug money spread into the heart of the Mexican government's establishment.

This included the officers and agents of the Centro de Investigación y Seguridad Nacional, or National Security and Investigation Center, CISEN.

Forty-eight hours earlier a high-placed official in CISEN sold out the location of an undercover team of agents from the American Drug Enforcement Administration to members of the hyperviolent and brutally sadistic Juárez Cartel.

The bodies of the American law-enforcement officers turned up in a ditch near the border.

Their heads turned up hanging from light poles throughout the city.

Now the CISEN agent responsible for the betrayal was meeting with his cartel contacts to receive his payment.

Thanks to the digital intercept capabilities of the National Security Agency, Stony Man's Able Team would also be attending the meet. Except the elite counterterrorist team would be gate-crashing.

THE ABANDONED FACTORY of the now defunct company Servicious Plasticos Ensambles stood alone in a massive dirt lot cluttered with garbage and rubble. Once the factory sweatshop had closed down, the city cut the power to that section of the grid.

Now the structural skeleton of the factory, along with the shantytown neighborhood surrounding it, lay covered in an utter darkness broken only by the occasional lantern in some black eye of a window. The lights of the better sections of Juárez glittered in the background.

Somewhere several blocks over, a woman began screaming in long, looping shrieks. A man's voice broke in, shouting angrily.

Seconds later a staccato burst of automatic weapons fire
broke out.

Then there was an abrupt silence broken a heartbeat
later by the screech of tires.

Able Team emerged out of the darkness.

They moved fast, with a purpose and a lethal confidence
hard earned. Like one of the U.S. Army's small kill teams
hunting the lonely stretches of highway outside of Baghdad,
they emerged from the desert and disappeared again into
shadow.

Night-vision goggles, DARPA-supplied next-generation
AN/PVS-9 models, turned them into cyclopean silhouettes. Sound-suppressed M-4 carbines hung under jackets,
silencer-equipped barrels pointed downward. Muscular
torsos were sheathed in Kevlar-weave protective vests
boasting ceramic inserts.

They wore backup silenced 9 mm pistols in shoulder
rigs, and unmuffled .45-caliber Detonic Combat Master
handguns were nestled in holdout holsters at the small of
their backs. Fighting knives of surgical-grade steel were
clipped to calves or forearms as weapons of last resort.

The stench of industrial pollution was a constant background miasma. Halfway across the dirt lot the smell was
cut suddenly by the sharp putridness of rotting meat.

Alarmed, Carl Lyons, ex-LAPD homicide detective and
Able Team leader, turned his head in the direction of the
stink and saw a dead dog lying in a shallow depression.
The NVG's amplification of ambient light was so good he
could see the squirming white mass of maggots covering
the corpse.

Hermann Schwarz, former Army reconnaissance

specialist and electronics genius, turned his head and spit the taste out of his mouth.

"This place has really gone to the dogs," he muttered in a low voice.

Rosario Blancanales, former Special Forces soldier, opened his mouth to reply and suddenly froze. The unmistakable sound of a rattlesnake buzzed out of the bushes near his foot.

Lyons spun instantly, cursing softly. His head swiveled as he scanned with the NVGs, looking for the snake. Both he and Schwarz drew their Beretta 92-F pistols with 4-inch silencers screwed into the specially threaded barrels.

"Where is it?" Schwarz snapped.

"There." Blancanales pointed to the ground at his feet.

Both of his teammates lifted their pistols but were too slow.

The Western Diamondback rattlesnake uncoiled like a trap going off, striking even as Blancanales tried dancing backward. It stretched out four feet and its blunt head rammed into the Puerto Rican's leg with the force of a baseball bat.

"Jesus!" Blancanales grunted and staggered.

He felt the hot needle of a fang slide into his calf, and instantly agonized jolts of pain raced up and cut his breath off.

Schwarz and Lyons, using their NVGs, fired.

The snake blew into three separate chunks like a severed noodle. The squat, ugly head of the Diamondback hung for a moment from the top of Blancanales's boot, then dropped off.

"Christing hell!" Blancanales swore.

"Sit down," Schwarz said, moving to help his old friend.

"You have anything in the med kit to help?" Lyons demanded.

The ex-cop took a knee as he holstered his pistol. He swung his M-4 up and provided security. Blancanales sat heavily on the rubble-strewn ground and yanked his pant leg up out from where it was tucked into his boot.

"Like a snakebite kit? Antivenom?" Blancanales laughed. "Nope. Just the standard trauma stuff." Ironically, the ex-Green Beret was the one most often charged with medical responsibilities on Able Team. "This is supposed to be an *urban* area, goddammit."

Schwarz leaned over, turned on the IR penlight set on his night-vision goggles and illuminated the wound. Even in that uncertain light the leg was already obviously swollen. The puncture mark was a neat, red, raised hole leaking thinned-out blood.

"Looks like it only got you with one fang," Schwarz observed. "The other one got caught on the leather of your boot top."

"Let's get him up and back to the vehicle," Lyons said. "We'll scrub the op."

"Screw that, Ironman," Blancanales said in a raspy voice. "Only one dose? It's not that bad—I've got time. The poison isn't that fast acting. I'll be sick, sure. I'll wish I could cut off my leg, but I've got hours before it's really life-threatening. We are going to continue the mission."

Lyons frowned, silently debating his responsibilities.

"You don't have any antivenom," he pointed out. "It'll kill flesh."

"The *pendajos* we're here to hit put those DEA agents' heads on poles, man. They put their heads on poles," he repeated. "I'm not blowing this."

"Is there anything we can do?" Schwarz interrupted before Lyons could object further.

"Sure," Blancanales said. "Pressure dressing and an EpiPen. Shoot the Epi right into my leg above the bite."

"What freaking good is that going to do?" Lyons demanded. "You going into shock?"

"No," Blancanales denied. His body was covered with sweat. "But epi works as a vasoconstrictor. It'll slow the spread of the venom."

"I'm on it," Schwarz said.

He saw Blancanales suddenly shiver despite the oppressive heat and he prayed the man was right.

"Fine," Lyons agreed. "We'll do it your way. But I want us back in our vehicle and we'll swing around and come into the building on the other side. We're not going to have you walking any more than necessary."

Already sweating, Blancanales nodded. "Whatever you say, boss."

# CHAPTER TWO

*Pan African Cross-Country Rally*
*Kenya*

The dirt road cut a dusty brown seam through the rough terrain.

The Nissan 4x4 pickup tore along the road at breakneck speed, sheets of dust streaming behind it. The engine growled as the driver gunned it hard, putting it through its paces like a trainer working a racehorse.

The heavily modified off-road vehicle was painted black and yellow with heavy grilles placed over enhanced headlights. In the back, two extra wheels, jerricans filled with reserves of high-octane gasoline, motor oil and pioneer tools of ax, shovel and pick were strapped down in the bed.

David McCarter took his foot off the gas, slapped the clutch and shifted up out of third gear. He stutter-stepped back on the gas and the tricked-out pickup lunged forward, gaining speed.

The left front tire dropped into a pothole on the dirt track and the steering wheel jerked in his hands. He rode out the recoil and guided the truck out of the hole, his teeth clenched under his helmet against the jolt.

"Jesus Christ!" T. J. Hawkins protested from the passenger seat. "I think I just tasted my own balls!"

"If that were true you wouldn't be complaining, mate!" McCarter shouted back.

The road turned in a brutal switchback, and the ex-SAS trooper casually used the emergency brake to slide around the turn. He released the brake and pushed the gas. The big knobby tires gripped the hard dirt, and the Nissan shot forward out of the fishtail.

"Screw you," Hawkins replied.

The Texan was an ex-Army Ranger and ex-Delta Force commando. He held a Audiovox Jensen NVXM 1000 GPS system and was furiously working applications on the unit's four-inch screen.

A Nexus Google phone set to speaker rested on his lap, providing communication uplinks to the support team. The device chirped and Gary Manning spoke up.

"How's your engine temp, David?" the burly Canadian demanded. "My diagnostic uplink shows it climbing into the red."

"Don't be a bleeding wanker, you mother hen," McCarter snapped. "I'm treating your baby fine."

"You sure are different when *you* own the vehicle Dave's driving instead of the U.S. government," Hawkins pointed out, laughing.

"I'm a consultant, not an owner," Manning argued. "But still, you blow an engine in the middle of the race and it's over."

"Mr. McCarter," said a cool and utterly feminine voice, "this represents a significant investment on the part of my company."

"*Your* company?" McCarter answered.

Up ahead a line of broken hills suddenly appeared in the windshield. To the west of the rocky ridgeline the terrain fell away into a deep, wide valley. A wall of dust cleared enough for the two Phoenix Force commandos to see the

French racers of Team Gauloises in their Citroën Méhari running full-out ahead of them.

"Yes, Mr. McCarter," Monica Fischer, CEO at North American, Inc., answered, "my company."

"Maybe so," McCarter snapped. "But I'm driving here!"

Just ahead of his pickup the French vehicle was a foot off his bumper. McCarter slammed the gas down and jerked his wheel to the side, running the Nissan up onto a wide shoulder. Rooster tails of sand spun out behind his grinding wheels as he gunned it past the Méhari.

He powered around the front of the French vehicle and snapped the pickup back onto the track, cutting off the Team Gauloises vehicle.

The Frenchmen shook their fists in anger but their shouted curses were lost to the roar of the big racing engines. Hawkins stuck his arm out the window and casually flipped them the bird as McCarter sped away.

"We're coming up to the first branch here," the Texan warned. "Have you got any better route intelligence to give us?"

There was a slight pause, then Manning, trailing behind the racing pickup in the team's matinee vehicle, a stripped-down Suburban SUV, answered.

"Negative," he replied. "I tried to get updated information about road conditions in the valley, but everybody around here is playing tight to the vest."

McCarter snarled in frustration as the fork in the road appeared. To one side lay the road running through the hills while to the other was the track cutting across the valley.

The dirt road winding through the hills meant slower speeds and some climbing; it had, however, been thoroughly scouted before the race and was shorter. There would be little in the way of surprises.

The valley was flatter, allowing for faster driving that should also be easier on the vehicle. It would have been McCarter's automatic choice in a race except that the racers hadn't been informed of the option until an hour before the starting gun had gone off.

As such, the route was poorly marked, unscouted and about the only thing they knew for sure was that the road was cut several times by the 440-mile-long Tana River.

"Screw it," McCarter mumbled and downshifted. "Let's do the hills."

"Ah, Christ," Hawkins replied immediately. "You're gonna shake my cherries right off their stem!"

"That's what separates the rock stars from the groupies," McCarter snapped.

He turned onto the hill road at the Y-intersection, going fast enough to fishtail sideways. Hawkins checked his passenger-side mirror.

"I guess you're right," he said, voice droll. "Because the French team just took the valley road."

THE SUN SLID RAPIDLY toward the horizon, bringing on a rapidly gathering twilight.

Monica Fischer swore.

She fought with the power steering of the big Suburban chase vehicle as they drove flat out in an attempt to keep within striking distance of McCarter and Hawkins. Beside her in the passenger seat Manning was downloading a weather report from a commercial satellite service.

"Damn," he muttered. "We're getting a build up of nimbi in the highlands."

"Nimbi?"

"Rain clouds. We have a pressure system stacking up against the mountains. There's going to be rain before the night is out."

"Great." Fischer laughed. She glanced at her dashboard, then added, "We're running low on fuel."

Manning looked up from his screen. "Fine. Pull over and we'll gas up while I tell David about the weather change."

Monica pulled the heavy steering wheel to the side and guided the SUV off the road and under the slight protection offered by a grove of acacia trees. She shut off the engine and hopped out as Manning finished relaying the weather information to the racers.

Walking around back, he stepped up next to Monica as she pulled open the rear cargo doors. He hesitated as her arm brushed his. He could smell her very clearly next to him. It was a good smell. They both reached for the same jerrican of fuel.

"I got this, muscleman," she teased. "You check the oil, we don't want our engine temp to spike."

"Sure," Manning agreed, feeling slightly flustered. "Use the strainer," he reminded her.

"This isn't my first rodeo, cowboy."

"Whatever you say, boss."

While Monica put the strainer in place over the nozzle as an extra protection against dirt clogging the fuel line and injectors, Manning popped the hood. Stuck behind the hood as he was he didn't see the accident—just the results.

Monica lifted the end of the jerrican and the greasy metal slipped in her grip. The jerrican dropped to the ground hard, knocking the strainer cap free and splashing high-octane fuel up in a spray.

Some of the gas splashed onto the still hot exhaust pipe and instantly ignited. The spilled gas lit in a flash with a small explosion, and Monica screamed in agony as she was burned.

Manning came around the side of the SUV in a rush. He saw Monica stumbling backward as flames began racing up the spilled gas on her jumpsuit. He struck her with a shoulder and knocked her to the ground.

Instantly he was on top of her, using his own body to smother the flames. The industrial jumpsuit, not unlike the kind worn by military pilots, was made of flame-retardant material, helping his attempts to put her out.

"Monica, Monica!" Manning demanded, voice on the edge of frantic. "Are you okay?"

"My arms, my hands," she said, teeth gritted against the pain.

She held her hands up for Manning to inspect and despite how red and puffy they looked, he was amazed the damage was so minimal. Despite this his practiced eye realized that soon, perhaps within minutes, the skin would first blister, then crack.

Such open wounds in the African bush were a guaranteed invitation to infection. On top of this, they had little in the way of pain medication in their medical kit. The chances of her slipping into shock were great, putting her life in danger.

"Hold on," he said.

Hurriedly he got the med kit from behind the driver's seat and began applying antiseptic cream to the wounds before wrapping them in loose, dry bandages.

"Gary, I'm so sorry."

"Shut up."

"But the race—"

"I said shut up," Manning repeated. "To hell with the race. I'll get you back to the checkpoint in the village we passed. We'll have you airlifted out to Nairobi in no time." He looked down the road and into the rough African terrain now cloaked in darkness. "Besides," he continued, "if anyone can finish this race without a chase vehicle, it's those two jokers."

# CHAPTER THREE

The Nissan pickup driven by David McCarter rattled like dice in a dryer as the Briton hammered the vehicle through the course. He and Hawkins were feeling the effects of so much vibrational trauma sapping their endurance.

Both men were silent for a moment after Manning had relayed his situation and intention to take Monica for medical help, leaving the racers without a chase vehicle. Hawkins looked up from his GPS device.

"Screw it, David," he said. "We're past the point of no return anyway. We might as well finish the race because it's just as short a distance to Nairobi as to turn around."

McCarter nodded. "Agreed. Tell Gary we're pushing on."

Hawkins relayed the information and for the next five minutes carefully calculated how far the fuel they carried with them would let them race.

"We don't have a choice." He looked up from his calculations. "We're going to have to risk the shortcut. Our fuel reserve is just too tight."

"Who Dares Wins," McCarter replied, using the motto of his old unit, the British Special Air Service.

Up ahead a lone baobab tree appeared in the Nissan's bouncing headlights and Hawkins immediately sat up.

"That's it!" He pointed through the dust-smeared windshield. "That's the marker for the shortcut."

"All right, mate," McCarter replied. "Don't get your panties in a bunch."

He slowed, downshifted, took the fork and gunned the vehicle back up to speed. Inside the cab the two Phoenix Force drivers were bounced against their safety harnesses like pinballs.

"Holy crap," Hawkins swore in his Texas drawl. "I didn't think a road could get worse than the one we're on, but this son of a bitch is tearing us up."

"It'll save us twenty minutes," McCarter reminded him.

"If it doesn't rip apart our axle," Hawkins shot back.

"You want to go back?"

"Just drive!"

For the next fifteen minutes the Nissan bounced across the open country course, leading them out of the foothills. Once a lone elephant standing calmly in the middle of the road appeared in their headlights.

McCarter swerved up out of the tire ruts and bounced across a rocky berm to avoid the multiton animal, then snapped the pickup back on the road before a pile of rocks almost tore off his front end.

Finally their first river crossing appeared in front of them.

*Mexico*

"THE AZTECS USED TO sacrifice about two hundred and fifty thousand of their own people every year," Schwarz said. "They would cut out their hearts while they were still alive."

"Okay, that provides us with a template on how to deal with this guy Chavez," Lyons pointed out.

Blancanales nodded from behind the wheel of the black

Dodge SUV. Around them a rambling shantytown sprawled outward from the edges of Juárez. The Stony Man crew kept the blacked-out windows on their SUV buttoned up tight against the smell.

The road they rolled along was made of dirt and heavily rutted, dotted with puddles of dubious origins. Bored, apathetic faces stared out at the expensive vehicle from the safety of clapboard and aluminum-siding shacks.

The poverty was appalling and left Carl Lyons uneasy. He was no stranger to Central and South American conditions. Able Team had made the lower half the Western Hemisphere a primary area of operations since the unit's inception.

Blancanales, already recovering, guided the big vehicle through narrow alleys while hungry dogs barked and chased them. Up ahead a line of railroad tracks divided the sprawling shantytown and massive warehouses began to line its length. Beyond these the silent mausoleum of factories built by American companies that had exported jobs to exploit cheap labor reared up like austere, prefabricated mountains.

Blancanales cut the SUV onto a single-lane dirt road that paralleled the train track. The Dodge's suspension rattled and hummed but inside the climate-controlled cab the ride was smooth and virtually silent. Up ahead a chipped and cracked asphalt lot opened up just past a broken gate in a dilapidated chain-link fence. A battered and rusted sign warning away trespassers in Spanish hung off to one side like a forgotten letter.

The building across the old parking lot was abandoned, dotted with broken windows and gaping emptiness where doors had stood. A line of crows had taken roost across the top, and Blancanales slowed the vehicle as he pulled into the old parking lot.

"How are we sitting for time?" he asked.

Lyons looked at his watch. "We're a good hour before the meet, according to the CIA stringer," he said. "We couldn't have got here any sooner with flight time anyway."

Blancanales guided the SUV around the side of the building. A pair of filthy alley cats hissed in surprise at the sudden appearance of the monstrous vehicle and scrambled for the safety of some overflowing garbage bins. Lyons eyed the building with a wary gaze as Blancanales drove around it. He reached under the seat and pulled an M-4 clear.

"Politics give me a rash," Lyons muttered. He snapped the bolt back on the compact carbine and seated a 5.56 mm round.

"I just wish we had more time to check out this set up," Schwarz said from the backseat. He pulled an identical M-4 from a briefcase on the seat next to him and chambered a round. "We don't know this guy from Adam."

Blancanales reached over and pulled his own prepped and ready M-4 from the inside compartment of his door. Each man on the team wore a windbreaker over a backup shoulder holster. They had no intention of hiding their firepower when they went into the meet.

As the team stepped out of the vehicle there was a thunderous roaring as a freight train began its approach of the rail yard off to the side of the building. Lyons looked around. This was the location of the meet with the man who was supposed to take them to where their target was hiding.

"This strike you as overly isolated for a simple meet-and-greet?" Schwarz asked.

"Why, whatever do you mean, Grandma?" Lyons asked.

The freight train began to slow even further. The

engineer popped its brakes with a deafening hissing noise accompanied by the screaming of steel on steel as wheels locked up on rails. Blancanales eyeballed the upper reaches of the building as they approached. The windows looked back at him, silent and dark.

Closer to the ground the building was taken up by a concrete loading dock and roll-up bay doors for almost two-thirds of its length. The other section was broken by a single metal door set at the top of a short flight of concrete steps. Spiky lines of graffiti covered the wall and doors. Displaced air from the sliding train pushed scraps of paper across the broken asphalt like stringless kites.

Juárez was one of the most polluted cities on the face of the earth and here, in its underbelly, the stench was sharp and chemical, coating the tongues of the three men as they approached the building.

The train pulled up next to the yard, arriving in a deafening din as boxcar after boxcar slowly rumbled by. Though they stood right next to each other the men couldn't have heard one another speak. Lyons frowned and made a gesture with his hand.

The other two immediately spread out, forming into a loose triangle as they finished their approach to the front of the building. Schwarz looked to one side and saw a line of gouts suddenly erupt in the earth. He reached over and shoved Lyons to one side, then flung himself in the other direction. The line of bullets stitched its way up the middle of them while off to the side Blancanales had lifted his carbine and began spraying it at the top line of windows on the building.

The compact M-4 carbine was designed for close-in range and ease of concealment, but the 5.56 mm rounds were more than powerful enough to cross the space between the ambush sniper and the men caught in the path of his murderous fire.

Blancanales's burst peppered the building.

Lyons rolled with the hard shove his teammate had given him and somersaulted over one shoulder. He came up and quickly scanned the building for the attackers. He saw nothing other than the single sniper trading shots with Blancanales and quickly crossed his stream of 5.56 mm rounds with those of the ex-Green Beret.

Bullets rebounded off the wall and shattered what slivers of glass still remained in their frames. He saw brilliant bursts of muzzle-flash and tried to bring his own fire to bear accurately as he continued racing toward the building. The freight train had formed a blanket of painful white nose on the entire area, and Lyons felt acutely strange, able to register the feel of his recoil and the heat of escaping gases but still almost entirely unable to hear the report of his own weapon in his hands.

Off to one side Schwarz bounced up off the parking lot and raced for the single pedestrian door set to one side of the building. Behind him Blancanales continued spraying successive bursts into the area of the sniper in an attempt to suppress his gunfire. The freight train continued to roll on past their position in an endless line of flatbed trailers and boxcars.

Snarling with the effort, Schwarz raced toward the building, his M-4 carbine up and at the ready. Closing with the short staircase, he let go of the carbine with his left hand and leaped up like a sprinter running hurdles. He caught hold of a metal safety rail running the length of the stair and vaulted over to the top of the steps.

He tucked his elbow in tight against his ribs and drew the M-4 in close to his body. With his free hand he grabbed the doorknob and twisted, jerking the heavy door open on protesting hinges. The sound of the train rolled into the building and echoed off it so that the racket was actually worse the closer the Stony Man crew got to the massive warehouse structure.

As the door swung open in his hands, he darted inside. Immediately, Schwarz found himself in a cavernous space some three stories high. He scanned the gloomy interior and let the door swing closed behind him. He had expected the structure to contain floors but he quickly shifted his tactics to compensate for the open space.

He pivoted and dropped into a crouch facing an erector-set formation of ladders and scaffolding set against one wall. Through a forest of metal bars and steel mesh he caught an impression of movement. He triggered a burst and heard the sniper do the same. Lead slugs ricocheted wildly inside the building and muzzles-blasts flared, casting crazy shadows.

Realizing he had to cut an angle on the sniper, Schwarz dived forward across oil-stained concrete and came up before triggering a second burst with his M-4. He saw a black-clad figure lean over a railing with a scope-mounted M-16, its black buttstock jammed tight into his shoulder.

The man fired down at Schwarz, and the Able Team electronics whiz threw himself toward the uncertain cover of a line of fifty-five-gallon barrels. One of the rolling bay doors directly beneath the sniper suddenly slid open to a height of about three feet and Schwarz had a brief glimpse of Rosario Blancanales lying flat on his stomach, M-4 held out in front of him.

Realizing Lyons was about to enter the abandoned factory, Schwarz raked the scaffolding with automatic fire, still desperately seeking an angle to catch on the sniper. He couldn't force a clear trajectory out of the mess and his rounds scattered in a wild pattern around the hunched and ducking man.

The sniper rose, straightened his weapon and returned fire, his assault rifle set to 3-round bursts. A flurry of rounds began to hammer into the barrels Schwarz crouched behind. Below the man Carl Lyons pinpointed his position and turned his own M-4 skyward. The chatterbox rattled in his hands and a stream of dull gold casings arced out like water from a hose and bounced and rolled across the concrete floor.

The 5.56 mm slugs began slamming into the mesh and metal framework at the sniper's feet and the man suddenly began sprinting toward one side of the platform above them while still trying to turn and return Lyons's fire.

Schwarz used the opportunity to merge his own stream of gunfire with Lyons's, only to have his magazine run dry.

He dropped the magazine from the well in the pistol butt, and curling gray smoke followed the empty box. He pulled a secondary magazine from his coat pocket and slid it home before chambering a round. In the brief time it took for the Able Team commando to switch out magazines, the faceless sniper had managed to reach the temporary safety of a double-girder overhead-bridge crane control panel and engine housing.

Schwarz cursed. The control area was like a fortress of metal squares and thick welded beams. He tried an exploratory burst but the M-4 was less than precise. He would have to settle for burst cover fire unless he could work his way in closer for a more accurate shot.

Off to one side Schwarz saw Blancanales enter the building, and three steady lines of 5.56 mm slugs now began converging on the sniper's position. The man disappeared behind cover only to reemerge and return fire.

The situation was fast approaching a stalemate, Schwarz realized. Without drawing closer, the M-4s were too inaccurate to pose a threat at the current range. But to get closer the Stony Man operatives would have to cross open space easily within the range of the man's assault rifle.

Carl Lyons sprinted out across the space between his position and the barrels Schwarz was using for cover. He rolled over and came up next to his teammate as Blancanales continued to fire from the edge of one of the bay doors. The train outside just continued rolling past, and the clatter rolled into the open space of the old factory through the open door and bounced around.

"This is insane!" Lyons yelled. "The asshole can't possibly think the CIA will let him get away with setting up a meet and then ambushing American agents!"

Schwarz lifted his M-4 and sprayed another quick burst. "He must think he can run."

The sniper poked the barrel of his M-16 around the edge of the panel and squeezed off an answering burst. Blancanales returned fire.

"The only way to find out is to take him alive," Schwarz said.

"You want to cross that open space and charge up a ladder?" Lyons demanded.

"No, but I was hoping you would, though," Schwarz retorted. "You are known for your temper."

"Kiss my ass, Schwarz!" Lyons muttered, the carbine bucking in his hands.

Schwarz scanned the wide-open floor space of the factory. He realized that with his elevated position and superior range the sniper still had every advantage—even though he'd blown his initial attack.

"Let's just go," Schwarz said.

"What!" Lyons shouted, voice incredulous.

"Lets just boogey out of here. I mean it. Let him think we ran."

"We need to know what that guy knows!" Lyons argued. "Our bad guy is a ghost—he's our only lead."

"To find out," Schwarz said, "we need him to come down."

Lyons opened his mouth to reply. He paused, then closed his mouth and cocked an eyebrow. He turned toward Schwarz and nodded once. "Okay, let's do it," he said.

"Blancanales!" Schwarz shouted.

"What?" Blancanales shouted back.

"Get the car!" Schwarz yelled. "Trust me!"

Blancanales looked at him, then nodded. In a second he was out the door. Lyons dropped a magazine from the pistol grip of his M-4 and inserted a fresh one while Schwarz provided covering fire.

# CHAPTER FOUR

The fleeing sniper cranked the throttle on his street bike and raced out of the building. He was pretty close to panicked. He had gone too far, pissed off the Americans. There was nothing left but to run for it.

What had started out as easy money from influence peddling against the arrogant Yankees had quite suddenly backfired. The Juárez organization on the border was wrecked. Their commandant butchered. It was time to take the money and run. Too bad, so sad. Now it was time to go.

He gunned the powerful motorcycle across the abandoned asphalt parking lot of the old factory and out the front gate. The American investigating team had made their escape and it was time for him to do the same. He used the toe of his boot to push the bike into a higher gear and he cranked his wrist, holding the throttle wide open.

He shot through the gate and out onto the access road lined with shacks of aluminum siding and cardboard. Suddenly up ahead, next to the rusting derelict of a train engine parked and forgotten on the old tracks, the sniper saw one of the American agents, the big blond bastard, standing out in the open with his carbine. The man flipped him the middle finger and the sniper locked up his bike, sending it into a slide and changing direction before the fool opened fire.

His rear tire caught on the hard-packed earth and he felt

the motorcycle start to respond. Suddenly he saw movement and looked up. Too late he saw the American's vehicle, a massive SUV, rush out of a narrow alley and head directly at him. Behind the blacked-out visor of his helmet the sniper screamed.

Blancanales's face was a smooth, flat affect, as expressionless as a mask as he rammed the big vehicle into the man. The heavy bumper struck the Japanese bike and sent it skipping end-over-end down the road, tossing the rider like a rag doll in a spinning pinwheel of limbs.

The corrupt Mexican law-enforcement agent struck the ground and bounced, his limbs almost instantly folding into unnatural angles. Blancanales hit the brakes on the SUV to allow the motorcycle to bounce away and avoid becoming entangled with it. He watched the figure of the ambush assassin rebound off the ground like a rubber ball and sprawl in an ungainly slide onto the weed-choked railroad tracks.

"Oh, that's going to leave a mark," Schwarz muttered, and winced.

Blancanales twisted the wheel and threw the SUV into a slide as he brought the vehicle to a stop. He opened his door and bailed while across from him the Able Team electronics expert did the same. Both men brought their compact carbines up to provide cover.

From his decoy position Carl Lyons raced toward the fallen man, his own carbine covering the motionless figure. Blancanales sized up the situation and immediately turned to provide cover outward as his two teammates converged on the broken body.

Lyons knelt and put two fingers against the motorcycle rider's throat while Schwarz covered him. Lyons pulled some clothing to one side and felt again. He looked up at Schwarz and shook his head.

"No pulse," he said.

"Yank the helmet," Schwarz said.

Setting the M-4 down, Lyons quickly undid the chin-strap and pulled the helmet free. The man's head bounced oddly and came to rest at an almost obscene angle. The neck of the assassin was clearly broken.

"Well, I guess we're done in Juárez," Lyons muttered.

"Shake him down for a cell phone or something, it might pay off," Schwarz suggested. "I'm sorry, guys. I know we needed him alive. I didn't realize he'd be riding a bike instead of driving a car when I set up the plan."

"Shit happens," Lyons said.

"Find anything?" Blancanales called.

Lyons looked up. "No, he was running clean."

"Let's get out of here, then," Schwarz said, looking around. "The natives are starting to get curious."

Lyons stood and nodded.

"Let's roll."

*Kenya*

"DOESN'T THAT JUST BEAT everything?"

McCarter's voice was so dull with disappointment it barely held a trace of his accent. Beside him in the SUV, Hawkins just slowly shook his head.

"It's the French," he said. His disbelief only served to thicken his Texas drawl. "Why did it have to be the god-damn French?"

McCarter didn't have an answer.

Their vehicle was parked on a bluff overlooking the river. Halfway across the dark brown waters they could clearly see the commercial ferry taking cars across to the other side.

Based on its current speed, the two Phoenix Force

members estimated it'd be another half hour before the ferry unloaded its cargo on the far side and made its way back to pick them up.

To make matters worse the ferry was loaded with the French racing team. The laughter of the other racers was clearly audible as they powered away across the water. One of the Frenchmen lifted up his arm and flipped off the two men.

"I guess I had that coming," Hawkins said.

"They started before us," McCarter pointed out. "So the fact that we've caught up to them again, means our times are good."

"Sure," Hawkins conceded. "But I'd feel a hell of a lot better with them at our six than running flat out ahead of us."

"What do you want to do?"

"According to the map there's another crossing down the river," Hawkins answered. "We get there and across, we could gain even more time."

"Better damned if we do than if we don't?"

"I sure as hell don't want to burn daylight just sitting here if we have another option."

McCarter released the parking brake and put the idling SUV into gear. "Let's hit it," he agreed.

The SUV powered across the open terrain.

McCarter navigated the riverbank for almost a mile until it twisted in a great bend. Reading the map beside him, Hawkins instructed him to cut straight cross-country to meet the waterway where it looped back.

Still battered by the lack of a road, the two men found the going relatively easy across a flat stretch of grassland. McCarter kept one eye on his watch while Hawkins used the dashboard compass, his much abused race map and the GPS unit to coordinate their position exactly. Soon he was plagued by a constant, low-grade headache. As they pressed on without an update on Monica Fischer's condition, their worry mounted.

Copses of trees proved the most difficult obstacle to navigate but the route called for them to ford several small streams along the way. McCarter gunned the vehicle through one such obstacle and clawed his way up the other side and the men found themselves on an immense plain.

"That's it," Hawkins said. "That's the last stream for a while and we're on the veldt before the river crossing."

According to their plan McCarter slowed and stopped the vehicle. Hawkins quickly got out, retrieved a grease gun from the cargo space and crawled under the vehicle to do his preventive maintenance.

As Hawkins worked, McCarter slipped out from behind the wheel to stretch. On a whim he crawled up onto the roof of the SUV and scanned his surroundings. The wild distance seemed vast as he scanned the terrain.

To the west he saw a small group of water buffalo wallowing in the mud beside the small stream they had just crossed. Beyond them a herd of giraffes moved easily across the grassland.

He felt at peace despite his exhaustion. The cares and worries of his singular occupation seemed far away. He felt the burden of his responsibilities lift off his shoulders like a bird taking flight.

He looked at his watch and noted how much time had passed. He was pleased. He calculated that their alternate route would put them in front of the Frenchmen in another hour.

"We might just win this thing, after all," he called down to Hawkins.

Hawkins answered from beneath the rear axle but

his reply was drowned out by the ringing of the satellite phone on McCarter's belt. The Briton pulled it free and answered, figuring it was Manning with an update on Fischer's condition.

He listened for a moment, then sighed.

"Hello, Barb. What can I do for you?"

*Brazzaville; Capital, Republic of the Congo*

THE NIGHT WAS HOT.

The heat was cloying, so humid it clung to the body in a blanket of damp. It made showering a superfluous activity. Despite this Rafik Bagdasarian had taken two in the past hour.

The first had been to wash the smell of the woman off him.

He'd been infatuated with her ebony skin and rich accent, but once he'd paid her, he'd come to the conclusion that whores were whores the world over. It didn't matter if it was Moscow, New York, Paris or Brazzaville.

He took the second shower to calm his nerves. This one the Armenian mafioso lieutenant took with an iced tumbler full of Ouzo. In his years as arms merchant, contract killer, drug smuggler and human trafficker he'd come to love the anise-flavored liquor.

Walking through the suite of the Olympic Palace Hotel, he toweled off his pale, lanky body then poured himself a second drink. His body was covered with swirling green ink tattoos that announced his résumé and biography to those who knew how to read them.

Skulls, daggers, horned monsters, Catholic iconography all twisted across his lean, muscular frame. He was a problem solver, which was why his captain had sent him to the Congo.

Taking his drink, he stepped out onto his balcony and looked across the dirty water of the Congo River at Kinshasa, the capital of the Democratic Republic of the Congo. The twin cities of Kinshasa and Brazzaville were the only national capitals sharing a river border or situated so closely together.

The unique circumstance had done nothing to help the two countries, however, Bagdasarian thought.

He stepped off the balcony, tossed back his drink and began to think. The civil war of Congo-Brazzaville in 1997 and the larger war in Congo-Kinshasa in 1998 had left the poverty-stricken nations and their capitals in ruins with political systems decimated.

From the power vacuum strongmen with guns had emerged.

It was a situation and environment Bagdasarian understood well. His own criminal clique had risen to prominence during and after the chaos of his own country's bitter, bloody and protracted war with neighboring Azerbaijan.

He lit a French cigarette and buttoned his shirt. His area of operations for the Armenian syndicate was Africa, but he wasn't just here for them. This time it was bigger; this time the Chinese principal had set him into motion.

Failure was not an option.

In the valise on the bed in front of him was a large amount of francs and a Walther PPK.

The woman he'd bought had served for something else beside sexual gratification.

Prostitutes were the elements of the criminal underground most readily available to foreigners in any country. They haunted the hotels and nightclubs promising sweaty miracles in exchange for cash.

But they were also conduits to the black market.

Prostitution went hand in hand with drugs and where

you found a drug dealer you found someone who could, if the wheels were greased, get you a gun or introduce you to all manner of nefarious operators.

Bagdasarian had the number of his own contact in Brazzaville but he wasn't about to go anywhere in the dangerous African city unarmed. Unwilling to risk his mission by attempting to smuggle a weapon onto a French airline, he'd used the hooker to secure a pistol.

Dressed, armed, and carrying twenty-five thousand dollars in francs, Bagdasarian went out of his room to find the police.

He needed some Americans killed.

# CHAPTER FIVE

Rafik Bagdasarian shoved a fistful of local currency over the battered seat to the cabdriver and got out. He leaned in the open window of the passenger door and instructed the driver to wait for him around the block.

The taxi sped away, leaving him standing on the edge of an unpaved street. There was an open sewer off to his right and the stench was ripe in his nose.

Bagdasarian looked around.

He was on the opposite side of Brazzaville from the international airport. The dirt street was lined with shanties and what light there was escaped from boarded-up windows or from beneath shut-up doors.

A pair of mongrels fought over some scraps in a refuse pile several dozen yards up the road. Other than those dogs fighting, the stretch of grimy road was strangely deserted.

Faintly, Bagdasarian could hear the sound of a lousy stereo playing and then voices raised in argument. A baby started crying somewhere and farther away more dogs began barking in response.

Bagdasarian looked up at the sky, noting the low cloud cover. The road was thick with muck from the seasonal rains and it clung heavy to the soles of his hiking boots.

He set the attaché case he was holding down and reached around behind his back and pulled his pistol clear. He jacked the slide and chambered a 9 mm round before sliding the pistol into his jeans behind his belt buckle, leaving it in plain sight. He leaned down and picked up the case. He shifted his grip on the attaché handle so that his gun hand remained free.

He took a quick look around before crossing the road and stepping up to the front door of one of the innumerable shacks lining the road. He lifted his big hand and pounded three times on the door. He heard a hushed conversation break out momentarily before the voices fell quiet.

"Kabila?" Bagdasarian asked, speaking French. "Rafik."

Bagdasarian felt a sudden damp and realized it had started to rain while he was standing there. Despite the wet he was still uncomfortably warm in his short-sleeved, button-down khaki shirt and battered blue jeans.

The short-sleeved shirt left his elbows and forearms exposed, revealing their thick covering of tattoos, his calling card.

The door opened slowly and a bar of soft, nicotine-colored light spilled out and illuminated Bagdasarian.

A silhouette stood in the doorway and the Armenian narrowed his eyes to take in the figure's features. It was a male, wearing an unbuttoned and disheveled gendarme uniform. His eyes and teeth were sharply yellow against the deep burnished purple-black of his skin.

He held a bottle of grain alcohol in one hand, and the other rested on the pistol grip of a French MAT-49 submachine gun hanging from a strap slung across his neck like a guitar. He leaned forward, crowding Bagdasarian's space.

Bagdasarian made no move to back up.

"You, Rafik?" the man demanded, also speaking French.

His breath reeked with alcohol fumes, and the light

around him reflected wildly off the glaze in his eyes. His words were softly slurred but his gaze was steady as he eyed Bagdasarian up and down.

The finger on the trigger of the MAT-49 submachine gun seemed firm enough.

"Yes," Bagdasarian answered. "Is Kabila here?"

"Colonel Kabila," the man corrected.

"Is *Colonel* Kabila here?"

"You have the money?"

Bagdasarian lifted the attaché case, though he knew the man had already seen it when he'd opened the door.

The gendarme ignored the displayed satchel, his eyes never leaving Bagdasarian's face. His hair was tightly cropped and Bagdasarian could see bullets of sweat beading on the man's forehead. The smell of body odor was acrid.

"Give me the pistol."

"Go to hell."

The drunken gendarme's eyes lifted in shock and his face twisted in sudden, instant outrage. He snapped straight and twisted the MAT-49 around on its sling, trying to bring the muzzle up in the cramped quarters.

Bagdasarian's free hand shot out and grabbed the submachine gun behind its front sight. The big man locked his arm and pushed down, preventing the gendarme from raising the weapon. The gendarme's eyeballs bulged in anger and the cords of his neck stood out as he strained to bring the submachine gun to bear.

"Leave him!" a deep bass voice barked from somewhere behind the struggling gendarme.

The man cursed and tried to step back and swing his weapon up and away from Bagdasarian's grip. The Armenian stepped forward as the man stepped back, preventing the smaller man from bringing any leverage to bear.

An ability to call up instant explosive anger and balls like brass fixtures was the way Bagdasarian had risen to the top in the hyperviolent world of Armenian organized crime. He didn't take shit. Even if it cost him his life.

They moved into the room through the door and Bagdasarian heard chair legs scrape against floorboards as men jumped to their feet. He ignored them, making no move for the butt of the 9 mm PPK plainly sticking out of his jeans.

The man grunted his exertion and tried to step to the outside.

Rafik Bagdasarian danced with him, keeping the gendarme's body between him and the others in the smoky room. His grip on the front sling swivel remained unbroken. Finally the gendarme dropped his bottle and grabbed the submachine gun with both hands. The bottle thumped loudly as it struck the floor but did not break.

Liquid began to gurgle out and stain the floorboards.

"I said *enough!*" the voice roared.

The gendarme was already using both his hands to snatch the submachine gun free as the order came.

The Armenian released the front sling swivel and stepped to the side. The gendarme found his center of balance around the struggle abruptly gone and overextended himself. Already drunk, he toppled over backward and struck the floor in the pool of reeking alcohol spilling from his dropped bottle.

Cursing and sputtering, the man tried to rise.

Bagdasarian surveyed the room. He saw four other men in the same soiled and rumpled police uniforms, each one armed either with a pistol or a submachine gun. All of them were gaunt and lanky with short hair except for the bear of a man bearing the gold braid epaulets of an officer.

The man rose from behind a table and hurled a heavy

glass tumbler at the gendarme Bagdasarian had spilled onto the floor. The glass struck the man in the face and opened a gash under his eye, high on a prominent cheekbone where Bantu tribal scars had been etched at puberty and rubbed with charcoal.

"I said leave him!"

The shock of being struck snapped the embarrassed man out of his rage. He touched a hand to the cut under his eye and held up his bloody fingers. He looked away from his hand and nodded once toward the man looming up behind the table before rising.

The officer turned toward Bagdasarian. "My apologizes," he said. "My men worry about my safety."

"Understandable, Colonel Kabila." Bagdasarian nodded. "I worry about my own safety."

"Come now, you are in the company of police officers."

"Yes, I am," Bagdasarian agreed.

"Foreigners are not usually permitted to carry weapons in our land."

Bagdasarian threw the attaché case down on the table. "That should more than cover any administrative fees."

"Is it in euros?"

"Francs," Bagdasarian corrected.

Kabila nodded and one of the gendarmes at the table reached over and picked up the attaché case. He had a sergeant's chevrons on his sleeve.

Bagdasarian saw there were two very young girls pressed up against the back wall of the shack. Their eyes were hard as diamonds and glittered as they took him in.

The gendarme sergeant pulled the case over and opened it. The sudden light of avarice flared in his eyes, impossible to disguise. Bagdasarian shrugged it off.

While the sergeant counted the stacks of French currency, Colonel Kabila reseated himself.

He snapped his fingers at one of the girls and she jumped to pick a fresh glass off a shelf beside her. She brought it over to the table and poured the colonel a fresh drink from an already open bottle. Bagdasarian could feel the intensity of her gaze.

Kabila regarded the Armenian through squinty, bloodshot eyes. He picked up a smoldering cigar off the table and dragged heavily from it. His men made no move to return to their seats. Kabila pulled his cigar out of his mouth and gestured with it.

"Sit down."

Bagdasarian pulled out the chair from the end of the table opposite Kabila and eased himself into it. The two men regarded each other with coolly assessing gazes while the sergeant beside Kabila continued counting the money. Kabila lifted his new glass and splashed its contents back without changing expression.

"Shouldn't a man like you be out selling drugs in the nightclubs?" Kabila asked.

"Shouldn't you be out in the delta or back east, fighting?"

Kabila shrugged. "That's what the army is for. I fight crime."

"How's it pay?"

"Not as well as you do, I hope." Kabila smiled. He wasn't smiling when he added, "For your sake."

The gendarme sergeant looked up from counting the money secured inside the attaché case. Kabila's eyes never left Bagdasarian. "Is it all there?" he asked.

"More."

"More?" Kabila asked Bagdasarian.

"There's a bonus in there. You're going to have to travel outside the city."

"Up river?" The colonel sounded incredulous.

"Yes."

"I am a policeman." Colonel Kabila smirked.

Bagdasarian followed the line of Kabila's sight across the room to where the gendarme he had scuffled with stood glowering.

"Any way you want it, Colonel."

"Yes. Yes, it usually is."

Kabila leaned back from the table and stretched out his arm.

The girl who had poured his drink slid into his lap. She regarded Bagdasarian from beneath hooded lids. Bagdasarian guessed she could have been no older than fourteen. She was beautiful, her eyes so darkly brown they were almost black, but still nearly luminescent. The effect was disquieting. In America she would be a freshman in high school. In Congo-Brazzaville she was the paramour of a corrupt warlord four times her age.

Bagdasarian forced himself to look away.

The sergeant on Kabila's right shut the briefcase and placed it on the floor of the shack underneath the table and at his colonel's feet. Bagdasarian looked around the room. An expensive-looking portable stereo played hip-hop music featuring a French rapper. A bar stood against one wall and a motley collection of bottles sat on it, devoid of import tax stamps. Cigar smoke was thick in the room, and Bagdasarian was surprised to see several of the gendarme officers chewing khat, a narcotic root he had always associated with the Horn of Africa, as well as the more common draggar.

The Armenian placed his hands palm down on the table and pushed himself up. He rose slowly and nodded to the colonel, who didn't bother to return the favor. Bagdasarian looked over at the gendarme who had opened the door. The man's eyes were slits of hate.

Rafik Bagdasarian crossed the room, keenly aware of how many guns were at his back. He placed his hand on the door handle and slowly turned the knob. Coolly he swung it open and stepped out into the falling rain.

*Nigeria*

THE QUONSET HUTS HAD BEEN dropped into the clearing by a Sikorsky helicopter. The cover story had to do with oil exploration for Chevron, which was a prolific presence in the Niger Delta region.

The electronic intelligence for the program hadn't been so lucky.

The four-man team had traveled upriver through snake-, crocodile- and pirate-infested waterways first by motor launch and then for four miles of bush breaking overland.

The satellite relay station was jointly funded through the NSA and the DEA for counterterror and antinarcotics trafficking operations throughout western sub-Saharan Africa. For the most part the marriage between law enforcement and raw intelligence gathering had proved successful.

The most glaring hole in the plan was the lack of a security element. The NSA, unlike its intelligence-gathering counterparts in the Central Intelligence Agency or the Pentagon, preferred a "below the radar" profile to one more centered on firepower.

Calvin Sloke, a six-year electronic-intelligence specialist, swatted a mosquito.

The flying bug was particularly big and had got that

way, Sloke suspected, by helping its vampric self to liberal portions of the American's blood.

"Got you, you son of a bitch!" Sloke shouted in triumph.

The bug was smeared like fruit pulp along his forearm just above his Timex Ironman wristwatch.

"Congratulations," Selene Hoffman replied from behind him.

Her voice was thick with sarcasm. She didn't much like Sloke after six weeks in the cramped quarters and had pretty much given up pretending otherwise.

"Screw you," Sloke replied, voice artificially pleasant.

"In your dreams, dork."

"Quitting smoking sure has done a lot for your personality."

"Sorry my not dying is inconveniencing you."

"Boy, has it."

"Stow the bullshit," Mark Ensign said as he entered the tech center.

The ex-Marine was the only one of the crew who'd been to Africa before, having served time in both Liberia and Somalia as a counterintelligence officer. He still kept in shape with daily routines of calisthenics that made the other techs nauseous just watching him.

"We get our signal today?" he continued.

"Coming up now," Sloke said.

Overhead, in geosynchronous near-earth orbit, a Dong Fang Hong satellite of the People's Republic of China made its daily pass. Like clockwork the Nigeria station would begin signals intercepts, or SIGINT, operations.

This operation, along with digital wiretaps of the satellite and cellular communications networks used by the criminal pipeline that moved cocaine and heroin from Mexico and South America through Africa, up to Armenia and into the European Union, was the primary responsibility of the Nigeria station.

"Where's Dex?" Hoffman asked.

"Getting some rack time," Ensign replied.

Jason Dexter was the hardware and systems engineer assigned to keep all the various highly classified components at the site working and working with each other. After six years with the U.S. Navy and then two more doing the same job with the Department of Defense's Defense Intelligence Agency, he'd been quietly recruited into the Puzzle Palace.

High-strung, type A and nearly anorexic, the specialist was a mission-first workaholic who'd run one marriage into the ground and didn't speak to his children. Despite this, or maybe because of it, he had a reputation as the premier field-operations guy in the Agency.

At that moment the door to the communications station opened and a figure appeared in the doorway, submachine gun held in his hands.

Ensign reached for the metal filing cabinet where he'd placed his holdout, an H&K MP-5. His fingers curled around the smooth metal handle of the drawer.

The figure in the doorway stepped to one side and a second form appeared in the entrance. Hoffman had time to look toward Ensign as he yanked open the drawer and reached inside. Sloke covered his head with his arms.

Ensign lifted the submachine gun, tried to turn as his thumb snapped the fire-selector off safety and onto full auto.

The men in the doorway opened fire.

Bullets streamed through the claustrophobic space in a hailstorm of lead. Rounds chewed through computer screens and electronics equipment, shattering cases and housing like sledgehammers.

Sparks flew in wild rooster tails and miniature columns of smoke spewed upward as shards of plastic and stamped metal ricocheted around.

The cowering Sloke caught a long burst that slammed into him with relentless force, gouging out the flesh of his side and back, shattering his ribs and scrambling his internal organs like eggs in a skillet. He screamed and flopped under the impact until a triple burst of soft-nosed slugs shattered his jaw, cracked his temple and punched two holes through the temporal bone of his skull.

He slumped instantly, banging his head on the tabletop before flopping onto the diamond-plate flooring panels. His blood spilled out like flood waters.

Hoffman rose to her feet in a half crouch, a hapless, helpless, terrified look freezing her face into a mask of fear. Her hands came up as if she could ward off the bullets with such a feeble attempt.

Her left hand lost the pinkie and index finger as the rounds sliced through her. Her right palm blossomed with blood as a round slammed through the muscle under her thumb and lodged in the bones of her wrist.

She opened her mouth to scream and a single round slid into her torso, slicing apart her diaphragm and venting the air in her lungs. She gasped weakly and folded like a lawn chair in time to catch six more bullets across her chest and throat.

The intelligence agent fell backward, her blood splashing her computer screen, and tripped over her chair. She struck the ground like a kid falling out of a tree and gasped, fighting for breath through ruined lungs and larynx.

Her eyes filmed gray in an instant and she fell slack. The oxygen-starved muscles of her abdomen spasmed once and a cascade of dark blood bubbled out of her mouth and streaked her face.

Ensign leveled the H&K, his finger tight on the trigger.

He felt two bullets strike him like the impacts of a base-ball bat, one in his thigh and a second low in his gut. He squeezed the MP-5's trigger and the submachine gun roared to life in his hands.

His rounds sprayed wildly in a loose pattern, most of them burning off harmlessly into the ceiling.

A second burst caught him in the chest and shoulder, smashing him back against the filing cabinet. The kinetic force jerked his arm, and the muzzle of the blazing SMG dropped.

Two rounds struck one of the attackers in his right arm, slicing through the biceps and cracking the humerus bone beneath, while the other sliced a gouge of meat an inch wide off the man's rib cage. The Nigerian killer grunted with the impact and staggered.

The second gunman hosed the ex-Marine down, stitch-ing a line of slugs in a diagonal pattern from hip to neck and unzipping the American's stomach in the process.

Ensign rebounded off the filing cabinet and dropped to his knees, the H&K falling silent. A final burst from the unwounded killer sliced his face off his skull, leaving only a bloody cavity in its place.

The corpse fell forward and struck the ground with a wet slap.

Colonel Kabila stepped into the hut, a bloody panga knife in hand, cigar burning in his mouth.

He looked at his wounded police officer and jerked his head to the side, indicating the man should go.

"Dress your wounds," he ordered, and the man hurried to obey.

Kabila took a deep drag and blew smoke out of his wide nostrils like a dragon. He looked at the other police officer and lifted his panga. The blade of the heavy bush tool was smeared black with blood.

"Get to work," he said.

Twenty yards away Dexter huddled in the bush, hidden from sight.

# CHAPTER SIX

*Suburbs, Washington, D.C.*

The phone rang.

Hal Brognola came awake instantly. The director of the Special Operations Group and head of Stony Man Farm sat up in bed and snapped on the lamp at his bedside table. His wife of some thirty years moaned in protest and rolled away.

The phone rang again.

Getting oriented, the director of America's most sensitive covert operation group looked at the table and tried to determine which of his two phones was ringing. The first phone was his home and it often rang when some matter from his position at the Justice Department needed urgent attention.

The second phone was a Secure Mobile Environment Portable Electronic Device, or SME PED. The combination of sat phone and PDA allowed the wireless transmission of classified information and conversations.

When that phone rang then Brognola knew without question that the call was in reference to the Stony Man program. It would mean that somewhere in the world something had gone very wrong and that a decision had been made at the very highest level that resolution was only to be found at the muzzle of a gun.

The Stony Man teams were the very best guns in the business.

Brognola blinked and phone chirped again. It was the SME PED.

Time to go to work, he thought, and picked up the secured device.

"Go for Hal," he said.

Things started to roll.

*Stony Man Farm*

CARMEN DELAHUNT HAD CQ duty at the Farm.

CQ was a military acronym for "command of quarters" and it simply meant that she had drawn after-hours duty. Despite not having the field teams on any active assignment at that precise moment, Stony Man was still a 24/7 operation and as such the Farm was fully staffed around the clock.

Secure in the Communications Room of the Farm's Annex, the fiery redhead and former FBI agent was monitoring updated intelligence situation reports, military communications traffic and twenty-four-hour cable news channels.

While monitoring all this sensory input, Delahunt casually whipped through page after page of challenging Sudoku puzzles. She was a multitasking machine driven by a sharp, type A personality engine.

On the top of the desk the duty phone blinked into life and then rang. Setting down her coffee cup, she snatched up the receiver.

"Farm," she said. Then, after a pause she continued, "Good morning, Hal."

She cocked a head as the big Fed began talking. Her fingers flew across the keyboard in front of her as she began pulling up the latest information on West Africa in general, the Congo in specific, focusing on the terrorist and criminal operatives in that area and a project known as Lazy Titan.

Satisfied she was up to speed, Brognola hung up in his suburban D.C. home and began getting dressed.

Once off the phone Delahunt made two priority calls, both to other locations on the Stony Man facility. The first was to inform Jack Grimaldi, chief pilot for the covert project, that he was needed ASAP to take a helicopter into Wonderland on the Potomac and ferry Brognola to the Farm.

The second call went to Barbara Price.

BARBARA PRICE, Stony Man's mission controller, opened her eyes.

She awoke clearheaded and alert, knowing exactly where she was and what she needed to do.

There was a war being fought in the shadows and like the ringmaster of a circus, she was at its epicenter. Her eyes went to the window of her bedroom. It was dark outside. She looked over to her bedroom table and noted the glowing red numerals of her digital clock.

She had been asleep for a little over four hours. She sat up and pushed a slender hand through her honey-blond hair. She felt revitalized after her power nap and with a single cup of Aaron "Bear" Kurtzman's coffee she knew she'd be ready to face another day.

She got out of bed and smoothed her clothes before picking up the copy of the *Washington Post* she had placed by her bed. The headline jumped out at her as she stepped out into the upstairs hallway of the Stony Man Farm main house.

Rebel Forces Invade Congo
Late yesterday afternoon the Congo was rocked by

violence as insurgents under command of the infamous Gen. Nkunda took control of a region on the upper river. Human rights groups are worried as communication with the area has been cut off…

Disgusted, Price stopped reading. She had too much on her mind at the moment to worry about politics as usual in Africa.

She frowned. The name "General Nkunda" was unfamiliar. If there was a new player trampling through national playgrounds then she needed to be on top of it. She resolved to have her computer wizard Akira Tokaido see if Stony Man had any files on the man.

As she walked down the hall and took the stairs to the main floor of the farmhouse she began clicking through options and mentally categorizing her tasks. She had men on standby, preparing to go into danger, and like the maestro of a symphony it was her responsibility to coordinate all the disparate parts into a seamless whole.

She was in the basement and heading for the rail system that connected to the Annex when the cell phone on her belt began to vibrate. She plucked it free and used the red push-talk button to initiate the walkie-talkie mode on the encrypted device.

"This is Barb," she said, voice cool.

"Barb," Carmen Delahunt began, "Hal called. We have a situation."

"Thanks, Carmen," Price told the ex-FBI agent. "I'm in the tunnel and coming toward the Annex now."

"See you in a minute," Delahunt said, and signed off.

Price put her phone away and got into the light electric railcar. The little engine began to hum and Price quickly picked up speed as she shot down the one-thousand-foot tunnel sunk fifteen feet below the ground of Virginia's Blue Ridge Mountains.

Things were starting to click, and Price could feel the tingle she had first felt as a mission controller for long-range operations conducted by the National Security Agency. It was there she had made her bones in the intelligence business before being recruited by Hal Brognola to run logistics and support at the more covert Stony Man operation.

It had been quite a promotion, she reflected as the railcar raced down the subterranean tunnel past conduit pipes and thick power cables toward the Farm's Annex, which was camouflaged underneath a commercial wood-chipping facility.

Stony Man had operated as a clandestine antiterrorist operation since long before the infamous attacks of September 11 had put all of America's military, intelligence and law-enforcement efforts on the same page. As such, Stony Man operated as it always had: under the direct control of the White House and separate from both the Joint Special Operations Command and the Directorate of National Intelligence.

Stony Man had been given carte blanche to operate at peak efficiency, eliminating oversights and legalities in the name of pragmatic results. It also, perhaps most importantly, offered the U.S. government the ability to disavow any knowledge of operations that went badly. Sometimes the big picture could provide a very cold and unforgiving snapshot.

This left Stony Man and its operators particularly vulnerable to certain types of exposure. One hint of their existence in a place like MSNBC or the *New York Times* could lead to horrific outcomes.

The electric engine beneath her seat began to power down and the railcar slowed to a halt. She pushed the morose reflections from her mind as she prepared to enter the Annex building.

Things were ready to roll hot; she could not afford to be distracted now. She stood and stepped out of the car. Fluorescent lights gleamed off linoleum floors and a sign on the whitewashed wall read Authorized Personnel Only. Price input the code on the keypad and reached over to open the door to the tunnel.

After passing through the door, she was met by the wheelchair-bound Aaron Kurtzman. The big man reached out a hand the size of a paw and gave her a steaming mug of coffee. She eyed the ink-colored liquid dubiously.

"Thanks, Bear. That's just what I've been missing—something that can put hair on my chest."

The pair of them had exchanged that same greeting so many times it came to feel like a *Groundhog Day* moment. Both took comfort from the repetition.

Kurtzman turned the wheelchair and began to keep pace with the female mission controller as they made for the Communications Room.

The former Big Ten college wrestler lifted a massive arm across a barrel chest and pushed his glasses up on his nose beneath a high forehead with a deep horizontal crease. Price had once teased him that the worry line was severe enough for him to be awarded a Purple Heart.

He'd earned his Ph.D. from the University of Minnesota. He was a Stony Man veteran who had been with the Farm since the beginning, and his wheelchair was a constant testament to his dedication.

"McCarter just called for Phoenix," he said, his voice a low rumble. "They've set up rendezvous with Encizo and James. Carl did the same for Able. They're in place and ready to transport if we need them. They've been informed of the attack on NSA station Lazy Titan and the possibility of a survivor."

"Good," Price said. She took a drink of the strong coffee and pulled a face. "I'll alert Hal, then. All we need is the go-ahead from the President."

The pair entered the massive Communications Room and into a maelstrom of activity. Price paused at the door like a commander surveying her troops. She liked what she saw.

Kurtzman glided over to his work area, where it looked as if a bomb had gone off. His desk was covered in faxes, paperwork and the exposed wiring of half a dozen devices. Next to his desk, fingers flying across a laptop while monitoring a sat com link, Akira Tokaido bobbed his head in time to the music coming from a single earphone. The lean, compact hacker was the youngest member of Stony Man's cybernetics team and the heir apparent to Kurtzman himself. The Japanese-American cyberpunk had at times worked virtual magic when Price had needed him to.

Across the room from Tokaido sat his polar opposite.

Professor Huntington Wethers had come to the Stony Man operations from his position on the faculty of UCLA. The tall, distinguished black man sported gray hair at his temples and an unflappable manner.

He currently worked two laptop screens as a translation program fed him information from monitored radio traffic coming out of France.

Carmen Delahunt walked through the door of the Communications Room. The ex-FBI agent made a beeline for Barbara Price when she saw her boss. The only female on the Farm's cyberteam, she served as a pivotal balance between Tokaido's hotshot hacking magic and Wethers's more restrained, academic style.

She finished her conversation and snapped her cell

phone shut as she walked up to Price. She pointed toward the newspaper in the mission controller's hand.

"Since we're on West Africa anyway you see the article about the new Congo player, General Nkunda?" she asked. "I started running an analytical of our files on that movement and him in particular."

Price smiled. "You read my mind, Carmen," she said. "Once we have Phoenix and Able taken care of, why don't you send me a summary in case anything comes of it."

"Will do." Delahunt nodded. "I have to double-check the South American arraignments we made for the team's extraction with the 'package'—if it comes to that. It's nice to be able to tap the resources of larger groups like the Pentagon's Joint Special Operations Command, but coordination is a nightmare."

"Let me know if anything goes wrong," Price said.

Delahunt nodded, then turned and began walking back across the floor toward the connecting door to the Annex's Computer Room, her fingers punching out a number on her encrypted cell phone.

Barbara Price smiled.

She could feel the energy, the sense of *purpose* that permeated the room, flow into her. Out there in the cold, eight men on two teams were about to enter into danger for the sake of their country. If they got into trouble, if they needed anything, they would turn to her and her people.

She did not intend to let them down.

She made her way to her desk, where a light flashing on her desktop phone let her know a call was holding. She looked over at Kurtzman and saw the man returning a telephone handset to its cradle. He pointed toward her.

"It's Hal on line one," he said.

"Thanks, Bear," she answered.

She set her coffee down and picked up the handset as she sank into her chair. She put the phone to her ear and tapped a key on her computer, knocking the screen off standby mode.

"Hal, it's Barb," she said.

"I'm outside the Oval Office right now," Brognola said. "Are the boys up and rolling?"

"As we speak," Price answered. "Tell him operations are prepped to launch at his word."

"All right. Let's hope this one goes by the numbers," the gruff federal agent said.

"As always," she agreed, and hung up.

"All right, people," she announced to the room. "Let's get ready to roll."

*Nairobi, Kenya*

PHOENIX FORCE MET UP in the capital and transferred to the Sikorsky MH-53 Pave Low helicopter. To them their mission was simple: go in and find a lone American survivor of a brutal attack. It didn't matter that an entire army of heavily armed insurgents had taken him into a city turned into a hellish fortress.

They would proceed, always moving forward.

FOR ABLE TEAM THE MISSION evolved in a more circumspect manner.

In the back of the Lear jet taking them to the Farm the three-man team relaxed, unwinding from the mission. Thirty minutes into the flight, Stony Man pilot Jack Grimaldi opened the cockpit door.

"I got Barb on secure communications," he told them. "I don't think you guys are going home yet."

"Perfect," Blancanales said, laughing.

*Nicaragua*

ABLE TEAM'S PLAN WAS simple.

They would come in on a commercial flight and make it through customs clean. Following that, they would pick up a vehicle and make their way to a safehouse used by a joint CIA and Army Special Operations Intelligence Support Activity operation to establish a base before starting surveillance of the target.

Things began to go wrong immediately.

Carl Lyons pulled his carry-on bag down from the overhead compartment just after the Unfasten Seat Belts sign popped up on the TWA commercial flight. They were flying first-class as part of their administrative cover, and the team leader had watched, bemused, as Blancanales had seduced the Hispanic flight attendant with his gregarious charm.

Team funnyman Hermann Schwarz had cracked one stale joke after another as the silver-haired smooth-talker had reaffirmed his membership in the mile-high club thirty thousand feet over the Caribbean with a dark-eyed Nicaraguan beauty half his age.

In a more regulation-orientated unit such behavior as stand-up sex in an airplane restroom would have been a scandalous breach of operational security, one that a team leader like Lyons would have had to treat severely as a discipline issue.

Not so in the shadowy world in which Able Team operated. Now there wasn't a person on the plane among the crew or passengers who didn't think the three men were anything but what they claimed; middle-aged divorced tourists on a Central American vacation. Blancanales's audacity was role-playing brilliance.

If there was anything bothering Lyons as he exited the plane after the flight attendant had slipped her cell number to Blancanales, it was that circumstances dictated they roll into the opening moves of the operation unarmed. Carl Lyons didn't like taking a shower unarmed, let alone enter a potentially volatile nation without a weapon.

"Okay," Schwarz murmured as they came into the big, air-conditioned terminal, "we can add a certain TWA flight attendant named Bonita to our roster of Stony Man local assets."

"Oh, yeah," Lyons replied. "I'm sure she'll be a big help. We can just send David and his boys down here sometime and they can all crash at her hacienda. It'll be like the Farm South."

"You see how it is, Gadgets?" Blancanales said, voice weary. "You try to take one for the team and management doesn't appreciate it. I try to show loyalty through service and all I get is cynical pessimism."

"Oh, buddy," Schwarz replied, voice dry as south Texas wind, "you just got a lot more on you than cynical pessimism."

"Yes," Blancanales replied seriously. "Yes, I did."

"Can you gentlemen come this way?"

The voice interrupted their banter with the certainty of undisputed authority. Able Team turned their heads as one to take in the speaker. He was a tall Latino with jet-black hair, mustache and eyes and was wearing the crisp uniform of a Nicaraguan customs officer. There was a 9 mm automatic pistol in a polished holster on his hip but the flap was closed and secured.

However, a few paces behind him the assault rifles of

the military security guards were right out and open as the soldiers stood with hands on pistol grips and fingers resting near triggers.

Lyons scowled. Schwarz gave the officer his best grin in reply to the summons. Then he turned his head slightly and whispered to Blancanales out of the side of his mouth, "Any chance you want to take one for the team now?"

Blancanales fixed an insincere grin of his own on his face. "Nope. This time we move right to cynical pessimism," he replied. He turned to face the stern uniformed officer, face suddenly serious. "This isn't about that flight attendant, is it?"

# CHAPTER SEVEN

Nicaraguan customs separated the three men quickly, hustling them into separate rooms. There they sat, isolated, for two hours. Carl Lyons found himself sitting in front of a plain metal table on an uncomfortable folding chair while the customs officer pretended to read official-looking papers he'd taken from a blue folder with a government seal at the top.

Fluent in Spanish, Lyons easily read the pages he set on the tabletop and saw that they were merely quarterly flight maintenance reports being used as props. Warily, Lyons decided to relax a bit; this seemed a more random occurrence than he had first feared. The Farm had considerable resources, but the operation was minuscule compared to other government agencies and Stony Man operatives were often forced to rely on logistical support from larger bureaucratic entities. Whenever that happened, security became a prime concern, but for now this seemed a more typical customs roust than anything more threatening.

The officer, whose name tag read Garcia, picked up Lyons's passport with his free hand and opened it. "Mr. Johnson?" His English was accented but clipped and neat.

Lyons nodded. "That's me."

Garcia regarded him over the top of the little blue folder. "What brings you to Nicaragua?"

"Sunny weather, beautiful women, the beaches. All the usual. Is there a problem with my passport?"

The customs agent carefully put the blue folder down. He ignored the question and tapped the passport with one long, blunt-tipped finger. "There are many countries in Central America with beautiful beaches and women."

"But only one San Hector Del Sur—it's world famous," Lyons replied in flawless Spanish, referencing Nicaragua's most popular tourist destination.

Garcia's eyes flicked upward sharply at the linguistic display. His eyes looked past Lyons and toward the large reflective glass Lyons knew from his own experience as a police officer was where the customs officer's superiors were watching the interrogation. Garcia let his gaze settle back on Lyons. He offered a wan smile.

"I'm sure this is just an administrative error," the officer said. "My people will have it sorted out in no time." Garcia rose to his feet. "Please be patient."

"Okay." Lyons nodded agreeably. "But, man, am I getting thirsty."

GARCIA LEFT LYONS and walked toward the interrogation room containing Hermann Schwarz. As he moved down the hallway he saw the tall, cadaverous figure in a dark suit standing off behind his commanding officer. The man met Garcia's gaze with cold, dead eyes, and the Nicaraguan customs officer felt a chill at the base of his spine. What was *he* doing here? Garcia wondered. He stifled the thought quickly—it didn't pay to ask too many questions about the internal security organization, even to yourself.

As he entered the room he saw a burly sergeant had Schwarz pinned up against the wall, one beefy forearm across the American's throat. The officer was scowling in fury as Schwarz, going by the name Miller, smirked.

Schwarz looked over at Garcia as the man entered and grinned. "Hey, Pedro," he called. "You know why this guy's wife never farted as a little girl? 'Cause she didn't have an asshole till she got married!"

The sergeant rotated and dipped the shoulder of his free hand. His fist came up from the hip and buried itself in Schwarz's stomach. The Stony Man operative absorbed the blow passively and let himself crumple at the man's feet. He looked up from the floor, gasping for breath.

Schwarz looked at Garcia. "You know what this *pendejo's* most confusing day is? Yep—Father's Day."

His cackling was cut off as the sergeant kicked him in the ribs. Garcia snapped an order and reluctantly the man backed off. "Leave us!" he repeated, and the officer left the room scowling.

Garcia moved forward and dropped Schwarz's passport on the table. He looked down as the American fought his way back up to his feet. Garcia watched dispassionately as the man climbed into his chair.

"This is a hell of a country you got here, pal," Schwarz said. "Tell a few jokes and get the shit kicked out of you. I should get a lawyer and sue your ass."

"You'll find Nicaraguan courts unsympathetic to ugly Americans, Mr. Miller."

"Yeah, well, your momma's so fat when she walks her butt claps."

"Why have you come to Nicaragua, Mr. Miller?"

"I heard a guy could get a drink. I think it was a lie. Seriously, I'm here with some buddies to check out the sites, maybe see the senoritas on San Hector Del Sur, but instead I get this?"

"Perhaps you shouldn't insult my officers?"

"Perhaps you shouldn't lock an innocent *turista* up for two hours in a room with a trained monkey like that asshole."

Garcia sighed heavily, a weary man with an odious task.

"I'm sure this is just an administrative error. We'll have it sorted out shortly."

"You're damn well right you will," Schwarz snapped, playing his role to the hilt.

"In the meantime perhaps you could refrain from antagonizing my officers? Yes?"

"Hey, Pedro—is that your stomach or did you just swallow a beach ball?"

Officer Garcia turned and walked out of the room, studiously ignoring the thin man standing outside in the hall next to the doorway.

"Hey, who do ya have to screw to get a drink around here?" Schwarz demanded as the door swung closed.

From behind the two-way mirror the thin man watched him with inscrutable curiosity.

As CUSTOMS OFFICER Garcia entered the final interrogation room, Blancanales, whose own passport was made out under the name of Rosario, rose from his seat, manner eager and face twisted into a mask of hopeful supplication.

"Listen," he began babbling, "I'm really, really, *really* sorry about what happened on the plane. I know I should have waited till I got to San Hector Del Sur but this is my first vacation in years and I guess I got carried—"

"Shut up and sit down!" Garcia snapped. "Yes, I know, I know. You are all here innocently. You are all planning to go to San Hector Del Sur, you are all thirsty and need a drink because you are just typical ugly American's here to screw our women and drink tequila!"

Face frozen in a look of sheepish innocence, Blancanales settled back in his chair. He blinked his eyes several times. "Well, er, I guess…yeah."

Face red, Garcia spun on a heel and tossed the blue passport on the table in disgust. He left the room and slammed

the door behind him so hard it rattled in its frame. Blancanales called after him, "Actually, I am kind of thirsty,
amigo."

OUT IN THE HALLWAY Garcia marched up to his superior,
who stood waiting next to the thin man in civilian clothes.
"Sir, their paperwork checks out. Everything checks out
perfectly. They've obviously rehearsed their story—or it's
the truth. Should I toss them in a holding cell?"

   "That won't be necessary," the thin man said. "Let them
go. Apologize for the mistake, wish them well."

   Garcia slid his gaze over to his commanding officer,
who glanced over at the man next to him, then nodded.
"Yes, we have enough. Let them go."

*Brazzaville, Republic of the Congo*

THE ROTORS OF THE Blackhawk helicopter were still turning slowly as the side door to the cargo bay opened and
the men Colonel Kabila had been sent to greet emerged.
He surveyed them with a critical eye, noting the athletic
physiques, flat affects and nonregulation weaponry hanging
off their ballistic armor and black fatigues.

   Kabila had seen enough special operations soldiers in
his life to recognize the type, French, American, British.
As much as they might have liked to think otherwise,
nationality mattered little—the elite always had more in
common with each other than even with others of their own
country or military. Kabila was wise and realistic enough
to know he himself did not belong among their ranks. It
was no matter of ego for him; his interests lay in other
directions.

   At the moment it remained focused on gaining these
mysterious commandos' trust, leading them into hostile

terrain beyond the reach of help, and then betraying them—
making himself a little wealthier in the process.

The first man to reach Kabila was tall and broad with
fox-faced features and brown eyes and hair. Having spent
the past five years operating alongside British forces in
Brazzaville the rebel police officer recognized an Englishman even before he spoke and revealed his accent.

"You Kabila?" David McCarter asked.

Kabila nodded, noting the man did not identify either
himself or his unit. Behind the Briton his team paused: a
tall black man with cold eyes, a stocky Hispanic with a
fireplug build and scarred forearms standing next to a truly
massive individual with shoulders like barn doors and an
M-60E cut-down machine gun.

Behind the tight little group another individual, as tall
and muscular as the rest, turned and surveyed the windows
and rooftops of the buildings overlooking the secured helipad. There was a sniper-scoped Mk-11 with a paratrooper
skeletal folding stock in his hands. The eyepieces on the
telescopic sight popped up to reveal an oval peep sight
glowing a dim green.

"We were briefed on the flight in," McCarter continued.
"You get us past the Congolese security checkpoints and
militia crossings until we're within striking distance, then
fall back with the reserve force should we need backup."

"Just so." Kabila nodded. "I'm surprised you agreed to
having only Congolese forces as overwatch. Did you work
with us in Brazzaville before?" The question was casually
voiced but still constituted a breach of etiquette in such
situations.

"Has there been a change in the situation since our initial
briefing?" the black man asked, cutting in.

Kabila turned to face Calvin James, noting the H&K
MP-7 submachine gun dangling from a sling off his shoulders down the front of his black fatigue shirt. In his big,

scarred hands the man casually cradled a SPAS-15 dual-mode combat shotgun. Its stock was folded down so that he held it by the pistol grip and forestock just beyond the detachable drum-style magazine.

Just as with the rest of them, Kabila saw the man's black fatigues bore no unit insignia, name tag or rank designation. His voice was flatly American, however, the accent bearing just a trace, perhaps of the Midwest, but he couldn't be sure.

The Congolese pretended not to notice the pointed disregarding of his own indelicate question. Behind the team the Blackhawk's engines suddenly changed pitch and began to whine as the helicopter lifted off.

Kabila shook his head to indicate no to the black man's questions, then waved his hand toward the APC parked on the edge of the helipad's concrete apron. The Dzik-3 was a multipurpose armored car made in Poland and used by Congolese army and police units throughout the country.

The 4.5-ton wheeled vehicle boasted bulletproof windows, body armor able to withstand 7.62 mm rounds, puncture-proof tires and smoke launchers. T. J. Hawkins, covering the unit's six as they made for the APC, thought it looked like a dun-colored Brink's truck and doubted it could withstand the new special penetration charges currently being used as roadside improvised explosive devices. He would have felt a lot safer in an American Stryker or the Cougar Armored Fighting Vehicle.

He was used to stark pragmatism, however, and made no comment as he scrambled inside the vehicle, carefully protecting his sniper scope. Despite the rotation of special operations soldiers through Stony Man, the exact nature of the Farm and its teams remained clandestine in the covert community. There were enough special-access programs floating around the intelligence and military establishments performing overlapping and complementary missions that the true carte blanche under which Hal Brognola's Sensitive Operations Group conducted business was greatly obfuscated.

It had been easier to coordinate a blacked-out operation through local Congolese forces than to bring international authorities operating in the Brazzaville theater in on the loop because the deployment had been so frenzied. Hawkins accepted the situation without complaint.

Inside the armored vehicle the team sat crammed together, muzzles up toward the ceiling. Rafael Encizo sat behind the driver's seat holding a Hawk MM-1 multiround 40 mm grenade launcher. As Kabila settled in the front passenger seat beside his driver, he looked back at the heavily armed crew with a frown.

"I am in charge of my vehicle during transport and thus am commanding officer for this phase of the operation," he said, voice grave. "I'm afraid I'm going to have to insist that you put your weapon safeties on."

McCarter leaned forward, shifting his M-4/M-203 combo to one side as he did, the barrel passing inches from Kabila's face. He held up his trigger finger in front of the Congolese colonel's face and smiled coldly.

"Sorry, mate," he said. "I know you've heard this before but—" he wiggled his trigger finger back in forth in front of Kabila's eyes "—*this* is my safety." He settled back into his seat. "End of story."

Kabila turned around, face gray with fury. He slapped the dash of the vehicle and curtly ordered his driver to pull away from the tarmac of the helipad. As the vehicle rolled out into traffic he forced himself to calm. It was as the old African proverb, claimed by the English as their own, said: who laughs last laughs best, and Colonel Kabila planned to be laughing very hard indeed at the end of the next few hours.

PHOENIX FORCE REMAINED alert as the Dzik-3 left the main traffic thoroughfares surrounding the airport and pushed deeper into the city. They rolled through Congolese national army and police checkpoints without a problem, but as the buildings grew more congested and run-down and the signs of the recent civil conflicts became more prolific—in the form of bullet-riddled walls, the charred hulks of burned-out vehicles, gaping window frames and missing doors—so did flags and graffiti proclaiming rebel slogans and allegiance.

Now the checkpoints were manned by local force police officers who all wore subtle indicators of tribal allegiance in conjunction with their official uniforms. Phoenix Force was entering a section of the city where centralized authority had lost its influence and clan leaders and tribal warlords were the de facto power structures.

The checkpoint stops became longer and the night grew deeper. In the backseat Gary Manning used a GPS-program-enhanced PDA to plot their course as they moved through the city. After a moment he froze the screen and leaned forward to tap McCarter on the shoulder. "We're here," he said.

McCarter nodded and looked out a side window. They had entered an era of urban blight forming a squalid industrial bridge between two more heavily populated sections of the city. The dull brown waters of the Niger River cut through concrete banks lined with empty and burned-out factories, manufacturing plants and abandoned electrical substations. A rusting crane sat in a weed-choked parking lot like a forgotten Jurassic beast of steel and iron.

"Pull over," McCarter told Kabila.

The man looked back in confusion. "What—we still have two more checkpoints to go before the rendezvous point," he protested.

"Pull over. We have our own ops plan." McCarter repeated. "When we give the signal, you and the chase vehicle can meet us at the RP. We'll insert on foot from here."

"This isn't what I was told—" Kabila sputtered.

"Pull over."

Kabila scowled, then barked an order to his driver, who immediately guided the big 4.5-ton vehicle over to the side of the road. They rolled to a stop and Phoenix Force wasted little time scurrying out of the vehicle, weapons up.

Before he slammed the door shut, McCarter repeated his instructions to the Congolese police officer. "Get to the RP. Link up with the chase vehicle and hold position as instructed. When I come across the radio we'll be shaking ass out of the AO so expect hot. Understood?"

Kabila nodded. His face was impassive as he replied, "I understand perfectly, Englishman."

"Good," McCarter answered, and slammed the Dzik-3's door closed.

As soon as the man was gone Kabila had his cell phone out. He could feel his laughter forming in his belly and he bit it down. He'd save it for when he was looking at the bloody corpses of the Western commandos.

*Managua, Nicaragua*

ABLE TEAM STEPPED OUT into the equatorial sunlight from the cramped depths of the customs station on the far side of the international airport. Hermann Schwarz's eye was swollen slightly and he had a bemused look as he used a free hand to rub at his sore ribs.

He turned toward Lyons, who was squinting momentarily against the hard yellow light of the sun. "Next time *you* play the asshole," he said.

Blancanales chuckled to himself. "It does come more natural to you," he pointed out.

Lyons shrugged and slid on his shades. He stood in the doorway of the customs station and smiled. "Quick, use your cell phone to take a picture of me."

Pretending to laugh along with the joke like ugly American tourists, Blancanales quickly opened his Samsung cell phone and thumbed on the video function. He started rolling, capturing the scene.

Immediately he saw a cadaverous man in a business suit watching them from beside their interrogator as he pointed the camera over Lyons's bulky shoulder. The man frowned as he saw the Americans taking pictures, and then he turned and walked away.

"Something to remember Managua by," Schwarz said loudly.

"Oh, that was great acting," Lyons muttered, walking forward.

"Thank you. Thank you very much."

"Did you get it?" Lyons asked.

"You mean, tall, skinny and corpse-looking?" Blancanales asked. "You betcha. I'll see what Aaron's crew can do with it." He hit a button and fired off the short video clip to a secure server service that would eventually feed it into Stony Man.

*Stony Man Farm, Virginia*

THE EMAIL TRAVELED with digital speed through security links and into Carmen Delahunt's computer. Seeing the priority message beeping an alert, she quickly raised her sensory-glove-encased hand to her left and pantomimed clicking on the link with a finger. Inside the screen of her VR uplink helmet the short cell phone video played out.

"Just got something from Pol," she said. "They want an ID on what appears to be a civilian who's buddy-buddy with Nicaraguan law-enforcement officials."

From behind her in the Annex's Computer Room Aaron Kurtzman's gruff voice instructed, "Send it over to Hunt's station. His link to the Roadrunner is more configured to that kind of search than your infiltration and investigation research algorithms."

The head of the Stony Man cyberteam referred to the blade farm IBM Roadrunner supercomputer used as the primary workhorse of the Farm. The IBM Roadrunner was considered the fastest supercomputer in the world, though Kurtzman, much like the NSA, preferred using a Blue Gene/L archetype for defensive counterhacking operations. The Stony Man Roadrunner model was every bit as efficient as the one in Las Alamos Laboratories, provided them digital espionage options equal to any agency in the American government or overseas.

Tapping the stem of a briarwood pipe against his teeth, Professor Huntington Wethers froze the video image on a single shot, then transported it to a separate program designed to identify the anatomical features on the picture then translate them into a succinct binary code. He ran the program four times to include variables for age, angle and articulation, then ran a blending-sum algorithm to predict changes for bad photography, low light and resolution obscurity. He grunted softly before firing off double emails of the completed project, one back to Carmen Delahunt and the other to Akira Tokaido.

"There you go," Wethers said. "I would suggest simultaneous phishing with a wide-base server like Interpol and something more aimed, like Nicaraguan intelligence."

"Dibs on Nicaraguan intel," Tokaido called out.

The youngest member of the Stony Man cyberteam

slouched in his chair using only his fingertips to control the mouse pads on two separate laptops.

"That's just crap," Delahunt replied. "I already have a trapdoor built into Interpol. Dad, Akira's stealing all the fun stuff!"

"Children, behave," Kurtzman growled. "Or I'll make you do something really boring like checking CIA open agency sources like your uncle Hunt is doing."

"Your coffeepot is empty, Bear," Wethers replied, voice droll.

"What?" Kurtzman sat up in his wheelchair and twisted around to look at the coffeemaker set behind his workstation. To his relief he saw the pot was still half full of the jet-black liquid some claimed flowed through his veins instead of blood.

"Every time, Bear. I get you every time," Wethers chided.

"That's because some things aren't funny," Kurtzman said. "I expect such antics from a kid like Akira, but you're an esteemed professor, for God's sake. I expect you to comport yourself with decorum."

"Brother Bear," Wethers said, his fingers flying across his keyboard, "if you ever did run out of coffee you'd just grind the beans in your mouth."

"Bear drinks so much coffee," Delahunt added, her hands still wildly pantomiming through her VR screen, "that Hector Valdez named his donkey after him."

"Bear drinks so much coffee he answers the door before people knock," Tokaido added. He appeared to be hardly moving at his station, which meant he was working at his most precise.

Stony Man mission controller Barbara Price walked into the Computer Room just in time to catch Tokaido's comment. Without missing a beat the honey-blonde former NSA operations officer added a quip of her own.

"Bear drinks so much coffee he hasn't blinked since the last lunar eclipse."

Kurtzman coolly lifted a meaty hand and gave a thumbs-down gesture. Deadpan, he blew the assembled group a collective raspberry. "Get some new material—those jokes are stale, people."

"Bear drinks so much coffee it never has a chance to get stale," Delahunt said calmly. She tapped the air in front of her with a single finger and added; "Ortega, Dan—"

"Daniel," Tokaido simultaneously chorused with the redheaded ex-FBI agent.

"Of the General Counterintelligence Agency," Wethers finished for them. All humor was gone from his voice now. "The Nicaraguan military intelligence agency."

Sensing the tension immediately, Price turned toward Kurtzman. "What does this mean for Able?"

Kurtzman pursed his lips and sighed. "Trouble."

# CHAPTER EIGHT

*Brazzaville, Republic of the Congo*

Phoenix Force became as ghosts.

They crossed the rubble of the abandoned parking lot until they could squat in the lee of a burned-out warehouse. Hawkins, who had perfected his long-range shooting as a member of the U.S. Army's premier hostage rescue unit, scanned their back trail through his night scope. The other four members of the team clicked their AN/PVS-14 monocular night-vision devices over their nonshooting eye.

McCarter waited patiently in the concealed position for his natural night vision to acclimate as much as possible before moving out. A stray dog, ribs visible under a mangy hide, strayed close at one point but skittered off in fear after catching the scent of gun oil.

The group maintained strict noise discipline as they waited to see if they had been observed or compromised during the short scramble to their staging area. After a tense ten minutes McCarter signaled a generic all clear and rose into a crouch. He touched James on the shoulder and sent the ex-Navy SEAL across the parking lot toward a break in a battered old chain-link fence next to a pock-marked cinder-block wall.

James crossed the open area in a low, tight crouch, running hard. He slid into place and snapped up the SPAS-15 to provide cover. Once he was satisfied, he turned back to McCarter and gave the former SAS commando a single nod.

McCarter reached out and touched Encizo on the shoulder, and the veteran combat swimmer sprinted for the far side of the lot, his dense, heavily muscled frame handling the weight of the Hawk MM-1 easily. He slid into position behind James and swept the squat, cannon-muzzled grenade launcher into security overwatch.

McCarter leaned over and whispered into Hawkins's ear, "You go after me."

Hawkins nodded and flipped down the hinged lens covers on the scope of his Mk-11 Enhanced Battle Rifle. He took up the EBR in both hands and slid up to the edge of the wall while Gary Manning took his place on rear security, using the cut-down M-60E machine gun to maintain rear security.

McCarter checked once with Encizo then slid the fire-selector switch on his M-4 to burst mode. There was a fléchette pack antipersonnel round loaded in the tube of his M-203 grenade launcher and he had attached an M-9 bayonet just after entering his forward staging area. He got a second clear signal from Encizo and immediately sprang forward.

He covered the distance fast, feet pounding on the busted concrete with staccato rhythm, then quickly slid into position behind Encizo. The muzzle of his weapon came up and tracked left to right, clearing sectors including rooftops with mechanical proficiency.

Satisfied, he turned and caught Calvin James's eye. He made a subtle pointing gesture with his left hand, and the ex-SEAL turned the corner and scurried between the break in the fence next to the cinder-block wall. As soon as he was gone, McCarter slapped Encizo on the shoulder and the former anti-Castro militant followed James through the opening.

McCarter scurried up to take his post next to the breach and then gave Hawkins the all clear signal. The man raced across the parking lot with his weapon up and plunged through the opening to disappear behind the bullet-riddled wall.

McCarter waited a moment, giving Hawkins a chance to take a good position beyond the wall, then waved Gary Manning over. Trusting McCarter to cover him, the Canadian special operations soldier took up his machine gun and crossed the danger area.

Once Manning was past, McCarter scrambled backward through the opening, remaining orientated toward the open parking lot the team had just crossed, carbine up and ready.

On the other side of the breach he found the unit in a tight defensive circle. A single-story outbuilding lay inside a concrete enclosure. A metal placard in red and white showed the universal sign for electrical danger above black French script. McCarter looked at Hawkins, who immediately moved to lie down and take up a position in the breach.

Gary Manning set his machine gun down and quickly opened the Velcro flap of a pouch on his web belt. He pulled an electrician's diagnostic kit from the container while Rafael Encizo pulled a pair of compact bolt cutters from the field pack on his back.

"Right, mate," McCarter whispered, "don't electrocute yourself, then."

Manning didn't look up as he quickly assembled his gear. "Do I tell you how to act like a complete jackass?"

"Not once," McCarter admitted, but the corner of his mouth crept upward.

"Then perhaps you can let me do my job wisecrack-free?"

"Not a chance, mate," McCarter replied with complete seriousness. "Your ego's already too well developed for my liking."

Manning looked steadily at McCarter for a moment, then nodded toward Encizo. "Ready."

Encizo quickly used the bolt cutters to snap the locking arm of the rusted old padlock connecting the panel access doors. The muscles on his forearms jumped out in stark relief next to his elbow and ran in cables down to thick wrists. The lock popped free with a sharp crack and dropped to the lens at his feet. Encizo picked up his MM-1 and scooted quickly back.

James helped him stow the bolt cutters as Manning replaced Encizo in front of the access panel. He reached up and pulled the metal hatches apart to reveal a wall of exposed wires, relay switches and conduit housings.

From behind them Hawkins suddenly hissed a low warning.

McCarter instantly moved to his side and sidled down low to present a minimal profile as he eased around the corner. Beside him the former Army Ranger lay his finger in the gentle curve of his trigger, taking up the slack. Out on the parking lot a dry wind pushed dead weeds and loose trash around. The area was an island of dark between two better lit areas of population so the headlights of the approaching vehicles were easily visible.

Hawkins lay the scope on the convoy, quickly working the dampener on his light amplifier to compensate for the brilliant illumination of the vehicle's high beams. The images of the Congolese police squad in three Dzik-3 armored personnel carriers filled the crosshair of his reticule. M-2 .50-caliber machine guns were mounted on the roofs of the APCs.

"Who are those guys?" McCarter demanded. "That wanker Kabila's boys? This isn't part of the plan."

Hawkins carefully zeroed in his scope and scanned the crew as they parked their vehicle patrol in a wedge formation facing the abandoned warehouse Phoenix Force had used to shield their initial movements after disembarking from the first wheeled APC minutes earlier.

"They're police for sure," Hawkins answered. His voice was grim. "But to a man they're loaded for bear." He removed his eye from the sniper scope and looked over at the former SAS commando. "David, looks like Kabila went and got some reinforcements and came back. Looks like a double cross."

"Bloody hell!" McCarter swore.

*Managua, Nicaragua*

"GODDAMN IT TO HELL!" Lyons swore. "We're in-country ten minutes and we've got their head spook nosing up our asses."

His big hand slammed the steering wheel of the rental SUV, a black Ford Excursion. His eyes darted to the rearview mirror, scanning the flow of traffic behind the automobile for any obvious tails or suspicious patterns. Managua was a teeming, modern city of almost two million people and the streets around the unit were packed with automobiles, motorcycles, service trucks and pedestrians. Around them office buildings rose in prototypical urban canyons. They would have to be sharp if they were going to spot a surveillance team in that kind of environment.

"At least the Farm was able to get us the information quickly," Schwarz pointed out as he slipped his PDA into a pocket. "It'd be much worse if we weren't aware *el douche* was hot on our ass."

"Having Nicaraguan internal security meeting us right there at the airport is a bad, bad sign," Blancanales said.

He sat in the backseat and was using a PDA of his own to download a software upgrade created by Schwarz into the vehicle's indigenous GPS system. "Something got SNA-FUed right from the beginning."

"We can't roll on the agent till we get to the safehouse," Lyons said. "But we can't lead a team of secret police right to a U.S. safehouse, either. Freakin' fine mess."

"I guess we have to identify the shadow unit, then out-drive them." Schwarz shrugged his shoulders. "I mean, the CIA does everything the CIA can do. The Farm does what the CIA can't."

"Or the FBI," Blancanales agreed. He caught Schwarz's eye in the rearview mirror and winked. "Or the LAPD," he added, voice casual.

Lyons, an ex-LAPD detective, stiffened in response to the inclusion. "Finest police force in the world. You can go to hell. Only reason I left is because SOG has a better dental plan."

"No, no. This is true," Schwarz said. "Absolutely. In fact, if you were to do an unbiased comparison of the three organizations I would say it's obvious the LAPD comes out on top." His voice was completely deadpan as he continued. "This is a no-bullshit story, heard it right from the big Fed, Hal himself. The LAPD, the FBI and the CIA were all trying to prove that they are the best at apprehending criminals. The President decided to give them a test. He released a rabbit into a forest and each of them had to try to catch it.

"The CIA goes in. They place animal informants throughout the forest. They question all plant and mineral witnesses. After three months of extensive investigations they concluded that rabbits do not exist.

"Then the FBI goes in. After two weeks with no leads they burn the forest, killing everything in it, including the rabbit, and they make no apologies. The rabbit had it coming.

"The LAPD goes in. They come out two hours later with a badly beaten bear. The bear is yelling, 'Okay! Okay! I'm a rabbit! I'm a rabbit!'"

"Ten will get you one that bear had done *something,*" Lyons snapped back as his two teammates laughed.

Instantly, Hermann Schwarz stopped laughing. "Pol, does that qualify as an actual joke from the Ironman?"

"Close enough, as far as I'm concerned," Blancanales replied in a sober voice, sounding slightly bewildered.

"Screw you both," Lyons replied. He then promptly ran a red light. "Got the bastards! Green current-year Impala, looks like three of them in the rig."

Blancanales turned and quickly looked over his shoulder. "I got 'em. Looks like three in the vehicle," he repeated. There was a sudden blare of horns, squealing brakes and a chorus of angry shouts around them in the intersection. "They just ran the red, too," Blancanales added.

"We're on now," Schwarz said. "Of course, if we actively lose these ass clowns, then they'll know we're up to something and we'll have to go completely black instead of trying to maintain cover."

"Good," Lyons muttered, and pushed the accelerator to the floor. "I was getting goddamn tired of all the bullshit sneaking around we've been doing."

"Oh, yeah, we've been real below the radar." Schwarz smirked. Then he put his seat belt on.

*Brazzaville, Republic of the Congo*

DAVID MCCARTER SCOOTED quickly backward, leaving Hawkins in his low-profile overwatch position. Once away from the opening, he turned to check on the rest of the team's progress. Manning was coolly using a stylus to work the touch pad on his diagnostic server.

"How we coming, mate?" McCarter asked.

"More time," Manning replied.

"We kind of have company."

"Look, I've got to uplink this substation to the urban power grid, then trace the connection to our neighborhood. *Then* I can shut out the lights. I need more time."

"Right." McCarter turned to the rest of his men. "Enciso, get into position next to Hawkins. If T.J. decides he needs to take a shot, I want you to bring the noise."

"Copy." Encizo nodded. The Cuban lifted the MM-1 grenade launcher and slid in next to the prone ex-Delta Force sniper.

McCarter lifted his left hand and pointed at Calvin James. "We're advancing the plan by ten minutes," he said. "I want you to open the sewer entrance right now and hold the position until we can get Manning through this sabotage gig."

"They're rolling this way." Encizo spoke up for Hawkins. "Moving slow, but it seems obvious they're spooked and looking for something, not just patrolling."

McCarter turned back to the massive Canadian. "Gary?"

"Need time."

"Right, then." He twisted around. "Hold the line," McCarter instructed Encizo, who leaned over and relayed the information to Hawkins. The Phoenix Force leader turned toward James and nodded once.

The ex-Navy SEAL rose into a crouch and glided into

the narrow space between the relay station Manning was working on and the cinder-block wall that encircled the work area. McCarter heard the whisper of cloth and leather on the concrete, then James was over the top of the far wall and gone, disappearing into the night.

James hit the ground on the other side of the wall, his boots making a crunch on the loose gravel as he landed. He was in a small access alley running behind a line of empty buildings. At one end of the lane a worn and deteriorated industrial wharf jutted out into the Niger River waterway. In the distance the lights of a garbage scow moved slowly away, gulls circling it, their night cries sharp against the low rumble of its engine.

James swung around to look the other way. He let the SPAS-15 dangle from his strap and pulled a silenced Beretta 92-SB from a holster on his thigh. Down at the end of the alley opposite the pier, a larger secondary road intersected the alley where a commercial gas station had once stood. The fuel pumps had been blown clean off their moorings at some point in the war, and the burned-out building was still covered in soot.

Moving carefully, pistol up, James jogged up the alley toward the former service station, heading for a manhole cover that was set in the ground. He covered the backs of the buildings fronting the alley, but he saw only empty windows, dark doorways and tight, twisted openings leading inward between the structures like tunnels.

Coming up to the manhole cover, James quickly went to one knee and holstered his Beretta to pull a thick-bladed diver's knife from a sheath on his combat boot. A diving knife was, by design, intended to be a pry bar and was built with full tangs and reinforced steel.

Working quickly, James slid the knife into the lip of the manhole cover and levered it. Instantly a foul miasma wafted up from the opening, causing him to yank his head back in sudden disgust.

As he turned his face to the side, nose wrinkled against the stench, a rebel army militia member stared out at him from a weed-choked causeway between two deserted maintenance sheds made out of corrugated tin and aluminum siding. The man had a unlit cigarette dangling from his lips with a blue, cheap plastic lighter held up with his free hand around the flickering flame.

Slung over his shoulder was an AKM.

James popped up out of his crouch like a jack-in-the-box. The Congolese's eyes grew wide and his mouth sagged open in surprise. James pushed his feet hard into broken ground, springing forward. The militia gunman's cigarette tumbled from his lips and the flame on the lighter winked out as it dropped from his hand.

James crossed the road in a flat sprint, knife up and ready, face twisted into a snarl of rage. The plastic lighter hit the ground at the Congolese's feet and bounced next to the forgotten cigarette. The man scrambled for the assault rifle slung on his shoulder, fingers fumbling in his fear.

The man tore the strap off his shoulder and swung the Kalashnikov down into his hands, fingers hunting for the trigger as he tried to bring the AKM barrel around. James swung his right hand down and knocked the weapon back into the man's own chest, blocking him like a defensive back on the line of scrimmage.

The man's fetid breath rushed out in a gasp, his spittle spraying James in the face. The diver's knife lunged up and plunged into the Congolese's torso just below the sternum, slicing through the membrane of the solar plexus. The man collapsed inward around the thrust, and James tore the knife free, blood gushing out to splash into the dust at their feet, making a sticky mud instantly.

James stepped backward to give himself room, then brought the knife back up in a murderous underhand slash. The triangle point of the blade caught the mortally wounded Congolese militia gunman in his throat just below the bobbing knot of his Adam's apple.

James felt the blade slice through flesh and cartilage. Hot blood gushed out over his fist, and the man croaked as a spasm rocked his body. James stepped in and shoved hard, pushing the corpse off the end of his knife to thump dully on the ground.

He whirled and ran back out into the street, slipping the blood-smeared knife blade under the web belt of his H-harness suspender. He drew his silenced Beretta and put a finger to his headset mike.

"Let's move this up," he said, breaking squelch without preamble. "I just had company at the secondary insertion point. There are bound to be more—he can't have been alone."

"Copy," McCarter replied. "Get cover—we have issues here, as well."

"Roger, out." James signed off.

He dropped to his knee and curled his fingertip under the manhole cover. He jerked upward and threw it clear. Once that was done he rose and quickly unholstered and transferred the Beretta to his left hand while taking up the pistol grip of his SPAS-15 in his right. He backed up quickly to the garbage-filled causeway where he had left the body of the rebel sentry.

In the distance he heard the sudden sharp crack as T. J. Hawkins unleashed with his sniper rifle. A second later Rafael Encizo let go with his grenade launcher and Calvin James realized hell had found Phoenix Force one more time.

# CHAPTER NINE

*Managua, Nicaragua*

Carl Lyons cut the Excursion hard to the right, shot across two lanes of traffic, threading between cars and trucks like a needle. The tires on the big SUV screeched in protest and the vehicle body leaned hard, threatening to roll at the sudden extreme angles.

"This isn't a Formula One car, Carl," Schwarz said, voice cool. "It will roll."

"It won't roll," Lyons answered flatly.

He snapped the wheel back hard in the other direction, cutting off a VW wagon then a red Audi. He crossed over the center divide, bouncing the wheels up and throwing the men around inside the cab.

"We're going to roll!" Blancanales shouted from the back.

"We're not going to roll," Lyons denied.

The Excursion bounced free and Lyons shot down the center of the busy St. Martin Grande roadway. Horns blared and a garish red-and-yellow tourist bus swerved out of the way. Lyons cut between it and a green Honda hybrid running close enough to scratch the paint on the Excursion.

He saw a side street and turned sharply, leaving a yard-long comma of rubber behind them on the pavement. He got the nose of the big SUV orientated correctly and floored the accelerator. He surged forward as more cars slammed on their brakes around him, but then he felt the back end shake loose and begin to drift.

"We're going to roll," Schwarz repeated.

Lyons didn't bother to answer but instead turned into the slide and eased off the gas for a moment. He cut the wheel back and just missed running up onto a crowded sidewalk before bringing the heavy vehicle back into line and shooting ahead.

He cut around a late-model four-door sedan and then back in front of it. He quickly looked in his rearview mirror but was forced to keep his eyes on the crowded road in front of him.

"Still there?" he demanded.

"Yep," Blancanales answered from the backseat.

"It's going to be damn hard to outmaneuver them in this behemoth," Schwarz said. "And if we keep this up for too long without losing them we'll have uniformed officers on our ass and it's right back to playing patty-cake with Customs Officer Garcia and his jolly crew."

"We're not going to roll," Lyons said preemptively.

The ex-LAPD detective slammed on the emergency brake, locking up his rear wheels, and spun the big SUV around in a half circle. The blunt nose of the Excursion pointed toward an alley. An ancient flatbed truck blocked half the narrow passage. In the back a lanky teenager handed boxes of ripe tomatoes down to a portly middle-aged man in a shopkeeper's apron.

The SUV rocked up hard on its suspension, leaning so hard toward the driver that the tires left the ground along the passenger side for several inches. The vehicle slammed back down and then the tires squealed as they grabbed traction on the asphalt.

The Excursion's big-block engine screamed as it lurched forward, barreling directly for the delivery truck. The shopkeeper turned and gaped in surprise, and the teenager on the flatbed dropped a box of tomatoes and leaped clear. The Excursion shot past them and there was sharp, metallic pop as the driver's side mirror was ripped clean off the door.

Lyons risked a glance back and saw the green pursuit car charge into the alley. He swore violently, then asked, "Can we take them out?"

"Our rules of engagement are pretty liberal," Schwarz said, his voice tinged with dry sarcasm.

"Are we sure we want to?" Blancanales asked. "They're just a surveillance team."

"They're agents of a secret police unit designed to keep an aggressive totalitarian despot in power. This country is about thirty-six hours away, at any one time, of going the Night of the Long Knives route. Hell, how many journalists and political dissidents has the local Gestapo already jailed, tortured and killed?" Lyons argued.

"True enough," Blancanales said. "But until we get to the cache point, we don't have weapons."

"Don't worry—I have a plan," Lyons said.

"Oh God no," Schwarz muttered.

*Brazzaville, Republic of the Congo*

HAWKINS SETTLED HIS HEAD down and eased into a tight cheek weld with the buttstock of his weapon. His finger rested firmly on the trigger, eliminating any slack from the pull. Poised for the kill, he used the scope to evaluate the hunter-killer team sweeping toward his position.

Two men stayed behind in each of the Dzik-3 APCs—the driver and a machine gunner using the roof-mounted M-2 .50-caliber machine guns. A dismount police squad consisting of a three-man fire team from each vehicle patrolled the area in methodical motions of cover and movement. The unit commander, an obese and belligerent-looking soldier in a felt green beret, walked along beside the center Dzik-3 with a sat phone in one hand and a U.S. Army Beretta in the other, controlling the search grids of the foot soldiers.

Target number one was the officer, Hawkins decided. Targets two, three and four would be the exposed machine gunners. Encizo could use the AP rounds in his Hawk grenade launcher to attack the three fire teams. With surprise and aggressive use of tactical firepower, their ambush could decimate the platoon. He just wasn't sure if they could handle any reinforcements.

"Coming closer. Moving careful and being thorough," he warned in a tense whisper.

He heard Encizo pass the information along to David McCarter. There was a murmured reply and then the Cuban whispered the Briton's instructions into Hawkins's ear.

"They start crossing the parking lot between the last warehouse and our position, then go ahead and take 'em. If we can get to insertion point two we'll be good either way, but we have to be sure we can hold them off long enough for Gary to finish the electrical job."

"Understood," Hawkins replied.

Encizo gave McCarter a thumbs-up. The Phoenix Force leader nodded, then turned back toward the big Canadian. Manning nodded without looking up.

"I'm in the schematic pathway," he said. "There's enough juice in these coils to do what we need, but I have to link the nodes one at a time to connect with the utility power grid. It has to be done in order or the transformers will reject the current or overload."

"I understand. Do what you have to. There may be shooting soon, however. Just our normal FUBAR luck."

Manning nodded, apparently unconcerned, his attention

entirely focused on his diagnostic and interdiction equipment. He pushed the stylus into the screen then dragged it downward, scrolling the blueprint connection to the next open port. He tapped the target, then quickly used the miniature keyboard to type in a command.

The node flashed green and he began the process again, this time following icons to the left of his screen. Behind him he could hear the big engines on the Congolese Dzik-3 APCs growing closer. A deep, harsh voice shouted orders in French, and Manning heard others reply.

The undershirt beneath his NATO body armor was soaked with sweat, and beads of perspiration stood out on his forehead. He hummed a little tune to himself to aid in his focus, narrowing his concentration to a white-hot edge despite the assault of adrenaline on his system.

He heard Calvin James give his update over his earjack and McCarter reply with his instructions. His hand moved and shifted across the pad, sliding and scraping the electronic stylus like a conductor at the philharmonic waving his baton.

Over his shoulder he heard Rafael Encizo suddenly speak up in a conversational voice to David McCarter. "T.J. says he's going to go ahead and kill some people now."

"Grand, just grand," McCarter acknowledged.

There was the heavy supersonic crack of a rifle.

AT THE END OF Calvin James's alley a white Nissan pickup pulled up, blocking the scorched gas station from view. In the bed of the pickup four militia members with green headbands and AKM assault rifles jumped out and hit the ground. The sound of gunfire coming from several buildings over had the irregulars jumpy as junkies, weapons primed. In the passenger seat a sallow-skinned man in a police uniform directed the civilian-clad militia gunman.

James sank back against the wall of the maintenance shed. Held in a left-handed grip because of the angle, his SPAS-15 was up at port arms as one of the militia called out a name down the alleyway. James looked down at the mutilated corpse sprawled at his feet.

The man would not be answering.

Slowly the Stony Man commando sank into a crouch and then risked a quick look around the edge of the building as the militia squad continued calling out the dead point man's name. The gunmen had fanned out into a loose arrowhead formation and were coming down the alley, Kalashnikovs up and at the ready.

From across the opposite of the alley the sound of explosions punctuated the chatter of automatic weapons.

"I have a flanking element," James subvocalized into his throat mike. "I can hold our position but I'm outnumbered."

"Copy," McCarter replied. "I'm rolling backup right now."

"Go prone once you clear the wall," James warned. "You're jumping straight into the cooking pot."

"Out."

Letting go of the forestock of the SPAS-15, James reached over to a suspender on his H-harness and pulled a canister-shaped grenade free. He brought it down and hooked the thumb of his trigger hand into the ring, then pulled outward with his right. The spoon sprang from the smoke grenade and flew across the causeway to land in a pool of standing blood with a muted splash.

Without looking, James reached out around the corner of the building and tossed the canister in an underhanded lob. He heard someone shout in surprise and anger as the grenade landed and began spewing thick white smoke. He went to his left knee, pressing the hard plastic pad secured there into the broken ground, and swung the barrel of his weapon around the corner.

Thirty yards away a wide-eyed Congolese was moving toward the smoke grenade, AKM up in the crook of his shoulder. James triggered the semiautomatic shotgun. Double-aught buckshot tore into the man, knocking the assault rifle free, tearing off both hands at the wrists in a geyser of blood and smashing into the abdomen and lower chest of the militia irregular.

The man stumbled backward and went down. A Kalashnikov chattered and a hail of 7.62 mm lead rattled the corrugated metal above James's head. He pulled the trigger on the SPAS-15 twice more without bothering to aim as he ducked back around the edge of the building, spreading lethal buckshot across the alley in a merciless wall of lead. The recoil hammered backward into his wrist and the smoking shells tumbled outward as he dropped to his belly.

He heard screams and his hand went to his web belt for a fragmentation grenade. Hard steel slugs buzzed and burned around him, slicing through the metal siding of the maintenance shed as if it were paper. Dirt and bloody mud kicked up just in front of his position and bullets whined as they sliced through the air above him.

Without looking, James returned fire, aiming low and filling the narrow alley with more .12-gauge shot. He heard the Nissan pickup engine suddenly surge as the driver gunned it, and he knew they were charging his position.

THE CONGOLESE POLICE commander's head filled the reticule of Hawkins's scope. He put the crosshairs on the bridge of the man's patrician nose. The range was ridiculously close for the powerful sniper optic, and he could see the man was sweating freely. Slowly, Hawkins let the air ease out of his lungs. Steadily, he squeezed back on the trigger.

The pull was so smooth the rifle going off almost came as a surprise. The police commander's skull exploded like glass as the rifle recoiled firmly into Hawkins's shoulder. Jagged edges of skull-like eggshell mixed with the black syrup of the man's blood as his brains were scattered across the dun-colored armor of the Dzik-3.

Hawkins shifted slightly. The machine gunner in the first wheeled APC filled his scope. The man swiveled in his open turret, swinging the muzzle of the M-2 machine gun around in the direction of the shot.

Hawkins put a bullet through his larynx.

A red depression appeared in the man's throat and a fine red mist haloed his head as the back of his neck was blown out by the high-velocity round. Hawkins shifted his sniper rifle.

*"Madre puta,"* Encizo barked over his shoulder. A half a second later there was the distinctive bloop sound as the MM-1 fired. Then three more as the Cuban combat swimmer unleashed on the dismounted fire teams.

"You're in charge of this element," McCarter told Manning just as the 40 mm grenades landed. "Once you're done, over the wall you go."

The sharp crack and dull thump of the explosions drowned out the big Canadian's reply but he was nodding and McCarter took that as his cue to go. He slid between the substation housing just as Hawkins killed the second machine gunner. As he went over the wall, the third weapons operator managed to open up on the Phoenix Force position and suppress them at least momentarily. The .50-caliber rounds blasted the cinder-block wall into fragments and sent all three Phoenix force commandos into a nosedive under the onslaught. Dirt kicking up into his face, Gary Manning continued his tedious task.

MCCARTER LANDED HARD on the other side of the wall and went to ground. One whole end of the alley was choked with thick white smoke, obscuring his movements from the militia squad. He saw green tracer fire knifing out of the smoke and heard the screaming of a V-6 engine.

Arching his back, McCarter lifted the upper half of his torso from the hard-packed alley dirt and twisted his M-4 carbine sideways. His left hand grabbed the weapon by its shoulder pad and his right went up to the 30-round magazine that served as the pistol grip for the trigger to his M-203 grenade launcher.

The combination weapon recoiled hard in his hand, and the 40 mm HE round shot down the alley and into the smoke toward the clarion call of the vehicle engine. The explosion was instantaneous and a ball of fire like a vol-cano blast billowed out and rolled forward, tossing bodies in pinwheels ahead of it.

A flaming figure emerged from the smoke, and Calvin James stepped out of his position and knocked it down with a blast from his SPAS-15. For a second there was only the sound of the burning vehicle in the alley. Then chunks exploded out of the concrete wall beside McCarter and rained down on him in jagged shards.

On the other side of that wall Gary Manning curled into a fetal position around his handheld. He lightly touched the electronic stylus to the last node icon, then began typing the final command.

He started singing the song he had been humming during his process. "'That's the night the lights went out in Georgia...'"

A single bar graph metric appeared on the screen. The cinder-block wall above him exploded. The bar turned from green to red and flashed. Heavy-caliber rounds began to hammer the structure in front of him. The red bar suddenly began to drain and a percentage number appeared on the screen just to the left of the plunging line. It dropped from 100% to 40% to 6% to 0% in the blink of an eye.

Then the neighborhoods of southeast Brazzaville went dark.

# CHAPTER TEN

*Managua, Nicaragua*

Hector Ramon Casella fought his car back under control. Driving, shooting silenced weapons, arranging wiretaps and wielding a rubber hose during interrogations were among the premier skills utilized by the General Counterintelligence Agency. The American was good—too good for a mere tourist—but in the clumsy and massive SUV he could never hope to evade a skilled driver in a quicker, more nimble automobile.

Trying to lose them in the parking garage was a mark of desperation, Casella realized. His partner pulled a Glock-17 pistol from a shoulder holster as the agent sped up a ramp and into the structure after the Americans. Hitting the second story, he turned the car smoothly and aimed for the curved ramp leading up to the next level. His knuckles were white on the steering wheel as he threaded the needle at fifty kilometers per hour.

BLANCANALES LEAPED from the back of the Ford Excursion and slammed the door shut. "Now!" he snarled.

Carl Lyons shoved his foot down on the accelerator. The transmission was in four-wheel drive and all the wheels suddenly lurched backward and started spinning in reverse.

The bulky battering ram shot back down the access ramp as the much lighter automobile raced upward toward it.

Ambush set. Ambush sprung.

THE HURTLING SUV of Detroit steel slammed into the undercover unit's street car in a heavy metal landslide. The thick rear bumper crumpled the smaller car's grill like an empty beer can and bludgeoned into the engine block at terrific velocity. The oil pan cracked and burst apart and fluid lines tore loose, dumping flammable liquids across the ruined front end of the car.

The dashboard inside the cab buckled under the impact, instantly spiderwebbing the safety glass of the windshield. The passenger, not wearing his seat belt, was thrown forward into the weakened glass and used his face to punch a hole in it. Instantly his flesh was peeled off his face like the skin of a grape, and blood poured down to bubble and sizzle on the heated metal of the exposed engine. The man's lower jaw came away, scattering his teeth like dice, and the jagged glass deeply gouged through his carotid arteries. Blood rolled in a scarlet flood.

A heartbeat later the man in the backseat was also catapulted into the windshield and fell limp.

Casella was thrown forward against his seat restraint and felt his ribs along his left side break at the sudden, jerking concussion. His head snapped forward and the steering wheel airbag deployed with a sharp explosion so that his vision was filled with a sudden sheet of white.

His face bounced back from the pneumatic pillow, wrenching his neck so sharply flashes of light burst in his eyes and a scream was ripped from his lips. Vaguely he was aware of the blaring of his horn then the thump of something landing on the roof of his car.

He tried to rally himself but this wasn't like kidnapping a teenage college student from the old Contra protest movements. Suddenly he felt strong hands grab him by the point of his chin and the hair at the back of his head. He peeled open his swollen eyes and tried to raise a free hand to swat at the monstrous grip, but suddenly his hair was yanked in one direction and his chin shoved in the other.

He heard a soft muted pop then saw only blackness.

THE EX-GREEN BERET, Rosario Blancanales, pulled his hands free and the agent's head rolled loosely on his broken neck to hang at a bizarre angle. Quickly Blancanales patted the man down and found his Glock-17 pistol.

"Got a handgun here," he yelled over the horn. "Partner's got to have one."

Lyons jumped out of the driver's seat of the Excursion and jogged down the ramp as Schwarz did the same from the other side. Lyons regarded the grisly remains of the dead driver dispassionately. "We have to find a clean car and go completely black."

Schwarz pulled his head from the passenger-side door, the mutilated man's Glock-17 in his hands. "Pick your car," he said. He slid the handgun under his belt behind his back. "I got a vehicle appropriation kit through customs by breaking it up into pieces," he said.

"Great," Lyons said. "I'll drive."

"Lovely," Blancanales replied.

*Brazzaville, Republic of the Congo*

RAFAEL ENCIZO LIFTED the reloaded Hawk MM-1 as .50-caliber slugs tore through the air around him. He depressed the trigger and rode out the recoil as the weapon spit out a fusillade of 40 mm firepower. The rounds arced out and slammed into the ground in trip-hammer shock waves, tossing the corrupt Congolese police gunmen in the air and raking them with shrapnel.

The concussive force momentarily stilled the final machine gunner and Hawkins attempted a shot that rang off the roof just to the right of the man. Encizo fired another two quick shots with the grenade launcher but in the heat of the moment the Cuban's aim was wide with the imprecise weapon and they sailed to either side of the machine gunner and landed behind him.

The weapon, momentarily silenced, opened up again and the withering fire of the heavy-caliber machine gun drove the members of Phoenix Force down so their noses were in the dirt.

"Phoenix," Manning said, "we are leaving!"

"It's about time," Encizo replied.

Small arms fired from the surviving police unit poured into the narrow substation, the 7.62 mm rounds forming a roof of lead above the cinder-block enclosure while the M-2 continued punching holes through the concrete.

"Oh, Christ," Hawkins muttered as he crawled toward the other two men. "This is starting to remind me too much of Mogadishu, guys."

"Sure, that or the Alamo," Manning answered, raising his voice over the din of gunfire.

Encizo rolled over in the dirt on his back and pointed the blunt muzzle of the MM-1 into the air so that the rounds would just skim the top of the wall. Rounds punched through the rim of the enclosure until it looked like a row of broken teeth. He triggered the Hawk grenade launcher and sent two more rounds over the top of the wall.

The 40 mm grenades landed hard, one right after the other and the explosions stilled the small-arms fire. However, the machine gun continued hammering away until there were enough baseball-size holes in the cinder block to let the three Phoenix Force members see the surviving Congolese police approaching their position.

From behind them where James and McCarter held security on the insertion point white smoke was billowing up. AKM fire popped up again in ragged bursts, green tracer fire knifing through the air.

"There's no way we're making it over that wall!" Manning yelled.

"Then go through it," Hawkins yelled back.

The ex-Army Ranger threw his Mk-11 rifle to his shoulder and started putting match-grade 7.62 mm NATO rounds downrange through the bullet holes in the wall.

Manning snatched up his M-60E and cut loose through the wall with a sudden long burst.

"Do it!" he yelled.

Hawkins pulled a HE grenade from his web gear and primed it. Encizo rolled away from the sound of Manning's machine gun and spoke into his throat mike. "We can't go over the wall, so we're going through—you clear?" he demanded without preamble.

"Do it!" McCarter answered instantly.

"Do it!" Encizo shouted.

Manning let the M-60E cut loose and just run through the 200-round belt as Hawkins let the spoon on his grenade fly loose. He lunged forward and slapped the high-explosive bomb around the corner of the substation building and into the tight space between it and the wall.

He threw himself back and all three men turned their body armor toward the explosion. It went off with a deafening boom that popped their eardrums. They scrambled to their hands and knees and snatched up their weapons, crawling for the breach they'd created.

They shoved themselves down the cramped passage as

bullets continued firing around them. The high-explosive charge of the hand grenade had created a chasm in the metal housing of the substation conductor and it smoked heavily, sparks showering as an electrical fire flared up.

The cinder block had burst outward under the force of the explosion, leaving a gaping hole three times the size of a man in the wall. Manning came to his feet, scooping up the heavy M-60E machine gun and charging out into the alley. Encizo and Hawkins scrambled through right behind him, weapons up and ready.

They entered a wall of choking, blinding white smoke that swirled around them as they jogged forward. Still moving forward, Encizo turned at the waist and lobbed the last rounds in his grenade launcher back over the wall in the direction they'd come from, and a portion of the small-arms fire went silent.

"This way," McCarter called to them from out of the smoke.

Rafael Encizo ran up to where David McCarter crouched beside the open manhole cover. "This wasn't the plan," he said, and grinned.

"You got to use your BFG, didn't you?" McCarter laughed back. "Down you go. Cal's holding security in the tunnel."

Encizo's biceps swelled as he lifted the MM-1 by the pistol grip so that the muzzle was pointed acutely vertical. He dropped down to his butt and thrust his legs into the opening until the soles of his combat boots hit the rungs of the service ladder. He ignored the stench of shit that enveloped him and scrambled down.

Gary Manning turned and held his machine gun in one hand and repeated Encizo's motions, dropping down into the hole. As his head dipped below the lip of the manhole, he looked over at McCarter.

"You always take me to the best places," he said, climbing down.

"Everyone in this chicken shit outfit is a bleeding comedian!"

He snapped his M-4 up and began holding security as Hawkins slung his Mk-11 and pulled a second smoke grenade free from his web gear. Behind him in the breach out of the derelict substation created by the HE grenade, a Congolese emerged, AKM up.

McCarter shot him through the face, tossing a loop of black blood up into the air from the man's head as he crumpled like a slaughtered steer in a stockyard. Hawkins let the armed grenade rolled down the alley, intensifying the weakening smoke screen already in place. Gray-white smoke immediately began billowing out, obscuring the breach point from view.

With Hawkins down the hole McCarter triggered an AP round out of his M-203. It shot through the smoke and exploded in a bright flash. Immediately he let the weapon fall to the end of its sling so that it hung by his waist, and reached out for the manhole cover. He jumped onto the iron bracket ladder set into the sewer line and scrambled down, dragging the heavy steel lid toward him.

The swirling smoke above his head twisted and cycloned as rounds sprayed down the alley. Green tracer rounds buzzed like hornets around him as the corrupt Congolese police unit fired blindly. He heard the sound of the lone Dzik-3 as it approached.

Then the manhole cover settled into place and for a second all of that was gone in the tomblike atmosphere of the reeking hot sewer. He clambered downward several rungs, then stepped back and dropped to the ground. Landing in a tight crouch he reached up and engaged his IR monogoggle—turning the impenetrable dark into a green-tinged black-and-white vista.

He saw the rest of his team strung out in a loose Ranger file along the catwalk next to a river of offal and sludge. He saw the body of a dog in the mess, legs stiff with rigor mortis, and twisted his face into disgust. Then he saw the partial body of the baby and he went cold.

He turned his face away and hurried toward where Calvin James crouched at the beginning of the line. He slid past the other members and knelt next to the ex-SEAL.

"You able to get a signal in here?" he asked.

"Negative," James replied. "I sent a text communication into the repeater service after I couldn't get contact. The server will keep trying to deliver the message so if we get near an open area as we move it should give our sit-rep."

"All right." McCarter raised his voice so all the members of Phoenix Force could hear him. "We go down fifty yards to a Y-fork. We can hold security there until we see if these evil bastards figure out how we escaped. Let's go. Gary, you have rear security."

Instantly the commando squad was up and moving. They shuffled along quickly, heads bent low in a toe-heel gait designed to maintain purchase on the slippery strip of stained concrete. They used IR flashlights set next to their monogoggle to help illuminate the catacombs. Hawkins ran his gaze across the domed ceiling and saw a mass of crawling cockroaches and squirming worms. Running point, James routinely kicked squealing rats out of his way or stomped the more aggressive ones to a jelly when they refused to give way.

Moving in an awkward, sidestepping shuffle, Manning kept his machine gun up and pointed back toward the insertion point as he moved, covering rear security. After a moment of travel the team reached the Y-juncture and took the right-hand fork, disappearing from view.

They went to ground and shut down their IR flashlights, relying on passive feeds only for illumination. Manning crouched at the lip of the turn, watching the back tunnel with keen interest.

"This thing has been bollixed up," McCarter said flatly. "Someone sold us. Probably that blood-ass Kabila. We have to assume our target knows we're coming after him."

"Maybe so, maybe no," James said. "Safe bet says yes, but that doesn't mean he's gone from the area."

"You want to Charlie Mike?" McCarter asked, using military slang based on the phonetic alphabet for "continue mission."

"Gary trashed light and power so the bad guys are living in the dark right now," Encizo said. "We never told the Congolese liaison our true insertion plan, so they have no idea that we're coming up from beneath them. We lost strategic surprise but we still have tactical surprise on our side."

"To do what?" Hawkins asked. "Still pull the snatch? I'd have to say that might be just a bit more ballsy than brilliant, Pescado."

"Maybe we don't get a snatch." Manning spoke up from the end of the line. "But maybe we could do a soft probe and call in an air strike or do a hard probe and get a sniper shot off. Plan B may have to be good enough."

"We're risking getting cut off deep in Indian territory," McCarter said. He couldn't keep the smile out of his voice, however. "This snake-out-of-a-hole insertion we came up with, though, seems too good to waste without a try."

"Agreed," James said.

"Agreed," Encizo and Hawkins echoed.

"Gary?" McCarter asked.

"Let's do it," Manning replied. "It doesn't seem like the Congolese have figured out how in the hell we got away. They could be chasing us all over the neighborhood right now. We should exploit that."

"Then let's roll," McCarter said.

# CHAPTER ELEVEN

*Stony Man Farm, Virginia*

Aaron Kurtzman clicked the icon to accept an instant message. His eyes scanned the screen in rapid movements as he took in the text message. He swore out loud and slammed his coffee cup down on the desk next to his wheelchair. Carmen Delahunt looked up from the computer printout she was reading as both Wethers and Tokaido spun in their chairs at the sudden cursing.

"What happened, Bear?" Wethers asked.

Kurtzman opened his mouth to speak, and the door to the Annex's Computer Room swung inward and slammed against the wall. All eyes from the Stony Man cybernetics team swung around as Barbara Price rushed into the room.

"Able is compromised," she said without preamble. "They're going deep black to Charlie Mike but we need to get them a new safehouse in a less populated area and arrange resupply."

"When it rains it pours," Kurtzman said.

"What?"

"I got a message from James on the ground in Brazzaville, text based."

"Why text?"

"He couldn't get a signal out so he put a communication in the system for the repeater relay. It's twelve minutes old.

They were compromised on initial insertion. They think their Congolese police counterpart might have set them up."

Akira Tokaido leaned back in his chair and whistled. "Phoenix under fire, Able on the run—this mission is screwed out of the gate."

"Reshuffling logistics for Able shouldn't be too much of a problem," Wethers said. "As long as they stay out of the Nicaraguans' hands they should still be able to move on the target. But I'm not sure what we can do for Phoenix. Grimaldi can be rotors up out of the Brazzaville International Airport as soon as we call him, but it was supposed to be a joint Congolese mission at British insistence. The Congolese were supposed to take the credit for nabbing a terrorist cell."

"Seems shortsighted for them to risk us finding their plant just to wipe out this team," Delahunt pointed out.

"Not if they're so ensconced they think they own the territory." Price shook her head. "We'll figure out the devious motivations later. For now we need to figure out how to support them."

"They've made it into the Trojan Horse insertion point," Kurtzman said. "For now they're going to continue with at least the recon phase of the op. They're going to see if plan B is at least an option."

Price nodded. "Akira, call Jack. Have him go ahead and prep the JSOC Predator he's staged with. Once the satellite links are hot and you have control of the drone, put it in high altitude and circle the AO. We'll be ready when they call."

The Stony Man mission controller turned to the other members of the team. "Akira, hack the Nicaraguan system. I want every communiqué in whatever form it might take on what they're trying to do about Able. If a janitor writes a note on a paper napkin, I want to read it.

"Carmen, you do the same for the Managua police. Hunt, I want you to get a hold of Agency, Joint Special Operations Command, the DEA and try to get me a new safehouse for Able.

"Aaron, try to establish contact with Phoenix and then arrange a backup resupply drop for Nicaragua. I'll have John Kissinger assemble their weapons and explosives. Think of every contingency they could face and then give them two of everything they'll need. Let's spend some taxpayer money, people." She turned and walked out of the room calling out over her shoulder, "Now I've got to go call Hal."

Behind her the Computer Room exploded into activity. Men's lives hung in the balance and the cyberteam had never failed before. They didn't intend to do so now.

*Managua, Nicaragua*

ABLE TEAM MADE poor time. Forced to act clandestinely, they avoided the main highway and took secondary streets toward the northwest of the city. There the urban center ran up against the Nicaraguan coastal mountain range known locally as Cordillera de la Costa, a stretch of the Mosquito Coast.

The lower levels of that mountain range were arid and steep. The Farm had provided Schwarz with the street address and GPS coordinates of a safehouse used by a U.S. Army Intelligence unit tasked with electronic surveillance and digital interdiction nestled in the rugged terrain.

The house was isolated and set on property at the end of a dirt road. The headlights of the stolen car illuminated the structure, revealing a modest stucco, adobe-style hacienda accented by a small courtyard behind a wrought-iron gate. The landscaped garden was filled with cactus plants, aloe, silver sword bushes and agave.

As Carl Lyons stepped out of the Subaru Outback's driver's side something heavy scuttled across his foot. Cursing, he jumped back and looked down in time to see a softball-size tarantula scurry off under the car.

He spun and saw Hermann Schwarz looking at him, single eyebrow arched.

"Not a word," Lyons warned.

Rosario Blancanales approached the gate to the dwelling's courtyard and worked the security code given him by Barbara Price. The series of miniature lightbulbs set across the top switched from red to a flashing dull amber, then blinked a muted green.

He hit a second three-digit sequence and a small drawer popped out of the bottom of the alarm housing like a feed tray on a CD player to reveal a master key. The Puerto Rican ex-Green Beret quickly unlocked the gate as Lyons and Schwarz carried their luggage in behind him.

They crossed a modest courtyard of terra-cotta tile to the heavy wooden door, which the master key unlocked, and they entered the nondescript hacienda. Just to the left of the inside hall through an open door was a small office set up with four desktop-size CCTV screens showing the outside of the property through live digital feeds. In the upper-left hand monitor they could see their vehicle sitting in the drive.

Blancanales moved quickly toward the back of the house to where the master bedroom was located. Once there he pulled up first a corner of the carpet, then two specially crafted sections of flooring to reveal a digital floor safe.

Sitting under the CCTV station, Schwarz fired up a Mac laptop, which he slaved to the U.S. Army portable computer he carried in his kit. Behind him Lyons grabbed a sat phone off a charging port and wandered into the kitchen. He opened the fridge and stood looking at the contents of the commercial-size appliance and grimacing at the supplies.

He shrugged as the connection was made and let the door swing shut—it beat the hell out of MREs. Absently he counted the seven distinct clicks as the signal was routed around the globe in a security shuffle before connecting to the Shenandoah black site.

"Ironman, I presume?" Barbara Price's cool, well-modulated voice answered. She sounded as aloof and poised as a Wall Street banker, Lyons thought.

"It's me, boss," he answered. "As you can tell, we have arrived."

"No more close calls, I hope?"

"None to speak of."

"You guys are now completely black," Price warned. "Delahunt got into the Managua PD and the Nicaraguan intel has given them your pictures and they have a general 'be on the look out for' on you guys. You have detectives and uniforms girding the city. The airports and all public transportation are on alert. And of course all that doesn't count the spooks at Nicaraguan intel and their pet commando unit they've called in."

"Commando unit?"

"The Guardia Puerto Cabezas. A special unit used to shut down dissenting voices in the media, kidnap political agitators and train narco death squads in the mountains to increase regional instability."

"More people to knock over the head." Lyons shrugged. "Whatever. You got any good news for us?"

"Yes," Price replied. "Your boy Chao Bao is completely oblivious to the fact that three *el norte gringos* have arrived in town to see him. He's taken no extra security precautions and is blithely unaware of his impending doom."

"I just had that warm, tingly feeling you always give me when you talk like that, Barb."

"I'm very happy for you, Carl. How's the safehouse?"

"Food in the fridge sucks and—wait a second. Here comes Pol with our ordnance."

Blancanales walked into the room with several firearms in his hands, which he set on the table. "Pretty generic. All silenced H&Ks and Berettas. Five total of each gun with ammo and night-vision goggles, as well as some tactical communications equipment. This was obviously a primarily defensive operation prior to us."

Frowning, Lyons looked down at the arsenal on the table. He saw three Heckler & Koch MP-5 SD-3 silenced submachine guns and three Beretta 92-F pistols.

"Barb, dammit," he said into the phone. "All we have are MP-5s and some Berettas."

"So?"

"They are both 9 mm. I've said this before but I'll say it again. The 9 mm was designed for killing Europeans. For serious people you need at least a .45, 'kay?"

There was silence on the end of the sat connection, followed by a long sigh. "Carl, do your recon. If you need an elephant gun, I have Bear working on a logistic link. Probably a night drop."

"That's all I needed to hear," Lyons said. "I'll call you again after we've been eyes on with the target."

"Farm out," Price said, and killed the connection.

Lyons set the phone on the table and picked up a suppressor-equipped submachine gun. He inspected the lethal weapon with a critical eye. "I guess every firearm doesn't have to be my AA-12." He sighed, referring to the Military

Police Systems updated version of the Atchisson automatic shotgun. "Let's eat and roll."

*Plaza de Sombra*
*Managua Nicaragua*

HUGO DANIEL ORTEGA paced the floor. His hands were held behind his back and his head was down as he calmly contemplated his options. Hector Gutierrez, commanding officer of the Guardia Puerto Cabezas, sat in a chair in the corner. At a word from Ortega the burly man would launch his death squad in an instant, but in the meantime there was nothing to do but wait for an update as the Nicaraguan agent coordinated the sweep of the city on the lookout for the three American spies.

The door to the office swung open and Ortega drew himself up as a short figure in a dark suit entered the room. Ortega instantly recognized the inscrutable features of the only Asian face in the entire building.

"General," Ortega said carefully in acknowledgment.

General Xi-Nan nodded in reply and casually swung the door shut behind him. Xi-Nan was the living embodiment of China's attempt to spread its international influence into the Western Hemisphere. An extremely high-ranking member of the People's Party, the Chinese military intelligence officer was fluent in Spanish and an expert in secured communications, digital espionage and passive intelligence-gathering activities.

Xi-Nan was here as a political courtesy from China to assist Nicaragua in its national security efforts against the United States. He brought resources and techniques far beyond any Nicaragua could hope to manufacture domestically and though, for himself, Ortega knew the deal was Faustian, he also knew Xi-Nan was invaluable.

"I have something for you," Xi-Nan said. "Something potentially about your current problem."

Ortega stepped closer, his face glowing with an eager light. In his chair Gutierrez leaned forward. "The gringos?" Ortega asked. "You have something on them?"

"I think so," Xi-Nan said.

He produced a computer printout from the inside pocket of his military-cut suit jacket. Ortega took it eagerly and opened it, eyes darting back and forth as he scanned the information on the page.

"Members of Chinese special operation mountain reconnaissance troops operating along our border with Afghanistan managed to…acquire…certain pieces of highly encrypted field radios from a U.S. Navy SEAL sniper team," Xi-Nan explained. "In Beijing we were able to disassemble and reverse engineer those radios."

"You can listen in on the Americans' communications?" Ortega was stunned. "The spies here, in Managua? You have eavesdropped?"

Xi-Nan shook his head sharply once. "No," he replied in perfect Spanish. "We have not. Cracking the connection is not possible. However, once you told me about your predicament I instructed my staff to begin searching for signature frequencies."

Ortega lowered his eyes to the paper and eagerly continued reading. "You were able to catch the signal."

Xi-Nan nodded. "Just so. We have no idea where the signal ended up, since the rerouting technology is too advanced. However, we do have a point-of-origin possibility. If this spy team makes contact again we should be able to triangulate their position. Already we know it came from the north of the city."

Ortega turned to Gutierrez. "Restage your men at the helipad we have in the security site. Be ready to move by air or ground as soon as our great friend General Xi-Nan gives us the information."

Gutierrez nodded. His eyes were the cold, dead orbs of a marine predator, soulless and without mercy. "It will be done," he said.

# CHAPTER TWELVE

*Brazzaville, Republic of the Congo*

The blast from an artillery had knocked a hole in the street. The explosion ripped up the asphalt and punched a hole in the ground deep enough to reveal the sewer line. Workers had managed to clear enough rubble out of the crater to keep the sewage stream flowing, but there had not been enough security or money for complete repairs. A line of rubble like a gravel-covered hillside led up out of the sewer to the street.

While the rest of Phoenix Force crouched in the shadows, T. J. Hawkins eased his way up the uncertain slope to reconnoiter the area. He crawled carefully, using his elbows and knees with his weapon cradled in the crook of his arms. As tense as the situation was, there was a large part of him that was grateful to escape the stinking claustrophobia of the tunnel.

He eased his way up to the lip of the blast crater and carefully raised his head over the edge. The neighborhood appeared deserted at the late hour. Tenement buildings rose up above street-level shops, the structures nestled right up against each other. Rusted iron fire escapes adorned the fronts of the old buildings. Brightly colored laundry hung from windows and clotheslines. The roofs were a forest of old-fashioned wire antennas. The street was lined with battered old cars, some of them up on concrete blocks and obviously unusable. Across the street feral dogs rooted through an overflowing garbage bin.

Carefully, Hawkins extended his weapon and scanned the neighborhood street through his scope. He detected no movement, saw no faces in windows and doorways, silhouetted no figures on the fire escapes and rooftops. He looked down to the end of the street and saw nothing stirring, then turned and checked the other direction with the same result.

Satisfied, Hawkins turned and looked down. He gave a short, low whistle and instantly McCarter appeared at the foot of the rubble incline.

"All clear. Come have a look," Hawkins whispered.

McCarter nodded once in reply and then reslung his M-4 carbine before scrambling quickly up the rubble. He slid into place next to Hawkins and carefully scanned the street, as well.

"There," he said. "That building." He indicated a burned-out six-story apartment complex with a thrust of his sharp chin. "That's the building. That'll give us the entry point into the compound."

Eighteen months before the building had been assaulted by a Congolese national army unit with British SAS advisors after intelligence had revealed it served as an armory and bomb-making factory for the local rebel militias.

"I haven't noticed any sentries yet," Hawkins said. His gaze remained fixed on the sniper scope as he scanned the building.

"They're there," McCarter said. "That's the back door to the militia complex holding our boy Dexter."

"Heads up," Hawkins suddenly rasped.

Instantly, McCarter attempted to identify the threat. Up the street a Toyota pickup turned onto the avenue and began cruising toward their position. The back of the vehicle held a squad of gunmen, and there were three men in the vehicle cab.

McCarter and Hawkins froze, nestling themselves in among the broken masonry of the bomb crater. Moving slowly, the vehicle cruised up the street. Carefully McCarter eased his head below the lip of the crater and transferred his carbine into a more accessible position.

Beside him Hawkins seemed to evaporate, blending into the background as the pickup inched its way along the street. The former U.S. Army counterterror commando watched the enemy patrol with eyes narrowed, his finger held lightly on the trigger of his weapon.

The vehicle rolled closer and both Phoenix members could hear the murmur of voices in casual conversation. Hawkins watched as a pockmarked Congolese in the back took a final drag of his cigarette and then flicked it away.

The still smoking butt arced up and landed next to the prone Hawkins with a small shower of sparks that stung his exposed face. The cigarette bounced and rolled down the incline to come to rest against McCarter's leg.

A gunman in the back of the vehicle said something and the others laughed as the pickup cruised past the two hidden men. Playing a hunch, Hawkins risked moving to scan the burned-out building across the street with his scope. His gamble paid off as a man armed with a SVD Soviet-era Dragunov sniper rifle appeared briefly in a third-story window to acknowledge the patrol rolling past his position.

Hawkins grinned. The pickup reached the end of the street and disappeared around a corner. "Got you, asshole," Hawkins whispered. "I got a gun bunny on the third floor," the Texan told McCarter.

"Does he interfere with movement?" McCarter scooped loose dirt over the burning cigarette, extinguishing it.

"He's back in the shadow now. I might have a shot with IR," Hawkins explained. "But he's definitely doing over-watch on this street."

"He the only one?"

"Only one I saw," Hawkins said. "But he could have a spotter or radio guy sitting next to him who'll sound the alarm if I put the sniper down."

"What's our other option?"

"I guess send the team across and hope he doesn't notice until we can be sure of how many we're dealing with."

"The clock is ticking," McCarter pointed out.

"Then I say let me take him."

"Enciz and I will cross the street to try to secure the ground floor before the rest of you come over."

"It's your call, Dave," Hawkins said simply. He clicked over the amplifier apparatus on his night scope and scanned the windows. A red silhouette appeared in the gloom of the third-story window. "I got him. No other figures present themselves from this angle."

"That'll have to do," McCarter said.

Hawkins held down on his target as McCarter called Enciz up and the two men slowly climbed into position. Enciz had left his Hawk MM-1 behind with Calvin James and held his silenced MP-7 at the ready. McCarter slid his M-4/M-203 around to hang from his back and pulled his own silencer-equipped weapon, the Browning Hi-Power, from its holster.

"Jack and Jill went up the hill," Hawkins softly sang under his breath. "Jill fell down, skinned her knees and Jack killed some fucking Congo rebels…"

THE MK-11 SNIPER RIFLE discharged smoothly, the muzzle lifting slightly with the recoil and pushing back into the hollow of Hawkins's shoulder. The report was muted in the hot desert air, and the subsonic round cut across the space and tore through the open window.

In his scope Hawkins saw the figure's head jerk like a boxer taking an inside uppercut. There was an instant of red smear in his site as blood splashed, then the enemy sniper spun in a half circle and fell over.

"Go," Hawkins said.

McCarter was instantly up and sprinting. Behind him Encizo scrambled over the edge of the hole and raced after him. Both men crossed the street in a dead run, weapons up and ready as Hawkins began shifting his weapon back and forth in tight vectors to cover the building front.

McCarter crossed the open street and spun to throw his back into the wall beside the front door of the building. Half a second later Encizo repeated the motion, his MP-7 pointed down the street.

McCarter checked once, then went in through the gaping doorway. He charged into the room, turning left and trying to move along the wall. Encizo came in and peeled left, coming to one knee and scanning the room with his muzzle leading the way. Both men scanned the darkened chamber through their low-light goggles.

The front doors to the building had been blown out during the Congolese raid and the room saturated with grenades and automatic weapons fire. The two Phoenix Force members found themselves in a small lobby with a cracked and collapsed desk, a line of busted and dented mailboxes, a pitted and pocked elevator and two fire-scarred doorways. One of the interior doors had been blown off its hinges, revealing a staircase leading upward. The second sagged in place, as perforated as a cheese grater.

McCarter carefully moved forward and checked both doorways before turning and giving Encizo the thumbs-up signal. The combat swimmer turned and went to the doorway so that Hawkins could see him. He lifted a finger and spoke into his throat mike.

"Come across," he said. "We'll clear upward."

"Acknowledged," Hawkins replied.

Encizo turned back into the room just as he heard footsteps on the staircase. Booted feet pounded the wooden steps as someone jogged downward, making no effort to conceal their movement. Encizo blinked and McCarter disappeared, moving smoothly to rematerialize next to the stairway access, back to the wall and silenced Browning pistol up.

Wearing a slouch hat and American Army chocolate-chip-pattern camouflage uniform, a rebel militia member with an AKM came out of the stairway and strolled casually into the room. On one knee Encizo centered his machine pistol on the irregular.

Oblivious to the shadows in the room, the man started walking across the floor toward the street. McCarter straightened his arm. The Browning was a bulky silhouette in his hand, the cylinder of the silencer a blunt oval in the gloom.

There was a whispered *thwat-thwat* and the front of the Congolese's forehead came away in jigsaw chunks. The man dropped straight down to his knees, then tumbled forward onto his face with a wet sound.

Encizo kept the muzzle of his machine pistol trained on the doorway in case the man wasn't alone, but there was no sign of motion from the staircase as McCarter shifted his aim and cleared the second door.

Behind Encizo, James entered the room and peeled off to the left to take cover, followed closely by Manning and then Hawkins. Each member of the unit looked down at the dead Congolese, his spilling blood clearly visible in their monogoggles.

"We take the stairs," McCarter said in a low voice. "There's no way to clear a building this size with our manpower so it's hey-diddle-diddle-right-up-the-middle until we reach the roof, then over and in. Stay with silenced weapons for as long as we can."

The ex-SAS trooper swept up his silenced Browning Hi-Power and advanced through the doorway as the rest of Phoenix Force fell into line behind him in an impromptu entry file. Hawkins took up the final position with his silenced Mk-11, replacing Gary Manning as rear security.

Weapons up, Phoenix force continued infiltrating Brazzaville.

*Managua, Nicaragua*

THE CENTRAL COMPLEX occupied the heart of downtown Managua. Twin residential towers rose up out of a huge complex of office buildings, entertainment galleries and civil amenities structures. The complex was the iconic soul of the modern Nicaraguan capital, all sleek steel, gleaming glass and streamlined design.

On the upper level of the west tower Mara Salvatrucha had purchased an entire floor for his personal use. The level was made up of posh business offices close to the elevator bank and a succession of grand suites growing progressively more ostentatious.

Chao Bao had been given use of a VIP luxury suite halfway down the avenue-wide hallway. Hip-hop music blasted from the most advanced stereo that money could buy, the American gangsta rappers talking about the perils of the hood, guns, drugs and the police along with how hard it was to run whores, earn your money and shoot your friends in the back. Bao found a lot of proletariat wisdom among the profane lyrics.

Three dozen people wandered around the luxurious apartment drinking from champagne flutes and snorting high-grade cocaine from hospitality bowls set around the suite. On a Louis XVI table of oak two European runway models writhed in a tangle of anorexic limbs sweating and naked as they enthusiastically wrestled themselves into a cosmopolitan 69 position.

Bao sat in a plush Gustavian divan sofa, his head spinning from the champagne. Two Nicaraguan sisters, ages fifteen and thirteen, their eyes glassy and red, sat on either side of him. His host had promised him that the girls had to be experienced to be believed. He had gone into great length describing the combined sensation of their oral talents, leaving Bao trembling inside his new Italian leisure suit.

Now he set aside his champagne flute and plucked up the platinum spoon on the chain around his neck. He leaned forward and dipped the utensil into the crumbling, flakey pile of cocaine set on the glass-top table in front of the twenty-thousand-dollar divan sofa.

He put the spoon to his nostril and snorted hard, leaning back into the couch as his head spun in a swirl of euphoric pleasure. The teenage sisters began rubbing their hands across his chest and thighs in mechanical motions, their young eyes never leaving the pile of drugs on the table.

Vision swimming, face numb, with 50 Cent blaring in his ears the Chinese intelligence agent looked across the table to his host, Nicaraguan narco kingpin and leader of the international clique of MS-13, Mara Salvatrucha. The man held a Diamond Crypto Smartphone to his ear, the Russian cellular device costing well in excess of one hundred thousand American dollars.

In his other hand he held a blunt the size of a Cuban cigar, the marijuana pungent as it smoldered. Over his shoulder the runway models switched positions and Bao reminded himself to take his Viagra pill soon.

Salvatrucha pulled his cell phone from his ear and handed it to a popular Spanish-language soap opera star. The former Miss Colombia boasted an eighteen-inch waist and gigantic breast implants. She held the drug dealer's phone without comment, white powder in a sticky residue on her left nostril. Rhinoplasty had crafted her nose into perfect symmetrical proportions. She had spoken as enthusiastically of the teenage girls' sexual talents as Salvatrucha had.

"My friend," Salvatrucha hollered across the table at the Chinese covert operator. "My associates have just informed me that the shipment was picked up from your Congolese freighter and brought by fast-boat to my warehouse in Puerto Negra." The ugly man grinned, revealing a mouth full of gold teeth. "Once again you have come through." The drug kingpin lifted a hand and snapped his manicured fingers. Bao saw the bulky frame of the Romain Jerome watch, crafted out of steel salvaged from the hull of the *Titanic*.

Instantly a steroid-enhanced gorilla with a military-issue Glock-18 machine pistol in a shoulder holster stepped from his post by the wet bar and crossed to Salvatrucha. The drug prince pointed at Bao and nodded before settling back in his seat and taking a gigantic pull off his blunt. The Colombian soap opera star whispered something in his ear and he grinned like a demented jack-'o-lantern, eyes glued to the deep valley of her improbable cleavage.

As the bodyguard handed the Chinese operative a padded manila envelope, Salvatrucha looked over at Bao. "Hey, friend," he said. "Did you know Marta has her tits insured with Lloyds of London for five million British pounds?"

Bao leaned forward and took the envelope from the bodyguard, his eyes following Salvatrucha's blunt-tipped finger as they waved at the beautiful woman's breasts. She giggled as the Chinese man stared and then thrust her chest forward and shook it at the intelligence agent. Lacking a bra inside her Halston dress, the globes bounced and jiggled.

"If the weapons are half as good as my man in Puerto Negra tells me," Salvatrucha continued, "I might let you do a line or two off them."

"It's better than a mirror any day." The television star laughed in a smoky alto. "Isn't that right, girls?" she asked the sisters book-ending the Chinese man.

Dutifully, with responses of zombies, the teenagers smiled and nodded. Bao put his glass down and opened the bubble-wrap envelope. Inside he saw a clear plastic shock case around a miniature 80 mm CD.

Illustrious would be pleased.

"That gives you what you need," Salvatrucha said. "That's my lifeblood right there. The information on that disk will give you everything you need to run along my network up through El Salvador into Mexico and as far north as Chicago. Most of the space on that disk is taken up by security ICE," he explained, using the slang acronym for intrusion countermeasure electronics. The man turned deadly serious. He sat forward and used a sharp elbow to knock the former Miss Colombia back away from him. "I want my submarine. I gave you what you said you needed. I gave you the underground railroad into America and all the support that goes with it." He kissed his fingertips like a French chef. "Those weapons that just came off your freighter? That's a good start—but I want the connection with the Russian navy. I want my motherfucking submarine."

Bao slid the envelope away. Illustrious would indeed be

pleased. He intended to inform his superior just as soon as he finished with the girls. Miss Colombia had confided in him that they worked harder if you spit on and slapped them. He was fairly tingling with his eagerness to tear into the teenagers.

The People's Republic seemed a far away place. Even with his comrade Xi-Nan running the other side of the operation with Nicaraguan intelligence, Bao still felt like a man who'd slipped into another world.

"We will get you the contact," Bao assured him. Rafik Bagdasarian and his Armenian syndicate were worth their weight in gold.

The Chinese agent's assignment to South America had already proved to be everything he'd heard. It beat the hell out of trying to run a cell in Islamabad or an assassination operation in Taiwan. He'd heard that working with the Russians was all parties and whores, but Bao hated vodka and the cold. He would give Mara Salvatrucha anything he wanted to stay in his position.

Around him the apartment erupted into frantic cheers as the runway models unveiled their sex toys. Bao snorted more cocaine and thought about how much the Party fathers in Tiananmen Square would disapprove.

HERMANN SCHWARZ GRASPED the TTY device in his left hand and the handle above the passenger window with his right. He spoke into the ISA-provided handheld device and his words were transferred to text, encoded and transmitted through satellite relay to the Farm.

"I appreciate the fact that Akira is flying one of the Farm's Predators for Phoenix, but the Agency confidential informant was wrong. I need the schematics for the west, not the east tower of the complex. Preferably before Carl kills me with his driving."

Barb Price's voice answered with cool proficiency over the earjack pickup. "Carmen's running it down right now. Using the IBM Bladerunner I think we can simply give you security and engineering overrides to the whole building. There's no way anything less than the hardware we're running is going to crack those firewalls anyway."

"Fine," Schwarz acknowledged. "What do I need to do to shut down the alarms and commandeer the elevators, then?"

"Bear is telling me that if you can manage to crack into the building through a local access port he can slave the commands to your PDA."

"Fine. That's not a problem," Schwarz replied. "Walk in the park. All I need is a computer inside the building and its AV in/out port."

"We're good to roll, then," Price said. "Stand by for transmission of west tower blueprints and electrical schematics."

"Copy. Able out," Schwarz said.

## CHAPTER THIRTEEN

Fourteen blocks away Xi-Nan entered Nicaraguan agent
Ortega's office. The Nicaraguan counterintelligence operative came to his feet instantly. The Chinese liaison handed
a second computer printout over to the secret policeman.

"You have them?" Ortega asked.

"Yes. Still no voice verification—that remains impossible. We do have a firm lock on the signal, however, allowing for triangulation," Xi-Nan replied. "They're in
downtown Managua right now and on the move. With the
codes I just provided you should be able to follow and track
that signal at will."

Ortega turned toward the stone-faced Gutierrez. The
commando leader rose smoothly from his seat. "Alert your
team," Ortega ordered. "Once you're in the air I'll have
tech services provide you with coordinates."

"Yes, Chief," the grim-faced killer replied.

*Brazzaville, Republic of the Congo*

RAFAEL ENCIZO OPENED his hand.

Greasy hair slid through his loosened fingers as he
plucked the blade of his cold steel Tanto from the Congolese militia member's neck. Blood gushed down the front
of the man's chest in a hot, slick rush and the gunman
gurgled wetly in his throat.

Standing beside Encizo, Calvin James snatched the

man's rifle up as it started to fall. The eyepieces of the two commandos' night optics shone a dull, nonreflective green as they watched the man fall to his knees. Encizo lifted his foot and used the thick tread of his combat boot to push the dying Congolese over.

The final rebel soldier on the building roof struck the tar paper and gravel as the last beats of his pounding heart pushed a gallon of blood out across the ground. As James set the scoped SVD sniper rifle down Encizo knelt and cleaned his blade off on the man's jeans before sliding it home in its belt sheath.

Seeing the sentry down, McCarter led the rest of the team out the stairwell and onto the roof and crouched next to a 60 mm mortar position that overlooked the cluster of buildings in the Brazzaville slum. Below them, in the shadow of the militia sentry building, a large flat-roofed home stretched out behind an adobe-style wall. Armed guards walked openly or stood sentinel at doorways. In the courtyard near the front gate a Dzik-3 with Congolese police markings stood, engine idling.

T. J. Hawkins took up a knee and began using the night scope on his Mk-11 to scan proximity buildings for additional security forces. As David McCarter took up his field com, Manning knelt behind him and began to loosen the nineteen-pound grappling gun from the Briton's rucksack.

"Super Stud to Egghead," McCarter said.

"That's so very funny," Akira Tokaido replied, voice droll.

"You have eyes on us?"

"Copy that," Tokaido confirmed.

At the moment the Predator drone launched by Jack Grimaldi from the coalition-controlled Congolese airport floated at an altitude high enough that it was invisible to either Phoenix or, more importantly, to the Congolese special groups HQ below. Despite that, the powerful optics in the nose of the UAV readily revealed the heat-signature silhouettes of Phoenix Force to Tokaido in his remote cockpit as they crouched on the Brazzaville rooftop.

It was a little known fact that most of the larger drone aircraft deployed in Afghanistan and, to a lesser extent, Congo were piloted by operators at McCarran Air Force Base in Las Vegas, Nevada.

As soon as Kurtzman and Price had seen the remote-pilot setup used by both the Air Force and the CIA, they had gone to Brognola with a request for the Farm to field the same capabilities using the Stony Man cyberteam as operators.

Both Kurtzman and Carmen Delahunt had proved skilled and agile remote pilots, but it had been Professor Huntington Wethers who'd proved the most adept at maneuvering the UAV drones and he had consistently outflown the other two in training.

But Akira Tokaido, child prodigy of the video game age, had taken the professor to school. The Japanese-American joystick jockey had exhibited a genius touch for the operations, and Kurtzman had put the youngest member of the team as primary drone pilot for the Farm.

Now Tokaido sat in the remote cockpit unit, or RCU, and controlled an MQ-1c Warrior from 25,000 feet about Brazzaville. He had four AGM-114 Hellfire missiles and a sensory-optics package in the nose transplanted from the U.S. Air Force RQ-4 Global Hawk, known as the HISAR or Hughes Integrated Surveillance & Reconnaissance sensor system.

From a ceiling of 29,000 feet Tokaido could read the license plate of a speeding car. And then put a Hellfire missile in the tailpipe.

Having seen the effects of the coordinated air strikes during training with the FBIs Hostage Rescue Team at a gunnery range next to the Groom Lake facility known as the Ranch, David McCarter was more than happy to have the air support.

The ex-SAS leader of Phoenix Force touched his earjack and spoke into his throat mike. "You see the wheeled APC at the front gate?" He asked.

"Copy."

"That goes. I want a nice big fireball to draw eyes away from us while we come in the back door."

"That should obstruct the main entrance to the property," Tokaido affirmed, voice calm. "That changes the original exit strategy Barb briefed me on."

"Acknowledged," McCarter responded. "But the truth on the ground has changed. Adapt, improvise, overcome."

"Your call, Phoenix," Tokaido confirmed. "I'll put the knock-knock anywhere you want."

"Good copy, that. Put one in the armored car and shut down the gate. You get a good cluster of bad guys outside in the street, use Hellfires two and three at your discretion. Just save number four for my word."

"Understood." Tokaido paused. "You realize that if you're inside that structure when I let numbers two and three go you'll be extremely danger close, correct?"

McCarter said, "You just bring the heat. We'll stay in the kitchen."

"Understood. I'll drop altitude and start the show."

"Phoenix out." McCarter turned toward the rest of the team. "You blokes caught all that, right?" Each man nodded in turn. "Good. Hawkins, you remain in position. Clean up the courtyard and stay on lookout for snipers outside the compound."

Hawkins reached out and folded the bipod on his Mk-11.

"I'll reach out and touch a few people on behalf of the citizens of the United States of America." The Texan shrugged and grinned. "It's just a customer service I provide. Satisfaction guaranteed."

"Just try to stay awake up here, hotshot," McCarter said. "I'll put the zip line on target. The rest of you get your Flying Fox attachments ready."

"I'm going first," Manning said. "You hit the mark with the grappling gun, but we'll use me to test the weight."

"Negative, I'm point," James said. "The plan calls for me to slide first."

Manning shook his head. "That was before we got burned. Those assholes down there know we're coming. We'll only get the one line. I should go first." He stopped and grinned. "Besides, Doc, if you fall who'll patch you up?"

McCarter lifted a hand. "He's right, Cal. We'll send Gary down first."

The ex-SWAT sniper took up his SPAS-15. "Doesn't seem right, a Canadian going before a SEAL, but I'll make an exception this time." He reached out a fist and he and the grinning Manning touched knuckles.

"Get set," McCarter warned.

He lifted the T-PLS pneumatic tactical line-throwing system launcher to his shoulder. The device sported 120 feet of 7 mm Kevlar line and launched the spear grapnel with enough force to penetrate concrete. Despite himself McCarter paused for a moment to savor the situation.

He felt adrenaline slide into his system like a bullet train on greased wheels. He knew that he was not only among the most competent warriors on the face of the earth, but he was also their leader. He could sense them around him now, reacting not with fear but with the eagerness of dedicated professionals.

They were exhausted from their hard slog through a stinking sewer and the sudden violence of their betrayal and ambush. They smelled like shit and sweat and blood and gunpowder. They had the brutal acumen of men about to face impossible odds and achieve success. McCarter smiled to himself in barbaric satisfaction as he recalled the motto of the SAS—Who Dares Wins.

As his men, other than Hawkins, slid on their protective masks McCarter's finger took up the slack in the grappling gun.

There was a harsh *tunk* sound as the weapon discharged followed by the metallic whizzing of the line playing out. The sound of the impact six stories below was drowned out by the sound of Tokaido's Hellfire taking out the Dzik-3 APC. A ball of fire and black smoke rose up like a volcano erupting. The blazing hulk leaped into the air and dropped back down with a heavy metal crunch that cracked the cobblestone court.

"Now we're on." Encizo laughed as Phoenix Force sprang into action.

THE MEN SLOWLY CHEWED their food as they watched the body hanging from chains set into the wall. The American Dexter had threatened Rafik Bagdasarian's operation with exposure. Now he was paying the price.

Battered, the American looked up and saw two men, one in the uniform of the Brazzaville police, calmly eating. The two men continued eating as other men caught his tongue in a pair of pliers and cut it off with a bayonet. They had continued eating as the torturers had taken a ball-peen hammer to first his fingers and then his toes. Then, when his naked body was slick with his own blood, they had driven the slender shaft of an ice pick into his guts, perforating the large intestine and allowing his own fecal matter to flood into his system, causing sepsis.

Then a vengeful god had rained fire from the sky.

Commandant Asira jumped out of his chair at the sound of the explosion. Around him his men scrambled to respond and he looked across the table to the Congolese police officer.

"It's them!" Bagdasarian retorted.

"Ridiculous. They never could have gotten close. It must be an air strike. I told you to leave the city," Asira declared.

Bagdasarian thought about the Chinese warlord Illustrious sitting in Beijing like a spider at the center of his web. He thought of telling the Triad leader how he had failed, how the Americans had driven him from the lucrative city of Brazzaville.

"No," the Armenian said simply. "I'm safer here."

"I'm not!"

Then they heard the gunfire burning out around them and they knew it was more than an air strike. They knew then that against all odds the unknown commandos had made it into the rebel slum, had come for them. They both realized that whoever these clandestine operators were they would never give up.

Instantly they rose and ran to rally their men.

"Fall in around me!" Asira snarled.

"To the roof and perimeter!" Bagdasarian said in turn.

Men were scrambling into positions and snatching up weapons.

THE LINE DIPPED under Manning's weight as he rode the Flying Fox cable car down the Kevlar zip line. He sailed down the six stories and applied the hand brake at the last possible moment. He lurched his feet up and struck the roof of the building on the soles of his combat boots.

Because of the size of his primary weapon, the cut-down M-60E, he couldn't roll with the impact and instead bled off his momentum by sliding across the roof like a base runner stealing second. With the last of his forward energy the big Canadian sat up and took a knee, swinging his machine gun into position and clicking off the safety.

Behind him he heard the sound as Calvin James hit the roof and rolled across one shoulder to come up with SPAS-15 ready. Above them they heard the muffled snaps as Hawkins cut loose with the silenced Mk-11 from his overwatch position. Below them in the courtyard around the sprawling house they heard men scream as the 7.62 mm rounds struck them.

Covering the exposed roof, Manning turned in a wide arch as Rafael Encizo slid to the roof, putting his feet down and his shoulder against the line to arrest his forward motion. The Cuban combat swimmer came off his Flying Fox and tore his Hawk MM-1 from where it rested against the front of his torso.

McCarter landed right behind Encizo and rushed across the roof, M-4/M-203 up and in his hand. Gunfire burst out of a window in a building across the road. Manning shifted and triggered a burst of harassment fire from the hip. His rounds arced out across the space and slammed into the building, cracking the wall and shattering the lattice of a window. Red tracer fire skipped off the roof and bounced into the street.

Above the heads of Phoenix Force in their black rubber protective masks, T. J. Hawkins shifted the muzzle of his weapon on its bipod and engaged the sniper. He touched a dial on his scope and the shooter suddenly appeared in the crosshairs of the reticle on his optics.

The man had popped up again after Manning's burst had tapered off and was attempting to bring a power scope on top of an M-16 to bear on the exposed Americans.

Hawkins found the trigger slack and took it up. He let his breath escape through his nose as he centered the crosshairs on the sniper's eyes. For a brief, strange second it was as if the two men stared into each other's eyes. The Congolese pressed his face into the eyepiece on the assault rifle. The man shifted the barrel as he tried for a shot.

The silenced Mk-11 rocked back against Hawkins's shoulder. The smoking 7.62 mm shell tumbled out of the ejection port and bounced across the tar paper-and-gravel roof. In the image of his scope the Congolese sniper's left eye became a bloody cavity. The man's head jerked and a bloody mist appeared behind him as he sagged and fell.

Automatic weapons fire began hammering the side of the building below Hawkins's position. He rolled over onto his back, snatching up his sniper rifle. He scrambled up, staying low and crawled through the doorway of the roof access stair. He intended to shift positions and engage from one of the windows overlooking the compound in the building's top floor.

Below his position McCarter found what he was looking for. He pulled up short and shoved a stiffened forefinger downward, pointing at a enclosed glass skylight that served to open up and illuminate the breakfast area. The opening had appeared as a black rectangle on the images downloaded from the Farm's Keyhole satellite, and from the start McCarter had seized on the architectural luxury as his means of ingress.

"We have control," Manning barked, and from half a world away Barbara Price and the Farm's cyberteam watched from the UAV cameras. "We have control," McCarter repeated.

To create a distraction on the hard entry Gary Manning had prepared an explosives charge. Being unable to precisely locate their target before the strike, nonlethal measures had been implemented. Working with Stony Man armorer John "Cowboy" Kissinger, the Canadian special forces demolitions expert had prepped a series of flash-bang charges using stun grenades designed to incapacitate enemy combatants in airplane hangars, factories or warehouses. In addition to the massive noise distraction device, Manning and Kissinger had layered in several devices from ALS Technologies that contained additional payloads of CS gas.

McCarter slipped into his own SAS model protective mask, then gave Calvin James a thumbs-up signal. "Five, four, three, two, one."

The ex-SEAL jogged forward and pointed the SPAS-15 at the skylight. The semiautomatic shotgun boomed and the double-aught shot smashed through the reinforced commercial-grade window.

"Execute, execute, execute!" McCarter ordered.

Instantly, Manning stepped up and threw his satchel charge through the hole. As it plunged through the opening the entry team turned their backs from the breach, shielding their eyes and ears. Instantly the booming explosion came. Smoke poured out of the opening like from the chimney of a volcano.

James spun and stepped up to the ledge before dropping through the hole. He struck the ground and rolled to his left out along the side of his body, absorbing the impact from the ten-foot fall. He came up, the SPAS-15 tracking for a target in the smoke and confusion.

A running body slammed into him, sending them both spinning. Ignoring the combat shotgun on its sling, James reached out with his left hand and tore the AKM out of the figure's grip, tossing it aside as he rolled to his feet. His Beretta appeared in his fist. He pulled the guy closer but didn't recognize the stunned terrorist, so put two 9 mm bullets through his slack-jawed face.

David McCarter dropped down through the breach into chaos.

He saw James drop a body and spin, his pistol up. Around him the whitish clouds of CS gas hung in patches but the interior space was large enough that the dispersal allowed line-of-sight identification.

The Briton was violently thrown into a momentary flash-back to his experience in the assault on London's Iranian embassy after Arab separatists had taken it hostage. He saw a coughing, blinded gunman in a Congolese police uniform stumble by and he shot him at point-blank range with the M-4.

The man was thrown down like a trip-hammered steer in a Chicago stockyard. McCarter went back down to a knee and twisted in a tight circle, muzzle tracking for targets. Behind him a third body dropped like a stone through the shattered skylight.

Rafael Encizo landed flat-footed then dropped to a single knee, his fireplug frame absorbing the stress of the ten-foot fall. His MM-1 was secured, muzzle up, tightly against the body armor on his chest, and his MP-7 machine pistol was gripped in two hands.

Through the lens of his protective mask Encizo saw two AKM-wielding men in civilian clothes stumble past. The Cuban lifted his weapon and pulled the trigger, firing on full automatic from arm's length. He hosed the men ruthlessly, sending them spinning into each other like comedic actors in a British farce. He turned, saw a Congolese police-man leveling a folding-stock AKM at him and somersaulted forward, firing as he came up. His rounds cracked the man's sternum, struck him under the chin and cored out his skull. The corrupt Congolese dropped to the ground, limbs loose and weapon tumbling.

Gary Manning dropped through the breach, caught himself on the lip of the skylight with his gloved hands and hung for a heartbeat before dropping. He landed hard with his heavier body weight and went to both knees. He grunted at the impact on his kneepads and orientated himself to the other three Phoenix members, completing their defensive circle as he brought up the cut-down M-60E.

Without orders the team fell into their established enclosed-space-clearing pattern. Manning came up and charged toward the nearest wall, clearing left along the perimeter of the room while James followed closely behind him, then turned right. Encizo tucked in behind Manning as he turned left, and McCarter, also charged with coordination, followed James.

Manning kicked a chair out of the way and raced down the left wall of the room. Weapons began firing in the space and he saw blinking muzzle-flashes flare in the swirling CS gas. He passed a dead man hanging by chains from the wall. A close-range gunshot had cracked the bearded man's skull and splashed his brains on the wall behind his head.

Manning suddenly saw Asira standing with a pistol, three men with Kalashnikovs in a semicircle in front him. The Canadian Special Forces veteran triggered the M-60E in a tight burst, and the 7.62 mm rounds tore the first police bodyguard away as he rushed forward. From behind him Encizo used the MP-7 to cut down the left flank bodyguard before the Congolese police officer could bring his weapon around.

Manning took two steps forward and shoved the muzzle of his machine gun into the throat of the final bodyguard as Encizo swarmed around him. The Congolese stumbled backward at the blunt-tipped spearing movement, his hands dropping his weapon and flying to his throat. As he staggered back Manning lifted a powerful leg and completed a hard-style front snap kick into the man's chest, driving him farther backward and into the Congolese.

Both men fell as Encizo reached the fumbling, corrupt Congolese police officer. The combat swimmer thrust the muzzle of his smoking hot machine gun into the coughing and half-blinded Asira's face, pinning it to the floor. With his other hand Encizo broke the man's wrist, sending his pistol sliding away.

## CHAPTER FOURTEEN

Hot shell casings rained down on Encizo as Manning cracked open the bodyguard's chest with a 5-round burst from the M-60E. Blood splashed Asira's face as he grimaced in pain and the stunned and terrified traitor squeezed his eyes tight shut.

Manning halted his advance and swung the machine gun up to cover them as Encizo flipped the Congolese over onto his stomach and used white plastic riot cuffs to bind his hands. Asira screamed in pain as the shattered bones of his wrist were ground against their broken ends by the Phoenix Force commando's rough treatment.

A block of light appeared in the gas-choked gloom. A knot of well-armed reinforcements surged through the open door from the outside. Manning shifted on a knee, swinging around the M-60E. He saw one of the reinforcements fall, the side of his head vaporizing, then a second fell, and Manning realized Hawkins had found his range even at this acute an angle.

Manning pulled back on the trigger of his machine gun and the weapon went rock and roll in his grip. He scythed the confused Congolese terrorists down, cutting into their ranks with his big 7.62 mm slugs. The men screamed and triggered their weapons into the ground as they were knocked backward. He let the recoil against his hand on the pistol grip climb the muzzle up and his rounds cut into the terrorist bodies like buzz saws.

"Phoenix, we have company," Akira Tokaido warned over the team's earjacks. "Hellfire number two is away. Danger close."

*Managua, Nicaragua*

FROM ACROSS THE STREET from the west tower of the plaza complex Able Team watched the building. Inside the vehicle, behind the steering wheel, Carl Lyons carefully slid the brochure on urban transportation in Managua into an inside pocket. Behind him in the back of the vehicle Schwarz was busy finishing up his daisy-chain linking of what explosives had been available at the safehouse, including the C-4 stripped from four Claymore mines and a small amount of Semtex.

"I think that'll do it," the former Green Beret said.

"Good," Lyons said. He turned to Blancanales. "You ready, Pol?"

The Puerto Rican looked up from his PDA, where he had been memorizing the building architectural plans. He tucked the device away and reached for the door handle on their stolen automobile.

"I'm ready. Create the distraction then get in hard on our six as I move through the building."

"You get a good copy on all that back on the Farm?" Lyons asked into his throat mike.

"We're picking you up solid," Carmen Delahunt replied. "It'll be myself and Hunt on the line tonight. Akira and Aaron are handling a Phoenix operation. I have zero official police chatter about you guys so far. Hunt is handling other government agencies."

"Let's roll," Lyons said. He reached down beside the steering column and hit the release on the sedan's gas tank.

The doors on the vehicle flew open and the Stony Man commandos slid their silenced H&K MP-5s beneath their jackets. The hour was late, past midnight, and there were only a few pedestrians, most in their early twenties, on the street.

Blancanales and Schwarz immediately left the automobile and began walking up the sidewalk. Lyons casually strolled to the back of the vehicle and unscrewed the cap to the gas tank. Behind him Blancanales and Schwarz crossed the street a full city block up from the entrance of the west tower.

Lyons let the gas cap dangle and reached into his jacket. Like a fisherman playing out line, he quickly unwound a yard of det cord attached to the firing system of one of the M-18 A1 Claymore mines Schwarz had stripped at the safehouse.

Blancanales, followed by Schwarz, stepped off the street and up onto the sidewalk fronting the side of the plaza west tower. They reached an ornate concrete divider holding heavy planters and leaped the barrier.

Lyons slid the silver metal blasting cap detonation trigger at the end of the det cord into the fuel tank of their stolen vehicle. Casually he backed away from the vehicle, playing out the cord as he strolled down the sidewalk.

Up the street Blancanales and Schwarz disappeared behind a wall of vibrant, blooming azaleas and arboreta shrubs. Lyons heard drunken laughing voices and looked up to see a young couple approaching his improvised explosives device.

"Oh, Jesus Christ!" he snarled, and pulled out his MP-5. Then in perfect Spanish he called out, "Excuse me, people—violence going on here." He triggered a burst from the silenced submachine that sent geysers of dirt from the sidewalk lawn into the air. The couple screamed and froze.

Growling, Lyons waved the muzzle of the H&K to shoo them away, and they both turned and ran.

"Carmen, I just had to play the big bad with some lovebirds. The Managua PD should be getting calls very soon."

"Copy, Ironman," Delahunt replied. "I'll monitor and delay as appropriate. This should help cement the action as a Salvatrucha rival's hit team."

"Absolutely," Lyons replied as he worked. "MS-13 has plenty of enemies. Getting ready to make some noise now."

He quickly unplayed the last of the det cord until he was left holding the prepped plastic Claymore trigger, often called a clacker. The Able Team leader took a knee behind the front of a conveniently placed Audi sports car and took a last look around before squeezing the lever action on the device.

There was a *whump* as the explosion sucked up the surrounding oxygen, then a brilliant ball of flame rolled into the sky, carrying the four-door sedan upward. The vehicle rolled up end over end, then crashed down in the middle of the street directly in front of the building's entrance.

Lyons casually rose, throwing the Claymore trigger down after wiping it clean of fingerprints on his shirt. He stepped out from behind the bumper of the Audi and casually strolled across the street as the burning automobile rolled over on its side and flaming engine fluids spilled out in a river from the blazing pyre.

Down at the doors of the west tower the ex-LAPD police officer saw a uniformed security guard appear, then three more. He hopped the concrete barrier and pushed his way through the bushes to come up against the side of the building.

Blancanales and Schwarz, MP-5s out and up, stood beside the first-story floor-to-ceiling window on this aspect of the west tower. Blancanales lifted his submachine gun and triggered a blast, raking 9 mm bullets down the length of the glass wall, unzipping it like a dress. The sound of the blazing vehicle muted the sound of shattering glass, and the leaping flames cast wild shadows in the window reflections, making the three Americans look like demons in the uncertain light.

Weapon up, Blancanales entered the building, stepping over the threshold of broken glass. Behind him Lyons pulled the pins on two smoke grenades and tossed them on either side down the building. The smoke canisters spit out their concealing fog and added to the overall confusion on the scene.

As Schwarz entered the building after Blancanales, Lyons stepped forward and followed him in. So far he could detect neither an audible building alarm nor the sounds of approaching response sirens.

Inside the building the team entered a labyrinth of office cubicles, computer workstations, copy centers and partitioned walls of the IT suites. Each member of Able Team reached up and pulled his NVD into place, transforming the office space into a surrealistic nighttime theater of muted greens and grays.

"Up ahead, on the left," Blancanales said.

The ex-Green Beret jogged forward, turned a corner, ran down three steps on a memorized route, then turned a right-hand corner. He lifted his MP-5 and fired on the move as he ran.

The single 9 mm round struck the glass of the interior door and shattered it. He ran up to the breach and used the silencer on his submachine gun to knock loose glass down to the carpet. Following behind him, Schwarz ran through the opening and entered the blade farm.

"I'll secure the access door," Lyons said, and peeled off.

He ran beside a transparent wall separating the building's CPU and blade server farm from the IT workstations. Inside the vault were several hard drives locked in transparent plastic cases and carefully stacked atop plasti-alloy filing cabinets. On the other side was a small rectangular box of polished Brazilian walnut. The containment unit was surrounded by a cluster of sophisticated electronics: climate-control sensors, humidity readouts, seismograph, gas analyzer, barometer and temperature gauge.

On the other side of the glass Schwarz used a sliver of his thermite to burn out a security door lock as Lyons raced for one of the doors in the office complex that opened up onto the nonpublic access parts of the tower.

"That was it, boys," Carmen Delahunt said. "We have the call. I'm moving to insert cross-channel traffic to slow the communications, but the clock is ticking."

"Understood," Blancanales said.

While Blancanales pulled security in the other direction Lyons cracked the door and looked out on the service hallway and toward the private elevator bank situated there. He looked back to see Blancanales covering the primary entrance to the IT offices.

Schwarz, speaking in a calm voice, broke squelch over the earjacks. "I'm linked up to the system, Stony Man."

"Copy that, Gadgets," Delahunt replied, using the team's nickname for the man. "I'm initiating our Trojan program now."

A burst of angry Spanish came from the front of the office and Lyons had to stifle his instinct to turn and spray the potential danger. They may have been trying to create the illusion that they were a drug cartel hit team, but they had no intention of murdering innocent civilians to perpetrate the charade.

Three security officers in brown uniforms rushed through the doorway. Each man had a radio on his belt with a handset attached to the epaulet on his shoulder. In their hands they carried side-handled batons and cans of pepper spray.

Blancanales stepped out of the shadows, lowered his MP-5 SD-3 and fired off three short bursts. The 9 mm slugs tore the red exit fire sign above the door into twisted pieces of metal and a shower of sparks. Further bursts punched holes in the Sheetrock on either side of the security officers as they crowded through the door.

"Jump back! Get back!" Blancanales yelled in Spanish, and the frightened men stumbled over themselves to make their escape.

"Able, listen, I have a sitrep from the professor," Delahunt broke in, using Wethers's nickname. "He's lifted an internal email from the Nicaraguan saying they're scrambling a squad of Guardia Puerto Cabezas. It doesn't say why or to where, but it's suspicious."

"The thug unit?" Blancanales asked. "The timing's not good for us, but it could be something else."

"No such thing as a coincidence," Lyons cut in.

"Trust an ex-cop not to believe in serendipity," Schwarz said.

"Seren-what? Is that even a real world?"

"Done!" Schwarz interrupted. "I have taken control of the building. Do not attempt to modify your vertical. Do not attempt to modify your horizontal. Let's get to the elevators."

A second later the building went black.

# CHAPTER FIFTEEN

*Stony Man Farm, Virginia*

Coordinating things at a hundred miles a minute, Barbara Price hurried into the Computer Room. She saw Hunt Wethers hunched over his workstation keyboard, fingers flying, while Carmen Delahunt was pulling her VR helmet back on.

"How's it going with Able?" Price demanded.

Wethers looked up and smiled. "The plaza firewalls were very good—but no match for our IBM Bladerunner. I negotiated primary control to Gadget's PDA interface just a minute ago. We'll still run all the software packages but our computers will take their cue from his gear."

"The Nicaraguan launched an elite unit by helicopter," Delahunt added. "It seems coincidental since Managua police are scrambling to the site, but we don't know what they're dealing with yet."

"I don't like coincidences," Price said flatly.

"Nobody does," Delahunt agreed. "But so far we have no indication that the commando unit is onto Able—just that they launched. There are a lot of dirty deals going down in country and even though local spooks are aware that Able is up to no good, that doesn't mean they know exactly what that 'no good' is."

"Fine," Price acknowledged. "Keep me informed, and I want to know the second they have the target."

"Understood," Wethers said.

Price left the room and pulled out her cell phone. She strode down the hallway toward the tramcar on the underground track connecting the Farm's Annex with the older structure of the main house.

Her encrypted cell phone rang as she climbed into the car and started the short ride. The walls of the tunnel flicked by as she picked up speed. At the other end of the signal Hal Brognola picked up on the third ring.

"Talk to me, Barb," he growled.

"Able has engaged, Phoenix is knee-deep in the hoopla as we speak. Akira's just dropped two Hellfires into Brazzaville."

"Christ," Brognola sighed, "when it rains it pours. We got lucky that it's this time of year, so that we have the necessary hours of darkness. To be honest I'm worried about Able's plan. It makes the President nervous."

"It makes *me* nervous," Price said. The open tramcar began to slow. "But that's Carl for you."

"True enough, but another firefight in Congo is nothing. They blow up the biggest landmark in Managua? That could be an international incident."

"There's something else," Barb said. The car came to a stop and she stepped out. A weathered-looking man she remembered had just rotated to the blacksuits held open a door as she breezed by and into the basement of the main house.

"Something else? What?" Brognola demanded.

"We're not sure if it's significant but one of Nicaragua's elite death squads got scrambled about the time

Lyons blew his distraction and the team made entry into the building."

"What's the chatter from the Nicaraguans? They made our boys? How?"

"We don't know. We just don't like the timing."

"You think they could have cracked our commo?"

"There's no way they busted our ice," Price said. "No one can bust our ice. Okay, maybe the British or the Chinese—but not that quickly and not even really that likely," the former NSA mission controller said. She stepped into the elevator and hit the button. "Though…maybe…"

"Maybe what, Barb?"

"Maybe if their gear was updated or augmented they could catch the signal itself. Not break the encryption or trace us through the cutouts, but maybe they could catch the initial beacon transmission."

"How much of a maybe is this?"

"Aaron doesn't think it likely of third world operatives. I tend to agree," Price said.

"But?"

"But I guess it's possible."

"So Able could be compromised?"

"Only as to a triangulation of their location, not to their actual mission objectives. Also the Nicaraguan spooks wouldn't know for sure that the people using the comm. unit were the same as the ones who shook them at the international airport. It'd be them throwing manpower at everything hoping to get lucky."

"I'll hold off telling the President then," Brognola said. "I want to know as soon as Phoenix and Able are both in extraction phase from their ops."

Price stepped out on the main floor of the farmhouse

and began walking toward the front door. "Understood," she said.

"Goodbye." The line went dead.

*Brazzaville, Republic of the Congo*

CALVIN JAMES SPUN, bringing up his SPAS-15.

The combat shotgun boomed like a cannon in his hands and steel shot scythed through the CS-tinged air to strike two AKM-wielding figures. The Congolese terrorists were thrown backward and spun apart, arms flying in the air, weapons tossed aside by the force of the blasts.

One of them tripped over a wastepaper basket and went down hard. The second bounced off a wall and tumbled into a chair. James moved between them, double-checking as he went. The one on the floor was leaking red by the gallon from a chewed-up throat and torn-open chest. The second was missing enough of his face that the ex-Navy SEAL could see his brains exposed.

There was a burst of rifle fire and the SPAS-15 was knocked from James's hands. Heavy slugs slammed into the ceramic chest plates of his Kevlar body armor. He staggered backward and grunted. His shoulder hit the wall and he went to one knee. Reflexively, his hands flew to his Beretta. As he drew the handgun David McCarter lunged past, the M-4 carbine up and locked into his shoulder, the muzzle erupting in a star-pattern blast.

He saw the figure wearing an expensive black silk jogging suit at the last moment and pulled his shot. The 5.56 mm rounds struck the man in his legs and swept him to the floor of the building. Bright patches of blood splashed in scarlet blossoms on the figure's thighs.

Behind them the front of the building exploded as another Hellfire struck.

McCarter was thrown to his knees. He grunted with the impact as something heavy and wet struck him between the shoulder blades. He looked down and saw a severed arm lying on the floor. He felt the heat of the raging blaze burning behind him.

He struggled to his feet.

"Talk to me, people!" Tokaido shouted over the line. "Talk to me!"

McCarter didn't answer but lunged forward. Rafik Bagdasarian was screaming from the pain of his shattered thighs but the Armenian mobster was pulling a Jordanian JAWS pistol from out of his attire. McCarter slashed out with his M-4. His bayonet caught the man across the forearm, slicing a long ugly gash. The Armenian screamed again as he dropped the pistol.

Still on all fours McCarter scrambled forward, the M-4 up in one fist by the pistol grip. The blade of the wicked M-9 bayonet jabbed into the soft flesh of the Armenian's throat and pushed the man backward.

"Freeze!" McCarter snarled. "Move one iota and I'll put your brains on the wall!" He lashed out with the bayonet again, lancing the tip into the meat of the man's shoulder and opening a small, harassing wound.

"Speak to me, Phoenix!" Tokaido hollered again.

"Manning up," Gary answered. "That was very danger close, my friend," the Canadian Special Forces veteran said.

"Pescado is good," Encizo said. "I'm knee-deep in tango guts, but that blast blew the front off the building."

"Copy that," Tokaido said. "They had two platoon-size elements as reinforcements at the door. Forty, fifty guys all bunched up at the entrance."

"McCarter up," McCarter said. "But Cal took a round

and I have our boy." He paused. "If we're clear, I need help."

Instantly there was a reaction from behind him and the bulky frame of Gary Manning appeared by his side as Encizo scrambled over to pull security near the prone Calvin James.

Encizo leaned in close, his eyes hunting for enemy motion from behind the lenses of his protective mask. "Speak to me, Cal," he demanded. "You okay?"

James turned his head and opened his eyes. He opened his mouth to speak but no sound came out. Encizo, ears still ringing from the Hellfire blast, shook his head to clear his hearing.

"Speak, bro!" the Cuban demanded.

James lifted his head and muscles along his neck stood out with the effort. His lips formed the words under his protective mask and his eyes bulged with his effort under the lens, but no sound came out. Finally there was a rush of air through the blunt nose filter.

"That *hurt!*" he wheezed. "Jesus, that hurt. I think I cracked my ribs."

"Is he good?" McCarter demanded over one shoulder. His weapon muzzle never wavered from Bagdasarian's face. "Is he good?"

Beside the Briton, Manning fired his M-60E in a short 4-round burst. A crawling Congolese terrorist shuddered under the impact of the 7.62 mm slugs and lay still. Encizo turned toward the Phoenix Force leader and shouted back.

"Yeah, he just had the wind knocked out of him, maybe bruised ribs, maybe cracked—we don't know, but he's ambulatory!"

"He's also right goddamn here," James snapped, sitting

up. "He doesn't need you talking about him as if he were incapable of speech."

"Good," McCarter replied, his voice echoing weirdly under the mask. "'Cause I got our boy but the bitch needs patching up before we yank him back to Wonderland." McCarter switched to his throat mike. "Akira, how we look out there?"

"You got vehicles coming up the street. You'll have more bad guys on site very shortly. I'm still sitting on Hellfire number three."

"Fine. Hit 'em at the gate and cause a further choke point but save number four for my direction."

"Understood."

McCarter pulled back as James moved forward, medic kit in hand. Bagdasarian looked at the black man with real hatred as the ex-SEAL ripped open the clothes and began to treat the Armenian's wounds.

"That's Dexter," Encizo said. "The dead guy on the wall. He matches the picture."

"We can give him a funeral pyre," Manning said. He looked at Bagdasarian. "I'd like to see you bleed to death, asshole."

"Give him morphine," McCarter told James as he rose. "We're going to have to carry him anyway with those leg wounds. It'll keep him docile."

"I'll keep him docile," Manning growled.

"I'll be the one to play doctor here," James said.

"Fine, Cal, you're the medic. What do you want to do?"

"Probably going to give him a heavy dose of morphine to keep him docile."

"Whatever you think is best," McCarter shook his head.

"What about the son of a bitch Asira?" Encizo spoke up. "He's Kabila's CO."

McCarter looked over at the Cuban combat swimmer. "You guys tag and bag him?"

"Yep," Manning confirmed as he rose. "We got him against the wall." The big Canadian began to move down the length of the room toward the blazing hole in the building, checking each of the downed bodies as he did so.

"Gary, watch out!" McCarter yelled and pointed to Asira.

The corrupt Congolese officer was rolling toward a nearby compatriot and reaching for a knife. Manning stepped back just as McCarter turned, lifted his M-4 to his shoulder and pulled the trigger. Across the stretch of floor broken by the rapidly thinning clouds of CS gas the corrupt Congolese police officer Asira caught the 3-round burst in the side of the head.

Blood gushed like water from a broken hydrant and the blue-gray scrambled eggs of his brains splashed across the floor with bone-white chips of skull in the soupy mess. McCarter lowered his smoking M-4.

The ex-SAS commando leaned down close to the wounded Armenian. "Rafik, you see the consequences of messing with me?"

The man paled under the scrutiny of the Phoenix pro. His eyes shifted away from the death mask McCarter's face had become. Then he jerked and winced as James unceremoniously gave him an intramuscular shot of morphine.

The black man's teeth shone very white as he smiled with ghastly intensity at the captured Armenian. "Don't worry," he said. "If we shoot you it'll only be in the gut."

Manning and Encizo reached down and jerked the Armenian to his feet. McCarter spoke into his throat mike. "Akira, how we look?"

"Clock's ticking. You got stubborn bad guys trying to dig their way through the burning barricade I made out of the first-wave vehicles. I'm still sitting on my last Hellfire."

"Good copy," McCarter said. "We'll be rolling out the back door in about ten seconds. Why don't you go ahead and blow me a hole out the back fence now?"

"One escape hatch coming up," Tokaido replied.

"Copy," McCarter said. "We are leaving."

*Managua, Nicaragua*

ABLE TEAM RODE in the elevator up the west tower.

With the building completely under Schwarz's control, he had shut everything down except for the back-of-the-building service elevator they had commandeered.

"Shall I hit the sprinklers and fire alarms now?" Schwarz asked. "Get everyone in the building running out just as the police and fire emergency show up?"

"Wait until we hit the floor," Lyons said.

"Sure," Schwarz replied.

The team stood in silence as the elevator smoothly rose. Time seemed to drag out to improbable lengths as the floor numbers grew steadily larger. Schwarz began to whistle a soft, distracted tune.

Lyons sighed and looked at his watch. Seeing the action, Blancanales leaned over and inspected the timepiece.

"That's nice. New?"

"Yeah, got it last week. Cracked the face on my other one when I took the hard landing on our training jump," Lyons replied.

"I got a new boat," Blancanales offered, looking at his own watch.

"Really?" Schwarz asked.

"Yep, little Bayliner," Blancanales said. "I got twin engines, though."

"That should be cool."

"Oh, yeah. I'll have you out on it. That extra outboard makes all the difference."

"Good enough weather we've been having," Lyons offered. "Back home, I mean—for boating."

"Oh, sure, super," Blancanales agreed.

The elevator slowed beneath their feet and slid to a stop at their floor. The doors parted with a pneumatic hiss to reveal a small, bone-white service area. Able Team stepped out, Schwarz using commands from his NSA-upgraded PDA to keep the elevator firmly in place.

Inside the service area there was an empty bucket with a mop and a silver metal room-service cart with an empty champagne bottle on it. The American commandos freed their submachine guns from beneath their jackets.

"Will that elevator hold even against a firefighter override key?" Lyons asked.

"We're in so deep to this building's control system that that elevator will hold until I say even if they cut the goddamn cables." Schwarz laughed.

"They have room service?" Blancanales asked. He pointed at the fancy wheeled cart with the empty green champagne bottle. The room smelled vaguely of disinfectant and the fluorescent lights were stark and industrial, casting everything in a bright, harsh light that Blancanales associated with hospitals.

"The building has a concierge service," Schwarz told him. "It's only available to the top five floors."

"Fine," Lyons said. "Go ahead and hit the fire alarms. When the authorities get here I want thousands of people streaming out. I want us to disappear in a real mob scene."

Blancanales reached out and pulled open the door to the service lobby as Lyons stepped forward, lifting his H&K MP-5. Behind them, Schwarz, grinning like a mischievous child, quickly typed a command into his PDA. The encrypted signal bounced along its traverse to the IBM Bladerunner under the Annex at Stony Man Farm, which interpreted the command and fed it into the building's network.

As they stepped out into the hallway all hell broke loose.

An electronic alarm began to screech. The lights on the top half of the tower went out just as the ones lower to the ground floor had. Red glowing emergency lights clicked on low to the ground. Overhead the sprinkler systems opened up and began to flood the area. An audio system of extensive power that had been blaring hip-hop music from behind one of the many hall doors suddenly cut out.

Able Team moved down the center of the hallway ignoring the chaos they had caused. They were in a luxurious hall of marble tile, titanium-gold fixtures and black walnut woodwork. Four burly Hispanic men in expensive suits came away from a teak desk and comfortable office chairs set in the middle of the hallway near the residential elevator doors decorated in gold filigree and Italian cut crystal.

Blancanales, the muzzle of his H&K submachine gun pointed down, walked forward, lifting his left hand up, palm out. "Good evening, my friends," he said in rapid-fire Spanish. "We have a fire in the kitchen of the restaurant on the top floor. Everyone must evacuate using the stairs because of the gas leak."

Ingram M-11 9 mm submachine guns appeared from beneath the desk.

"Why are you armed!" One of the bodyguards demanded. His face was adorned with an el Diablo–style goatee. "Who are you? Who is the gringo!" Water from the spewing sprinklers began to pool on the desktop and run over the edges.

Doors began opening up along the hallway, drunken partygoers stumbling out in confusion, men cursing and more than a few females screaming in fear. The blinking red emergency lights illuminated the scene with a surrealistic quality.

Lyons stepped from around behind Blancanales even as Schwarz floated out even farther to the left. The Americans revealed their silenced weapons and the narco-soldiers understood the situation instantly. There was a triple echo of harsh, sound-suppressed coughs as the German weapons fired, the three American commandos moving forward, heel-toe in a synchronized line.

Able Team's bullets tore down the wide hall in a pyramidal pattern designed to avoid the clusters of intoxicated partygoers stumbling out of the rooms. Bullets stitched into the bewildered bodyguards and the pooled water from the sprinklers turned a diluted crimson.

The dead men flopped to the ground as confused and intoxicated partygoers flooded the hallways. The fresh, leaking corpses were trampled on by a dozen different men and women in expensive party clothes and cocaine-induced tunnel vision.

Lyons lowered his submachine gun to make it less obvious and stepped in front of Blancanales and Schwarz. He turned a big shoulder to the press of hysterical humanity and began to rudely push his way through, searching faces as he made for the door to the main suite.

Behind him Blancanales and Schwarz threw punches to knock the cartel hangers-on away from them. Twice stoned soldiers produced pistols in a threatening manner and were executed, their bodies dropping to the cold, water-slicked tile.

A topless woman tripped over one such corpse and sat up screaming, her face and hands painted red. Reflexively, Schwarz stopped and grabbed her under on arm to help her. She shrieked and raked his exposed face with her nails, clawing for his eyes.

The ex-Special Forces soldier jerked his face back and shoved the screeching drug whore away, barking out his pain and surprise as three red stripes were gouged into his face. The hissing woman stumbled backward, eyes rolling wildly. The heel of her pump broke as she forced herself to her feet—then the crowd surged around her in the dark hallway and she was gone.

"What the hell," Schwarz swore, amazed.

"Hey, I wanted a building's worth of people clogging the halls and spilling out into the street when the police showed up," Lyons said. "But these guys are crazy."

"Cocaine and Johnnie Walker Black Label will do that to you," Blancanales replied.

# CHAPTER SIXTEEN

The team shouldered their way to the door, the thick crowd of partygoers thinning out steadily as the men approached the far end of the hallway. The door to the master suite foyer hung open and Able Team approached the entrance with caution, weapons held low but ready.

From inside, even over the scream of the fire alarm and the rushing howl of the sprinkler system, they could hear a man shouting angrily in Spanish. Lyons stepped through the door and stepped left, coming up against a table. Behind him Schwarz followed him through and peeled off to the right. Blancanales anchored the door just to the right of the opening.

Inside the room a man they recognized from their briefings as Mara Salvatrucha was snarling into an expensive cell phone. Standing close by, a group of bodyguards watched him, hair plastered against their heads by the sprinkler system. As if controlled by a hive mentality, the squad of gunmen turned to face the intruders, hands darting beneath jackets to dig for the grips of pistols.

Lyons stepped forward and lifted his H&K MP-5 as one of the bodyguards pulled a Skorpion vz. 83 machine pistol from inside a sky-blue suit jacket. The German-made submachine gun shook in the big American's hands and the 9 mm Parabellum unzipped the narco-soldier from belly to sternum.

Blood splashed the front of the man's shirt as his

stomach was opened up and he stumbled backward. Schwarz knocked the Nicaraguan gunman standing next to Lyons' kill down with a 3-round burst to the head. From the doorway Blancanales hammered a third kill down with his own weapon as the other two swiveled to deal with the remaining bodyguards.

The room flashed with light and cracked with the detonation of unsuppressed weapons returning fire.

*Brazzaville, Republic of the Congo*

PHOENIX FORCE SPRANG into action with the choreographed smoothness of a dance troupe on display or a surgical team in an O.R. Taking out the last three 40 mm rounds for his Hawk MM-1, Encizo laid his grenade launcher on the ground. He pulled a fragmentation hand grenade from his web gear, armed it, then trapped the spoon under the weapon's weight to create a high-explosive booby trap.

Gary Manning jerked their prisoner to his feet and threw a pillowcase like a hood over the frightened man's head as Hawkins snatched the man up under his arm. Still gathering himself after his close call, Calvin James readied two smoke grenades. David McCarter, waiting by the door to the terrorist redoubt, looked back at his team, then nodded once when he saw they were ready.

"Hit it," he ordered.

"Copy, danger close," Akira Tokaido responded immediately.

There was a long moment of silence. During the elastic minute the team's ringing ears recovered slightly and they could hear the shouts of men coming from the street outside the compound gate, the racing of engines and the stutter barks of automatic weapons. There was the crackling of vehicle fires clearly audible through the walls of the building. Inside the hazy room it stank of sweat and blood and fear. Their eyes watered and their noses ran as they stripped off their protective masks to facilitate their coming sprint.

Hawkins held the sweat-soaked Armenian under one sweat-drenched arm while the gigantic Manning held him tightly on the other side. For a moment the Texan had a very clear picture of the end of one of his favorite movies; an old Western called *Butch Cassidy and the Sundance Kid*.

In his mind's eye Hawkins could clearly see the climax of the film where the trapped Robert Redford and Paul Newman loaded their final rounds into their pistols before making a last, desperate charge against the Bolivian army. Legend had it the outlaws had survived.

Most historians disagreed.

"Here it comes!" McCarter shouted.

The ex-SAS trooper swung away from the open door and went to a knee. Outside there was a final heartbeat then the Hellfire slammed into the back wall of the compound. The missile shrieked in, screaming as it darted toward the cinder-block wall, it struck with the force of an automobile and detonated with a deep, resonate boom. The concussive waves rolled through the building and shook the team, threatening to knock them down.

Bagdasarian swayed and the Americans jerked him up right. Outside, through the open door past McCarter a cloud of smoke and dust rolled by. The Phoenix leader came up off his knee and turned toward the door.

"Go! Go! Go!" he yelled.

James ran forward and threw his two primed smoke grenades into the swirling mess toward the blocked compound gate where the armored car burned. Thick smoke began to pour into the already obscured area, reducing vision to inches.

McCarter slapped Enciso on the shoulder as James threw his grenades. The Cuban rushed out and ran toward the breach in the wall created by Akira Tokaido's Hellfire. Broken chunks of masonry and rubble were scattered across the courtyard, threatening to twist his ankles. He moved forward, weapon up, pushing through the smoke until he found a hole big enough to drive a truck through.

He rushed forward through the smoke until he broke out on the other side. He stood in a dirt lane running along one side of the compound. To his right he could see the building and street the team had used to infiltrate the enemy combatants' stronghold. Seeing no movement, he spun in the other direction and took a knee.

"Clear!" he hollered back.

"Coming!" Manning shouted through the swirling cloud of smoke and dust. A second later the big Canadian burst through the smoke. He and Hawkins were dragging the stumbling Armenian between them. The men spotted Enciso and approached him, walking fast, weapons up in their free hands.

A second later James emerged from the smoke, his submachine gun ready, and half a heartbeat after him came David McCarter. There was the sound of Kalashnikov fire from above them and gouts of dirt geysered up from the alley floor in a sloppy staccato pattern.

McCarter and Enciso spun as the bullets hammered toward the group. The Briton's carbine swung up and he cut loose with a series of 3-round bursts as Enciso joined in with his backup weapon. A Congolese in a third-floor window was driven back from the opening as the team's bullets hammered around him. In the brief lull McCarter triggered his M-203 and launched a 40 mm HE round through the opening. The black projectile lobbed upward, then sailed into the window.

The crack of detonation was followed by a surge of dark brown smoke, and body parts flew out the window.

"I'm overhead," Jack Grimaldi's voice filled their earjacks. "Three blocks due west is our LZ," the Stony Man pilot reminded them. "But the streets around you are crawling with bad guys," he warned.

Hawkins felt a chill surge through him as he was forcibly reminded of his experiences in Mogadishu, Somalia. He snarled in response and lifted his weapon as more Congolese gunfire began to be directed toward the fleeing team.

"Phoenix," McCarter shouted, "let's move!"

In the buildings around them Congolese awoken by the explosions and gunfire appeared in their windows, looking down on the chaos below while others tried to shepherd their families toward cover. The occasional militia member or armed neighborhood youth took the opportunity to snipe at the American unit below even as Bagdasarian's own militia foundered in confusion.

Overhead Jack Grimaldi's Blackhawk helicopter appeared. The Farm's premier pilot spun the aircraft around, the rotor wash beating down on the struggling men. He got the Blackhawk's nose pointed to the team's six o'clock and sent two 7-inch rockets down the alley behind them. The missile rounds flew like arrows through the tight passage for a hundred yards before slamming into the corner of the compound, pouring fire and smoke in a wild, wide pattern and driving the civilian gunmen for cover.

Running hard with one hand under the Armenian's arm, Hawkins saw movement and reacted without conscious thought. He pivoted at the waist and brought up his submachine gun. A Congolese teenager armed with a folding-stock AKM staggered backward in a doorway, red blossoms opening up his chest.

There was a blaze of gunfire from a second-story window on Manning's side and the big Canadian staggered as a round struck his vest. Two 7.62 mm rounds struck their prisoner in the hip and right leg. The rebel screamed out loud and staggered, trying to fall.

Hawkins swung around and put a shoulder into the Armenian terror master's gut, scooping the wounded man up in a fireman's carry. Manning let go of the prisoner and twisted toward the fire, swinging up the cut-down M-60E. He cursed savagely and cut loose with the heavy machine gun.

Red tracer fire lanced upward as he poured twenty rounds through the open window. There was a shrill, high-pitched scream as the heavy-caliber slugs ripped into the building and a shattered Kalashnikov forestock still attached to a nylon shoulder sling tumbled outward.

"I've got the bastard!" Hawkins yelled. "Just cover us!"

"Got it!" Manning yelled back.

Around them James and Encizo and McCarter were firing, as well. Above them a cascade of smoking, gleaming brass shells fell around them as the hovering Grimaldi worked the trigger on his chain gun.

"Phoenix." The pilot's voice broke squelch. "It looks like an anthill from up here. You've got men and vehicles pouring into this area from all sides. I have RPGs on the roof and snipers in almost every window."

"Another day at the office, Jack," McCarter replied. "Block and a half. We can do anything for another block and a half."

"Negative," Grimaldi replied. "Your primary route is

filled with Congolese gunslingers. You need to move to Route Bravo."

Hearing that, James shouted, "Plan B, people, we are switching to plan B."

"I thought this *was* plan B," Encizo shouted, his machine pistol chattering in his hand.

Bullets knifed through the air around them. Manning cut loose again with the M-60E, trying desperately to suppress the growing enemy fire. Above the team Grimaldi banked the helicopter hard and swung away to leapfrog one street over from their position. McCarter fired his last 40 mm grenade from his M-203 at a rocket team on a building above them.

The HE round arced up like a basketball sailing smoothly from the hands of a talented player in a fade-away jump shot. Just as the two RPG gunners knelt and shouldered their weapons the 40 mm grenade slammed into the roof. The round tore the ambushers apart, spraying chunks of their bodies out in a spinning whirlwind and punching a hole through the structure's ceiling. Both of the RPG-7 warheads were detonated and the resulting explosion ripped the roof off the building, scattering bricks in the air like raindrops.

"This way!" James shouted.

Manning sprayed the street behind them as the other four men quickly ducked down an open alley and cut across to the next street. With each step the burdened Hawkins took, the Armenian prisoner screamed in anguish and the ex-Delta operative was soaked in the man's blood.

Phoenix Force emerged on the next street over, McCarter leading the way. A bullet parted the hair on his head and tugged at the sleeves of his black fatigue shirt. A step behind him, James and Encizo both saw the gunner at the same instant and fired simultaneously. Their bullet streams crossed as they poured tight bursts into the man's body and he was scythed to the ground.

Up ahead of them by thirty yards Grimaldi swiveled the helicopter around in a tight pivot. His voice came over their earjacks, eerily calm in the din of the massive street fight. "It's the same as the sat photos showed," the Stony Man pilot reported. "We've got a chain-link fence bisecting the alley."

"Copy," McCarter replied. "Blow it."

A rocket sprang to life and leaped from the pod on the Blackhawk. A second later a ball of fire rolled up into the air, funneled like a chimney between two buildings. At the rear of the team Manning sensed motion and heard a high-pitched, almost rhythmic wailing from behind him. He spun, swinging the M-60E into position, the barrel so hot it showed red.

He paused, finger on the trigger. He felt his throat choke in shock and horror, his eyes bulging wide in surprise. From behind a heavy black cloth dress he saw a Congolese woman racing toward him, wailing her prayer. From behind her body two middle-aged Congolese men fired from the safety of a basement doorway. The woman's hands appeared empty at first glance and were held above her head as she raced, each step she took causing her ankle-length dress to flare outward.

Manning squinted in confusion as the men's AKM fire snapped and popped around him. Thrown hastily over the woman's concealing outfit was an OD green vest with multiple pockets. Red and green wires ran out of the pockets and up past her veils to a square black plastic detonation device in the woman's hand.

"Jesus Christ!" Manning swore in horror as he realized

the woman had to be wearing over twenty pounds of plastic explosives in her suicide vest.

His finger tightened on the trigger.

## CHAPTER SEVENTEEN

*Managua, Nicaragua*

Muzzle-flashes erupted like yellow blossoms from the barrels of the narco-soldiers. The three bodyguards cut loose with sustained blasts as they closed ranks to protect their boss. Carl Lyons went to a knee, his H&K MP-5 already up and firing as he dropped. Above him 9 mm rounds slammed into the ornate paneling of the luxury suite, gouging wood and drilling holes through the walls. He heard the buzz of a round cutting through the air next to his right ear and he felt his hair blow back from the bullet's passage.

The MP-5 danced in his hands as he triggered a hasty burst. Across the doorway from him Schwarz's weapon responded with its own *thwat-thwat-thwat* of suppressed fire. They both heard Rosario Blancanales grunt in pain as he was struck.

Lyons saw one of the bodyguards go down under his fire, the man falling backward, weapon spraying wildly as blood splashed out in inky scarlet jets. The falling thug struck his boss, Salvatrucha, in the shoulder and the intoxicated man staggered as he tried to bring a Beretta 92 to bear. On the other side of the cocaine kingpin the last bodyguard did a drunken two-step as one of Schwarz's 3-round bursts nearly decapitated him. Lyons surged to his feet and thrust his submachine gun to the full stretch of his arms and snapped his finger against his trigger three times.

The German submachine gun shook in Lyons's hand, sending vibrations up his arms as shells came spinning out of his ejection port. All nine 9 mm rounds hit the drug lord center mass, shredding his sky-blue silk shirt. The man folded inward under the impact of the pistol rounds, his shoulders slumping, his knees buckling. His face, frozen in disbelief, snapped forward as his head fell forward on a loose neck.

The man dropped straight down on his ass, pistol flying to the floor, then he flopped over onto his back. In an incongruous moment it registered with the American that the man's pants were unbuckled and open at the waist, revealing a flash of silk boxer shorts the same sky-blue as the man's shirt.

Operating on instinct and adrenaline, Schwarz's own fail-safe blast carved the Nicaraguan's jaw off and shattered the man's spine just below his skull. The former Special Forces commando spun toward his partner, finger easing off the trigger to lie along the guard.

"Pol!"

Blancanales was on one knee, his face twisted into a grimace and his left hand clutching his chest. With an exercise of sheer willpower the ex-Green Beret rose, bringing his weapon into play.

"I'm fine," he gasped. "Let's go!"

Lyons was already moving forward. He caught a flash of movement and spun, dropping the smoking barrel of his MP-5, his finger finding the smooth metal curve of the trigger. In the manner of all trained hostage-rescue experts the former LAPD detective's eyes went to the rushing figure's hands. The rule was a simply dichotomy: weapon equals shoot. No weapon equals no shoot.

His finger slacked off the trigger of his weapon just before he almost fired a tight burst. He saw empty, slim brown hands tipped by long, bloodred nails. He blinked out of his operational tunnel vision and saw the complete picture. The woman was nude, a sheer G-string revealing a bikini wax and silicon bags blowing her bare breasts up to the size of beach balls, the nipples and areolae very dark against her flawless skin.

In an adrenaline-stretched moment Lyons saw a glittering diamond necklace above the swaying, bouncing breasts and a beautiful face twisted in terror, brown eyes tinged red as she screamed past perfect pearl-white teeth. He saw her eyes find the bloody, mutilated corpses of Salvatrucha and his bodyguards and he saw something snap in her mind.

She screamed again and darted for the door.

Lyons stepped forward and thrust the heel of his left palm into her sternum and knocked her backward, tossing her anorexic frame onto a Louis Baptiste divan. She gasped at the impact and flew backward before bouncing into the cushions. He lowered the smoking MP-5 and trained it on her face.

She looked up, eyes white in terror, her lipstick smeared across her face. He leaned in close, menacing and huge, eyes angry slits. He spoke in perfect Spanish, his voice an angry bark.

"Where's the Chinese?" he snarled.

"In there," she sobbed. A skinny arm thrust out and one of those scarlet-nail-tipped fingers pointed toward a double set of ebony wood doors across the room. "I swear to God, he's in there with the girls."

"Go," Schwarz ordered. He jerked his weapon muzzle toward the door, indicating the path. "Get out of here."

The woman sobbed in relief and sprang up off the couch. She sidestepped in a skittish dance past the bloody corpses of her former lover and his men, then raced out of the room. Blancanales, still recovering from the impacts to his body armor, covered her until she left the room, then took a knee again to provide rear security.

"Get ready," Lyons told Schwarz, voice low.

Schwarz nodded and took a flash-bang from under his coat. Lyons moved forward toward the door. "Come out!"

From inside the room a pistol boomed five times. Able Team ducked as bullets slammed through the door, spraying splintered wood. The bullets cut through the room in wild, desperate patterns, none striking close to the Americans.

"Hard way. Always the goddamn hard way," Schwarz swore.

Lyons carefully lifted and aimed his MP-5. He triggered a 3-round blast. The 9 mm Parabellum rounds struck the handle of the interior doors, shattering the lock housing. Instantly two feminine voices screamed in terror from inside the room.

Schwarz and Lyons ran forward, each taking up a position by the door. Behind them they heard Blancanales's weapon cycle as he fired the suppressed submachine gun at targets outside the room.

Schwarz let the spoon fly off his flash-bang as he primed the grenade. Lyons leaned forward, reaching across the door and snagged the twisted metal handle connected to the shattered lock housing. He yanked his arm back and jerked the door open. A pistol fired three times from inside the room. Schwarz tossed the stun grenade through the opening and both men turned away.

The metal canister landed on thick carpet and rolled to a stop. The voices of the teenage girls screamed again and a man cursed in fear. There was a brilliant flash and a sharp, deafening bang as the grenade detonated.

The occupants of the room cried out in pain and fear as dozens of hard rubber balls exploded like shrapnel, cutting through the room and raising welts on naked flesh. There was the distinct sound of shattered glass, and Schwarz turned and charged through the bedroom door, his MP-5 up and ready. He darted inside and cut left as Lyons popped up out of his crouch and swung around the open door to enter the room and cut right.

Schwarz danced left in a sidestep like an NBA guard trying to cut off the center's drive to the basket. His own submachine gun up, Lyons sprinted right, the muzzle snapping through vectors as he cleared his assigned spaces. The room was dark but floor-to-ceiling balcony doors revealed a million-dollar view of the Managua skyline and provided light from the buildings around them.

Cold air rushed in through the shattered windows and sheer gauze drapes fluttered like flags. Schwarz saw a huge bed in the shape of a heart, the covers and blankets tangled into piles, a dozen pillows scattered around. To the left of the big bed, on his side of the room, he saw two skinny but eerily beautiful teenage girls, one dressed in jet-black lingerie and stockings, the other in gleaming white. He felt a queasy sense of disgust as his adrenaline-sharpened eyes recognized the girls as looking so alike they could only be sisters.

The two young girls huddled in the corner of the bed. "Stay down," he ordered in Spanish and put a burst into the bed, slicing the sheets and kicking up stuffing. "Clear!" he snapped in English.

Lyons charged forward on his side of the room, clearing his vectors. He saw a lean man in a pair of European-style, fire-engine-red briefs. The swarthy-skinned and black-haired man was laid out on his stomach. A 9 mm pistol lay on the floor several yards away.

Bao moaned, still blinded and deafened by the stun grenade, and attempted to push himself up on shaking arms. Lyons ran forward and kicked him in the gut. The man gagged, almost puking at the impact and sagged back down. The Able Team leader spun around and stomped the fingers of the Chinese agent's right hand, breaking three of them, then hopped forward and kicked the pistol across the room toward the shattered glass window.

Schwarz stepped closer, keeping his muzzle pointed in the general direction of the teenage girls but watching the downed Chinese intelligence agent with a reflexive, mechanical suspicion. Lyons moved closer to the man as he gasped for breath and let his submachine gun drop to hang from its strap. He dropped down, driving his knee into the man's unprotected kidney.

Bao shouted at the pain and spasmed up like a fish yanked into the bottom of a boat. Lyons snatched the man's arms while he was too hurt to resist and slapped on a pair of plastic riot cuffs. Once his hands were secure Lyons popped back up and dragged the Chinese agent to his feet. He reached down and squeezed the intelligence agent's fingers, grinding the broken fingers together in a viselike grip.

Bao screamed. Lyons leaned in close, maintaining pressure, and whispered in Spanish, "You are coming with us. If you give me a moment of problem I'll break your arm at the elbow. If you try to run I'll machine gun your kneecaps. Do you believe me?"

Bao didn't answer, panting from the pain. Lyons snarled and crushed his hands harder. "Do you believe me?" he repeated.

"Yes, yes—I believe you." He nodded.

"Good, let's go."

Lyons shoved the injured man forward, driving him out of the room despite the man being dressed in nothing but underwear. Kept up on his toes by the painful hold the ex-cop kept him in, the bewildered and overwrought agent meekly complied.

Schwarz danced backward toward the door, searching the room for possible intelligence or dangers. He saw the Chinese agent's clothes in a pile at the foot of the bed and he stooped to rifle the pockets quickly. He took the man's wallet, cell phone and a manila envelope containing a miniature disk. As he secured the finds he looked over at the girls. They had stopped crying and watched him with huge, dark eyes.

"Stay in school," he told them as he backed out of the room. "And 'just say no,' okay?"

The girls hugged each other until they were sure the killers were gone. Then they went out into the gore-painted suite to steal money and drugs from the dead men.

BLANCANALES LED THE WAY down the dark hallway. He moved quickly, stepping past the occasional corpse of a Salvatrucha bodyguard and ignoring the spraying sprinklers. The water was two inches deep on the floor and Able Team splashed as they hurried along the hallway toward the elevator.

Lyons initiated his throat mike. "Stony, we have the package. We're making our exit now."

"Copy," Price replied immediately. "Everyone okay?"

"Pol took a few rounds to the vest but he's mobile," Lyons acknowledged. "What's the status of forces at the moment? I can hear a whole shitload of sirens outside, even this far up."

"You have a massive police presence, according to Carmen," Price relayed. "However, the Managua fire service was not able to break Gadgets's lock on the elevators with their master override keys. The elevators are still shut down and under your control, so those police teams are going to have to climb up to try to find you."

"Good to hear," Lyons said.

"Americans!" Bao sputtered, outraged. "You dare—!"

Casually, Lyons squeezed tighter on the man's broken fingers. The spy went up on the balls of his feet in agony as shocks of anguish burst through his body. Nonchalantly, Lyons swung a big hand out and slapped the prisoner across the face, cutting off his words and outcry.

"You shut up," Lyons snapped. "There'll be plenty of time for you to talk later."

The man gasped at the pain but stopped talking. Schwarz pulled his sat-linked PDA clear as the team approached the service elevator room. Furiously he began typing on the miniaturized keyboard.

Lyons shoved the Chinese captive into a corner of the room, grateful to be out from underneath the constant deluge of the sprinklers. Blancanales kept the service room's door open an inch, watching the hallway outside with his weapon at the ready.

"What about that helicopter response crew Hunt picked up?" Lyons asked.

"Radio silence on that," Price told him. "Nothing going across the Nicaraguan intel network. If they're coming for you, they've gone operational quiet. The regular police and fire emergency services are screaming up a storm, but that's it for the moment."

"If they're screaming now, just wait," Schwarz said, grinning. He hit Enter on his pad. "Let's go!"

"Able over," Lyons said into his throat mike and shoved Bao into the elevator car.

"Stony copy," Price said, and went silent.

"Christ, heads up!" Blancanales said from the door.

"What do you have?" Schwarz demanded, finger on the button of the elevator.

"I got a SWAT team with flashlight-mounted shotguns and assault rifles just come out of the stairwell at the other end of the hallway," Blancanales replied into the dark room.

Lyons narrowed his eyes and squinted past Blancanales to look out through the crack in the door. The flashlight beams cut through the sprinkler drizzle and cut swathes through the dark hallway. "Impossible," he said, voice low. "No way a team in full helmet and body armor makes it up that fast. I don't give a crap how good they are."

"Helicopter from the roof?" Schwarz offered.

"Only way," Blancanales agreed. He eased the service door shut and began backing away.

"Help! He—" Bao shouted in Spanish, voice shrill from inside the elevator.

Lyons pivoted and punched the man in the stomach as Schwarz automatically threw a sharp elbow into the man's jaw. Bao folded then sagged, his voice cut off as Blancanales jumped into the elevator.

Schwarz closed the doors and emergency lights flickered on, casting weird shadows as the elevator lurched and began descending. "Going down?" he asked.

"You've been waiting to say that all night," Lyons said.

"I take it where I can get it." Schwarz shrugged.

"This asshole alerted that team," Blancanales said. "They'll come for the room, see us descending and radio down."

Lyons shrugged. "Nothing for it now. They aren't going to be able to guess what we're up to, no way. We just have to ride it out." He looked over at Schwarz. "You still got that hundred-mile-an-hour tape?" he asked.

Schwarz produced a small roll of the OD green military electrical tape from his fanny pack. "Always."

"Good, tape this asshole's mouth shut."

Bao started to protest and tried to rise up off his knees, but Lyons silenced him by pressing the still hot muzzle of his submachine gun between his eyes. "Shh," the ex-cop said. "You're already pushing my buttons, Mr. Chao Bao of Chinese origin. Now hold still while my good friend here tapes your piehole shut or I'll shoot you in the shoulder."

Bao went very still and with impersonal, utilitarian efficiency Schwarz wrapped several loops of the industrial-strength tape around the man's head, pinching his lips shut. "Tsk, tsk," Schwarz whispered. "A man your age in bed with two little girls like that? What would the Revolutionary Council back home say? Seems a little Western and decadent."

"We got other problems," Blancanales pointed out. "How the fuck did that team know to come down from the roof? You think regular Managua police got SWAT teams just flying around in a chopper in case someone tries to steal a Chinese spy from a local drug runner?"

"No, I do not," Lyons agreed. "Occan's razor makes me think that they were the Nicaraguan crew Hunt tripped onto. Has to be."

"Still doesn't explain how they knew about us," Schwarz said. "Nicaraguan intel might fly around, but mostly only to kill reporters and torture students—they don't roll backup on regular police operations."

"We have to assume they've been onto us from the airport," Lyons said.

"Then we can't go back to the safehouse," Blancanales said.

"No, we've got to adapt, improvise and overcome," Schwarz said. "Once we blow this building we've got to disappear 'cause they're going to pull out all the stops to get us—bring the military in, shut this city down."

"This mission hasn't gone the best," Blancanales pointed out, voice rueful. "But we don't say die."

"No, we just make other bastards die," Lyons snarled, and poked Bao in the head. He looked up at Schwarz. "Get the Semtex ready. Once these doors open I want to be ready to roll the hell right out of here."

"No worries, we'll be ready." Schwarz grinned.

# CHAPTER EIGHTEEN

The two point men of the heavily armed Nicaraguan commando unit came through the door hard and fast, weapons up and fingers poised on triggers. Right behind them a third man rushed into the room and then a fourth. Four gun muzzles swept tight vectors in the crammed space, four fingers tightened on the smooth metal curves of triggers. Adrenaline-charged hearts hammered in heavily muscled torsos as safety-visored eyes flicked around the room. Flashlight beams played through the suffocating dark, searching.

"Clear!" each man barked in succession.

Immediately, Ortega entered the room, pistol out and ready. Behind him his cohort of highly trained killers crowded in around him like hunting dogs at the foot of a cliff where a big cat has gone to ground.

The officer strode forward, face twisted with frustration, and stood next to the elevator. Above the doors a red digital light clicked off numerals in descending order as the car plummeted downward.

"How in the hell do they have control of the elevator!" he demanded. "How can we be locked out of the building like this?"

The men shifted uneasily, unable to answer and not liking the feeling of futility that ensnared them. They were action players, used to effecting changes on their environment. Now their initiative had been stolen, their energy subverted and their motivation rendered futile. It was an unaccustomed feeling and it undermined their morale.

"Open the doors!" Ortega snapped.

The members of the elite Nicaraguan unit leaped to obey. One man, tasked by designation as breaching specialist, produced a claw-ended crowbar in the shape of a comma from his kit. Two burly men hovered close, ready to leap forward and assist.

The breach trooper crammed the end of his crowbar into the seam between the elevator doors and worked it in. Once the tip was in the gap the big man threw his body weight against the resistance. The doors opened with a slight screech of metal on metal and a hydraulic hiss.

Weapons snapped to shoulders, the red cyclopean eyes of laser sights danced in the black opening. In front of the commando squad the elevator cables sped by as the lift car smoothly fell away below them. Ortega moved forward and peered down the shaft.

Seemingly satisfied, the man stepped back. His face was an ugly, brutal-featured mask of impassivity. His eyes were the dull brown, near black of a shark's, the cold dead eyes of a remorseless predator.

"Stop them," he snapped.

Instantly two men stepped forward and around their commander. Grenades were snatched off Kevlar vests and the pins yanked free. Lever safety catches sprang free and fell away. The two men looked at each other and nodded before stepping forward and tossing their grenades into the open shaft.

The black eggs arced out and then fell away, dropping

down the long pit. The men stepped back, waiting for the twin explosions to follow.

Standing with his hands folded behind his back, feet spread shoulder width apart, Ortega allowed himself a small, ugly smile.

*Brazzaville, Republic of the Congo*

The woman shrieked, her voice as penetrating as an air-raid siren. Manning, an explosives expert, automatically calculated the blast radius from the detonation of plastique in the vest as he hesitated to fire.

The sum of his calculation was obvious. If the woman wasn't stopped, then every member of Phoenix Force would die right there, strewed in chunks across the dusty Congolese street like bloody piles of garbage.

His finger spasmed on the trigger.

The shot wasn't smooth and his burst was ragged, but instinct and training ensured his accuracy even if he couldn't consciously bring himself to do what needed to be done. The woman took the rounds and fell to the ground, the detonator flying from her grip.

Manning shifted his still rattling machine gun and poured fire past the spot where the woman's body had been and into the doorway where the cowardly Congolese fighters crouched. The rounds from the heavy machine gun chewed through mortar and wood, bursting the structure apart into shards and splinters. The rounds chewed into the men like buzz saws and ripped them apart mercilessly.

"Come on! Come on!" McCarter screamed.

James raced past Manning and up to the dead woman. He reached down, snatched the det cord from the suicide vest and threw it away, rendering the device inert. "Let's go!" he shouted.

Bullets whipped and whined around them, tearing up the road and filling the air with angry lead hornets. Hawkins dug in hard, running for the alleyway in a stumbling sprint. McCarter led the way, his carbine up and barking. Congolese gunmen fell with each discharge of his weapon, Kalashnikovs spinning away and bodies tumbling into the dirt.

Encizo shuffled along directly behind the burdened Hawkins, covering him with his machine pistol as the man charged forward toward the dubious safety of the alley. The Cuban saw a flash of motion above him on the one-story roof of an earthen-brick business. Encizo lifted his MP-7 and fired on reflex as the sniper leveled his weapon. The man screamed as six rounds tore into his gut and he crumpled at the waist and pitched forward. The sniper fell, struck a cloth sun awning and flipped over to land in the middle of the street in a broken heap.

McCarter ran up to the edge of the alley and turned the corner. Immediately a Congolese neighborhood gunman reared up in front of him, the man screaming in angry surprise. The Congolese tried to lift his AKM and bring it to bear in the short distance separating the two men.

Directly behind the first Congolese a second man with an RPG-7 lowered his weapon and clawed for an automatic pistol in his belt, eyes wide as he watched his friend struggle with the lanky Englishman.

McCarter snarled and lashed out with his M-4 carbine, using his bayonet to catch the Kalashnikov just behind its fixed iron sights and knock it aside. The Congolese's hand came off the foreshock as the M-9 bayonet slashed the old Soviet weapon aside. The man triggered a frantic, useless burst, and the sound of the weapon firing echoed in the confined space of the alley.

McCarter stepped in close and swept his bayonet up

before thrusting it forward and catching the man in the throat just under his Adam's apple. The blade punched through skin and cartilage, spilling bright blood in a gush. The Congolese's eyes bulged in pain and terror, then filmed instantly in death as the tip of the bayonet shattered his spine at the back of his throat.

The Congolese militiaman tumbled backward and Mc-Carter's M-4 twisted in his grip as the stuck blade tried to drag his weapon down. Behind the falling Congolese the RPG soldier had his hand on his pistol and was yanking it clear. Desperate to clear his weapon, McCarter triggered a 3-round burst.

The 5.56 mm rounds tore through the dying man's throat at point-blank range, the muzzle-flash setting his shirt on fire as the high-velocity rounds shredded all organic material in front of them, freeing the tip of the blade from where it had become anchored in the man's spine.

The RPG gunner lifted his pistol as McCarter pivoted and jerked his assault rifle upward. The Congolese's finger tightened on the trigger as the ex-SAS trooper fired a second 3-round burst, then a third and a fourth. At the extremely close range all nine rounds smashed into the man with supersonic force.

The pistol went off with a single, sharp bark, then tumbled from slack fingers as the Congolese was cut open from belly to sternum by the blast. Blood exploded outward like water from a child's balloon. The bearded man went down and looked up toward the sky with fixed and sightless eyes.

McCarter looked beyond the RPG team and down the alley. He cursed violently as he saw the jumbled mess blocking movement for his team. Behind him the street was on fire and echoing with the sound of automatic weapons.

Bullets slapped the mud-brick wall above his head and burrowed into the ground with lethal force.

He spun and fired at a building across the street as Hawkins entered the alley, pushing their Armenian captive in front of him. Manning followed and immediately turned and began spraying the street behind them with withering streams of fire as James sprinted into the opening, closely followed by Encizo.

"Manning!" McCarter bellowed.

The big Canadian turned and looked toward his team leader, his machine gun still bucking and kicking in his hands, the belt-fed links spilling from the green plastic drum attached to the weapon. Empty shell casings poured in a shining stream from his ejection port as he let the weapon run and the barrel had begun to glow red-hot from the continuous barrage.

Making eye-contact acknowledgment with his demolition expert, McCarter jerked a thumb over his shoulder at the alley. Manning followed the gesture with his eyes and saw the old BMW sitting there, stripped of tires and doors. Crammed into the narrow lane beside the dented old vehicle were garbage cans, filthy mattresses, coils of barbed wire, rusted oil drums and piles of stinking garbage.

Manning stopped firing and rose up off his knee, dancing backward as bullets sliced through the air around him. He sized up the task in a moment's study and frowned as he looked at his team leader.

"That's not a precision job—it's a mess," he said. "No need to try to place my charges strategically. I'll just pile what I have at the bottom and hope they do the job."

"We can't go back out into the street to avoid the blast," McCarter shouted.

Next to them Hawkins had dumped his wounded prisoner on the ground beside the dead RPG team, splashing the already blood-soaked man in their gore. The ex-Delta Force trooper lifted his primary weapon and started laying down suppressive fire of his own.

"I can slide it to the other side under the car," Manning offered.

"Good enough!"

McCarter let his M-4 drop to the end of its sling and took Manning's piping-hot M-60E as the Canadian unhooked two OD-green cloth satchels from where they hung around his neck.

"Down!" McCarter hollered as he rushed forward to the lip of the alley. The members of Phoenix threw themselves down as Manning worked to arm his Semtex satchel charges.

A knot of Congolese militia began advancing up the street from behind the cover of a .50-caliber machine gun mounted in the back of a white pickup truck. On the rooftops armed figures scrambled into position or took hasty shots at the cornered commandos.

There was such a milling mass of humanity in the street that the Phoenix Force operatives hardly bothered to aim, instead simply pouring their fire into the congested mass of militia charging toward them, weapons blazing.

The .50-caliber opened up and tore baseball-size chunks of masonry from out of the wall above their heads. The stench of cordite hung in the air and stung their nostrils with every breath they took. Their empty shell casings rained down on each other and tinkled into piles on the ground like mounds of loose change.

Encizo looked over as Manning suddenly appeared and threw himself down. Instinctively the Cuban ducked his head and thrust his face into the dirt. James saw Bagdasarian blink his eyes in sudden lucidity and try to get up. The ex-SEAL dropped his weapon and threw himself bodily over across their prisoner.

Suddenly the air was sucked from his lungs and his eyes were stung by a searing flash of light, then a deafening explosion boomed out, the blast force channeled up and over the team's crouched forms followed by a rolling cloud of dark smoke and thick dust. Manning and Encizo and McCarter bounced instantly to their feet just as a burst of machine-gun fire sprayed the alley from the rooftop of the building across the street.

Manning grunted in a sharp exhalation as two 7.62 mm rounds smashed into his flak vest and NATO body armor. He staggered backward and fell from the concussion, his face twisted in a grimace as he hit the dirt for a second time.

Encizo cursed in sudden, shocked surprise as a heavy-caliber round struck his right shoulder and a second round gouged out a furrow of flesh on his biceps. He spun like a child's top and staggered against the alley wall, his arm going numb and turning red in a spilling splash of blood.

McCarter popped up, lifting his carbine to direct the team as the burst found him. Three machine gun rounds burrowed through his flak vest at the gut and were only slowed when they buried themselves in the Kevlar weave of his body armor. He folded up like a book closing, his breath driven from his body in ruthless fashion.

He went facedown on the ground hard enough to draw blood from his nose. His teeth went through his lip in a bright sensation of pain, and blood filled his mouth and funneled down his throat as he fought to breathe.

He gagged at the slippery rush of copper-tasting fluid and threw up into the ground as smoke and dust billowed around them. Green tracer fire lanced through the cloud of debris, burning paths around the huddled team.

James came up off Bagdasarian and jerked the Armenian terror master to his feet. "Go! Go!"

He snarled in adrenaline-charged anger and shoved the prisoner forward. Hawkins rose up off his belly and ran forward. He grabbed McCarter up under one arm and hauled the man to his feet. Beside him Manning stood, still gasping, face a mask of dirt while Encizo struggled to his feet.

Hawkins spun as he saw his teammates trying to gather themselves. His weapon erupted from his hip and he swung the muzzle in a loose figure 8, filling the street with loops of hard-jacket slugs. James came up behind the stumbling Armenian and roughly shoved him, pushing the man over the dented hood of the BMW wreck. As the Armenian flipped over to the other side the ex-Navy SEAL jumped the obstacle and hauled the man up.

Encizo ran forward, the first to recover, and hurtled over the obstacle, followed by the lumbering Manning. Hawkins felt a presence at his shoulder and suddenly McCarter was beside him, hammering out covering fire with Manning's M-60E. The barrel of the machine gun was so hot the superheated rounds came out sideways, rendering the weapon completely inaccurate but still putting out a wall of lead to cover the team's retreat.

"Go!" Hawkins yelled above the din.

"Get out of here! That's an order," McCarter yelled back.

Hawkins fired a last, long burst into the dust-choked street, then followed the rest of the team over the wrecked car and into the alley. McCarter kept the trigger of the machine gun wide open as he shrugged his shoulders upward and ducked his head underneath the strap, freeing himself.

The last NATO 7.62 mm round cycled through the

weapon out of the green plastic drum and the weapon bolt
froze in the open position. The Briton heaved the weapon
from him and turned, snatching up his own M-4 carbine.
A black metal sphere arced out of the smoke and landed
at his feet. McCarter lashed out with his foot in a soccer-
style kick and punted the grenade out of the alley. The little
bomb rose up off the ground and cleared the edge of the
building.

McCarter spun as a bullet caught him high on the back
and punched him to the floor of the alley. His M-4 skidded away, lost in the swirling dust as the grenade exploded
behind him. Instantly he went deaf from the concussive
force and razor shards of shrapnel shredded his black fatigue pants.

Bursts from assault rifles poured into the alley as smoke
from the hand grenade added to the obscuring cloud of
dust. McCarter came up to his hands and knees only to
realize his left arm was numb and useless. He tried to crawl
and tumbled back down to that side. With a soft pop his
hearing returned and his head was filled with a ringing
sound. He heard angry screams as if from under water
and turned to see two Congolese gunmen charge into the
alley.

Flat on his back McCarter drew his Browning Hi-Power
as the confused fighters searched for a target. He lifted the
pistol and shot the lead man first in the crotch then in the
throat. The second man turned as the other fell and Mc-
Carter squeezed the trigger on the Browning again. The
handgun jumped in his hand and the Congolese's throat
disappeared in a flash of red and pink, punctuated by white
shards of spinal bone. The man dropped down as McCarter
got his legs under him and heaved himself up, his left arm
still useless.

McCarter turned and ran toward the blackened BMW,

his Browning up in a port arms position while his left hand dangled limply from his useless arm. Running forward, the ex-SAS trooper leaped for the hood of the ruined vehicle and rolled across the top.

Hawkins appeared out of the dust on the other side of the vehicle, his weapon up. A star-pattern flash blinked from the American commando's muzzle and bullets struck targets behind the rolling McCarter.

The Phoenix team leader hit the ground on the other side of the car, grunting at the impact. Firing one-handed, Hawkins reached down and hauled him to his feet. McCarter saw movement at the hostile end of the alley and lifted his pistol, putting three rounds into the figure.

Hawkins turned and ran, pushing the Briton in front of him. Blood soaked McCarter's shredded trousers. A channel had been blown between the debris and trash choking the alley by Manning's satchel charges, and the two Phoenix Force commandos forced their way through.

Coming out into the street on the other side McCarter instantly saw Grimaldi. The Stony Man pilot lowered his helicopter into a vacant lot half a block down from their position. A building had been caved in and set on fire by the helicopter's rockets. Rotor wash sent billows of grit and sand and masonry dust rolling out in clouds.

McCarter squinted against the blinding sheets. He saw James and Manning running with the captured Bagdasarian between them, trussed up like a Christmas turkey, while Encizo ran just off to their side, firing his machine pistol in an almost futile attempt to cover their movements.

"Come on!" McCarter shouted to Hawkins, but he was already running forward.

The rifle in Hawkins's hand cracked and a bloody crater appeared in the face of a Congolese in a random doorway. McCarter turned and shot two men through the heart at thirty feet before he was even fully conscious of the threat.

The two men sprinted forward as James and Manning threw their prisoner into the helicopter cargo bay. The Armenian screamed as he landed and the two big commandos threw themselves in after him, battering him with their bodies. The pitch of the helicopter's engines changed as Grimaldi prepared for liftoff.

A screaming Congolese in soiled clothes popped out from behind a pile of brick and rebar, an AK-74 chattering in his hand. Encizo took the top of the man's head off with a wild burst from his machine pistol. The Kalashnikov rounds hammered into the Cuban combat swimmer, smashing the MP-7 apart and punching into his flak vest and body armor.

Encizo staggered backward and across the few short yards to the chopper. Hawkins saw his eyes roll up, showing whites as he was knocked unconscious from the heavy blunt-force trauma of the impacts. The Cuban toppled backward, falling flat out, his hands bleeding profusely from where broken parts of his weapon had sliced into them.

Suddenly, Gary Manning was there. Two strong hands reached out and snatched the falling Encizo up by his combat harness. A third hand, starkly black and belonging to James, appeared between Manning's, and Encizo was yanked up into the helicopter.

Bullets burned past Hawkins and McCarter, slamming into the body of Grimaldi's helicopter. Divots appeared in staccato patterns and rounds ricocheted wildly as the last two members of Phoenix Force ran forward. The landing skids broke free of the ground and lifted off. Hawkins dived forward and threw himself through the open cargo door. An RPG rocket burned past, missing the tail rotor by inches before sailing out into the lot and exploding.

McCarter put one foot up on the helicopter skid as it rose two feet off the ground. He lunged forward toward Calvin James, who leaned out, hands spread wide to catch him.

Then the bullet struck him in the side of the head and the world went black.

# CHAPTER NINETEEN

*Managua, Nicaragua*

Carl Lyons jerked his head upward in surprise.

Two metal thunks sounded, clearly audible overhead on the roof of the elevator car. The red digital readout on the floor indicator flashed past 1 as they dropped toward the building basement.

The twin hammer explosions came hard, denting the roof with intense bangs. The lights on the ceiling bulged outward and exploded from the concussive force. The elevator went dark and shards of plastic sprayed outward. Above them the explosion of the hand grenades snapped the cables instantly and the elevator car plunged downward.

Carl Lyons was thrown hard against the side of the elevator, but he rebounded wildly and his feet got tangled up in each other. He went down, landing hard on their prisoner. The man grunted in pain as the big American struck him.

Hermann Schwarz felt his center of gravity suddenly shift and his feet flew out from under him so that he landed hard on his ass, snapping his teeth together with the force of a trap. His out flung arm struck Rosario Blancanales, who was falling himself. Both men went down in a tangle of arms, weapons spinning out of their hands in the sudden, violent plunge.

Blancanales threw an arm up and grabbed for the side

railing on the elevator wall but a loose weapon struck him in the face and broke his nose in an instant, blood gushing across his face. He cursed out loud then heard Lyons doing the same.

The elevator car crashed down fifteen feet and slammed into the bottom of the shaft. Lyons was picked up and thrown forward by the force of the impact. He struck the front of the elevator with his back and his breath was bludgeoned from him. He gasped and flipped down on his face.

In the darkness a sharp, unwilling cry was forced out of Blancanales as his left leg, folded unnaturally beneath his body, was twisted at the ankle. Bao screamed at the impact, then gagged. Schwarz moaned and rolled over, pinning the Chinese agent's head down beneath his bodyweight.

"Jesus," Schwarz said. "We good?"

"As good as can be expected," Lyons replied. "Pol, you okay?"

"I hurt my ankle." His voice sounded nasal and thick from his broken nose. "We tape it up I can move no prob-lem, but we've got to get out of here before they drop any more grenades."

Lyons was already up, a wide-bladed fighting knife in his hands. He reached out in the dark and felt for the seam of the elevator doors. Blancanales was correct; they were sitting ducks at the moment. His searching fingers found what they were looking for as the rest of Able Team prepped themselves behind him in the dark, cramped space.

He dug in with his fingertips and slipped the point of the knife blade into the seam. He got a purchase then vio-lently prized them open. They slid back with a sluggish, unwilling motion revealing a concrete wall and the lip of the basement floor about a yard high. Red emergency lights cast shadows across the room. Lyons threw himself upward, caught the lip with his belly and scrambled over.

"Give me the asshole," he muttered.

Schwarz forced the moaning and disorientated Bao up to his feet, imagining more grenades falling down the shaft with paranoid clarity even as they worked. "They drop any more bombs," he warned in Spanish into the man's ear, "and you're a goner just like the rest of us."

"Yeah," Blancanales added as he helped shove the man up. "I'm guessing these guys aren't exactly 'hostage rescue' so much as 'search and destroy,' savvy?"

Bao didn't answer but went willingly into the viselike grip of Lyons. The ex-LAPD detective hauled the man up out of the elevator car then turned and pushed him to the ground. He held out his grip for Schwarz, who took it and stepped upward onto the basement floor. Then both men turned and pulled the injured Blancanales upward.

"Let's clear the area and get to the extraction site," Lyons said.

Schwarz put a hand under the Chinese's sweat-drenched armpit and helped the big blond team leader haul the prisoner to his feet. Behind them Blancanales used the wall as a crutch to hobble after them.

Twenty feet down they paused to activate their NVDs and after that they made better time.

ORTEGA WATCHED HIS MEN unfold into action with a cool disposition. His face remained impassive as the descent team secured their nylon ropes and shrugged into their rappel harnesses. He'd already sent fire teams down each stairwell to try to pinion any survivors but the rappellers would cover the vertical distance in two big leaps at ten times the speed. He would follow them down. Two SWAT troopers in black uniforms stood for a moment in the open elevator shaft, weapons secured on slings across their ballistic vests.

Faceless behind protective masks and night-vision monoculars, the men turned and nodded once to each other. In unison the two stepped off the edge and plunged into the darkness of the elevator shaft, leaving only the whisper of metal carabiners on nylon fibers to mark their passing.

Instantly a second pair moved forward and snapped into a second set of lines. Working quickly, they were over the edge and down their ropes in a matter of well-orchestrated seconds. After the second pair of rappel troops had dropped, Ortega stepped into position and hooked up to his line.

He counted off the seconds with patience. Then the team leader of the rappellers informed him in clipped tones that the relay point had been reached and the second set of ropes put into position. He acknowledged them and began his own drop into the black.

HERMANN SCHWARZ PULLED the two rolls of engineering tape from his belt pouch and stuck a single finger through the center of them. Using his finger like a dowel, he began quickly wrapping the tape around Blancanales's injured ankle over the outside of his boot while Lyons pulled security.

The Puerto Rican ex-Special Forces soldier set his mouth in a firm, thin line against the sharp pain of his injured ankle as he kept an eye on their prisoner. Behind them, across the vast expanse of the tower's basement, IR illumination beams, visible only through night-vision goggles, suddenly played across the pitch-black room.

"Company," Lyons warned. His finger rested on the curve of his H&K's trigger.

Schwarz played out the last of the tape in the makeshift cast and looked up at his teammate. "You good?"

Blancanales shifted his own submachine gun and nodded. "You bet. Let's finish this."

Moving quickly, Schwarz tossed aside the denuded cardboard tape rolls and produced a blocky object the size of a catcher's mitt from his pouch. Bao's eyes grew wide as he took in the digital display on the thermal detonator placed atop the PPC, or Precision Penetration Charge.

Seeing the man's fear, the Able Team electronics and demolitions expert grinned wickedly. *"Que pasa, jefe?"*

"Everybody belly down," Lyons ordered. "I've got to keep them off us."

Immediately his silenced submachine gun cycled in a series of 3-round bursts. From across the basement there was the sound of confusion and erratic movements followed by angry shouts. Then the return fire began to pour in.

Crawling on his belly, Schwarz moved up to the cinderblock wall of the basement. He held up a laser stud finder used by building construction crews and scanned the wall. Stray bullets took chips out of the concrete wall above his head. Behind him Blancanales added his own firepower to Lyons's while maintaining close surveillance of their prisoner.

Schwarz began peeling strips of industrial-strength two-sided tape off one aspect of the shaped PPC. He worked calmly to place the high explosive even as enemy fire peppered the room around him. He looked over at the panicked Bao and placed the PPC.

He then hit Enter and the digital numerical display changed from a subdued green to a dull red.

"We're ready!" Schwarz barked. "Everybody please move to my right."

Bao began moving without help even with his hands bound behind his back, scooting frantically along on his stomach as the digital readout began to count down. Lyons held his MP-5 up and burned off the better part of a clip to provide cover fire as the team moved farther down the wall away from the shaped charge.

Blancanales fired three ragged bursts, then pushed himself forward and somersaulted over one shoulder to spare his injured ankle. Behind them Schwarz snatched up the prisoner by the back of his shoulder and hauled him forward while crawling quickly. Despite the specific explosive trajectory of the shaped charge, where most of the force would be channeled through the wall in a blade to create the breach while the back blast was directed off in a specific funnel pattern, Schwarz did not want to press his luck by remaining in unnecessary proximity to the detonation.

"Move!" Schwarz barked.

IR flashlight beams scythed through the dark and off toward the other end of the room while unsuppressed muzzle-flashes flared in star patterns. Bullets whined around the frantically scrambling team. The lead slugs smacked into the wall, causing craters and spinning shards of masonry out in razorlike fragments.

Blancanales grunted as his injured ankle turned as he pushed off it, the pain causing white points of light to appear in front of his eyes. He threw himself down next to the cursing Bao and threw his hands over his head. Beside him Schwarz shoved the captured Chinese agent into the floor and rolled over on top of him.

Lyons dropped flat on his belly but stubbornly continued to fire, punishing the approaching SWAT unit for any bold motions. Then like the crack of a falling redwood the PPC breaching device detonated.

ORTEGA LET THE ROPE SLIP quickly through his gloved hands. His feet struck the devastated roof of the elevator car and he quickly unsnapped his carabiner. He dropped down through the elevator hatch and looked out. Ahead of him he could see his men fanned out across the basement in defensive positions, trading fire with the foreign gunmen.

He scrambled clear, brought his own weapon up and shuffled forward, throwing lead downrange in the general direction of his targets to add to the assault momentum. Red tracer fire zipped past and lit up his IR goggles like laser bolts, and he saw one of his men go down, the side of his head dented inward like a soda can.

Ortega snarled and barked the orders like an angry dog, driving his men out of their defensive positions and toward the enemy. His unit had the numbers and firepower on their side to drive what the Chinese suspected was an American commando team into a box trap and finish them. To utilize that advantage, he would need to be ruthless in his expenditure of resources.

Ortega got them up and moving forward, submachine guns, assault rifles and combat shotguns blasting out a wall of covering fire. Through his night-vision goggles he saw bizarre shadows twist in the winking bursts of muzzle-flashes.

His head twisted and turned even as his primary weapon jerked on automatic in his hands as he madly searched for targets. Two of his men executed a pincer movement and he held his finger off the trigger as they passed in front of him.

Off in the darkness behind a support beam he heard a man scream in agony and another start cursing horribly in Spanish. He twisted on the ball of his foot as the soldiers deployed to his left began to fire their weapons with renewed intensity.

He took three steps forward in a fast, crouched-over shuffle, weapon up at his shoulder. He stepped around the splayed legs of one of his fallen officers and ground his teeth in impotent fury. The American invaders would pay.

Ahead through the monochromatic lens of his NVD goggles, Ortega suddenly saw the heat signatures of his prey. He saw a broad-shouldered burly silhouette raise an arm and a submachine gun with glowing red muzzle spit a white-hot star-pattern burst. A black-clad soldier on the Nicaraguan commander's left was thrown backward.

Ortega twisted and leveled his submachine gun. His finger took up the slack on the trigger and the laser sight engaged. The red beam cut out like a searchlight, cutting through the black and cordite-stench-filled basement. The big man in Ortega's IR vision suddenly dropped his weapon and put his head down.

Ortega opened his mouth to bark an order when he had the sudden strange sensation of all the air in his lungs being sucked clean of his body. Some instinct made him squeeze his eyes shut in the heartbeat that followed.

The concussive force slammed into him like a freight train, driving him backward and jerking him off his feet like a puppet on a string. A burst of brilliant light flashed past his eyes, searing them white.

He grunted as the sledgehammer force slammed into him and his breath was pummeled from his body. He hit the floor of the basement hard enough to rattle his teeth and his jaw slapped upward like a trap. Blood poured as his teeth tore of a chunk of his cheek and a small piece of his tongue was bitten off. His skull smacked the concrete hard enough to put stars in his already dazzled eyes.

He felt nausea sweep over him in a tidal wave as his lungs fought to drag in a breath, then the darkness took him.

*Stony Man Farm, Virginia*

"DAMMIT!" Barbara Price snarled.

The Stony Man mission controller ripped her headset off and threw it on the desk. Around her Kurtzman and his cybernetics team looked grim as they waited for their instructions in the face of this new wave of successive crises.

"Bear," Price said, her voice coldly devoid of emotion. "Get on our back-door link and see if the Brazzaville UN commander is willing to give us a reactionary force. Tell them we need medical, our chopper is down and our Congolese counterparts may be compromised by tribal loyalists. We need armor or mechanized infantry and we don't have much time."

"I'm on it," Kurtzman replied, taking up a sat com unit and rolling his wheelchair toward an isolated corner.

Price turned toward Tokaido and Delahunt. "I need more information from Nicaragua," she said, shifting gears. "The response and speed of deployment to Able's snatch operation was too good, too smooth. Something is wrong. I want you to find out why we've been compromised."

"Will do," Tokaido said, turning to his screen and keyboard.

Delahunt didn't bother to verbalize her response, just tucked her chin in a nod of affirmation. She quickly slid her VR glove and helmet back on and began to navigate the encryption of the Nicaraguan intelligence agencies using the Farm's Cray supercomputer the way a talented surfer manipulates a long board.

Her troops deployed, Price walked past Hunt Wethers,

who was busy setting up a transatlantic two-way informational link, and pulled out her personal cell phone. She hit her speed dial and inside of three rings Hal Brognola had answered her call.

"This is Hal. Go." His voice was gruff as always.

"Just giving you an update," Price said. "It's not a happy one."

"Give it to me," he replied.

"Phoenix and Jack are down. Apparently, McCarter took a round to the head. He's alive but out. I don't how much time he has. Able has run into trouble in Managua. They're still on schedule but somehow Nicaragua's premier squad of bully boys managed to respond within minutes to their takedown. It's an impossible coincidence. Like Delta Force showing up to a drive-by shooting in Compton."

"We've been compromised, obviously. Have you got support rolling to Phoenix?"

"Aaron's on with the Brits now. We expect cooperation but the infiltration of the local police by tribal sympathizers brought a response on target completely out of proportion to what we initially briefed the area commanders on. They may feel like they were set up by us to be tricked into a massive display of unilateral force they were unprepared to deliver."

"Goddamn politics," Brognola muttered, voice dark.

In her mind's eye Price could see the big Fed sticking an unlit cigar in his mouth to chew on. There was a heartbeat of silence as the coordinator of the Justice Department's Sensitive Operations Group digested what his mission controller had just told him.

"I'm going to inform the President," he said. "If the UN gives you any flak let me know immediately and I'll see if I can put some executive weight behind the request. For now all we can do is watch and hope Able can get clear. Otherwise we'll have to punt in Central America."

"Understood," Price said. "But Phoenix is pinned down now. If the UN balk, it may not matter what the President does. It may just be too late."

"Can we get them artillery or close air support?"

"Negative," Price said. "Every rebel in that neighborhood is shooting at them, but if we go in with indirect fire there's going to be collateral damage. The rules of engagement were very clear on that."

"Understood. Keep me informed."

Both of the Stony Man officials hung up at the same time. Barbara Price spun on her heel and marched back through the door of the Farm's Computer Room to find Kurtzman.

The lives of Phoenix Force lay in the hands of gun-shy and politically entangled professional bureaucrats. She could feel her stomach tie into knots as she waited for the answer.

It wasn't long in coming. As soon as she entered the room Kurtzman waved at her and put his connection on speakerphone.

"Commander," Kurtzman growled. "You recognize the code paroles I gave you—the level they represent?"

When the voice on the other end of the line answered it was English with a heavy Pakistani accent and very collected.

"Yes, I do," the UN general replied. "I know exactly what they mean but that doesn't change the truth on the ground." His voice was strained enough under the surface that Price knew he was being sincere. "This isn't like the bad old days of the 1990s," the man explained. "This isn't 'my' sector or a 'UN' sector anymore. This is a Congolese-controlled city and province. We are no longer occupiers or authority—we are guests and advisors. I have no authority to use military force without direct Congolese approval, do you understand? Supplementing a covert op is a hell of a lot different than me rolling a tank platoon into a neighborhood to rescue people operating in a technically illegal matter."

"Dammit," Kurtzman snapped back. "That's not fair! When we started this we were going on the assumption that the Congolese forces were international criminals and not tribal militia."

"Welcome to the truth on the ground in Brazzaville," the general replied. "Look, I understand. But my ambassador is already fending off screaming attacks about murdered Congolese policemen and collateral damage in a city that's been mostly peaceful. I have my orders from on high—do not intervene.

"I'm sorry," the general said. "My hands are tied."

# CHAPTER TWENTY

*Brazzaville, Republic of the Congo*

Jack Grimaldi hung out of the helicopter door.

Blood flowed from superficial gouges in his shoulder and thigh, and exploding shards of glass had peppered his mouth and jaw in sharp slivers. Bullets streamed into the cockpit from enemy positions as a column of smoke roiled up from a smoldering engine.

As soon as the stray round had knocked McCarter down, the Stony Man pilot had powered down his bird to allow James and Hawkins to go after their fallen commander. Two seconds later a white pickup powered around a turn in the street, a Russian antiaircraft heavy machine gun mounted in the back.

The barrage had come from only fifty yards away, practically point-blank range for a weapon of the size and had ripped apart the helicopter until Encizo and James had put two rounds each through the gunner's head, vaporizing it simultaneously.

Jack Grimaldi suddenly lifted his head, and his hands came up and he found the release on his seat harness. He manipulated the device and dropped free, falling on all fours to the dusty, hard-packed earth. The amber light of dawn illuminated his motions and more fire was directed his way.

Hawkins had commandeered a Soviet AKM with

a folding stock and was using it now. He scooped the wounded Stony Man pilot up with one hand under an armpit and sprayed covering fire with the Kalashnikov held in his other.

"How bad is it?" he yelled.

"Not bad, but I'm hurt," Grimaldi said, the oxymoronic statement making perfect sense to the veteran commando.

Hawkins took Grimaldi's weight onto his shoulder and felt his clothes instantly soaked with the other man's blood. The ex-Delta Force shooter killed a gunmen who had popped up behind an abandoned hulk of a car to fire on them, then began dragging the pilot toward an almost adobe-style tenement building made of sun-dried brick that rose four stories.

Behind them the helicopter made a dramatic whoosh as the fuel tanks spilled out and splashed the burning motor mechanisms, igniting the aircraft like a bonfire. Gary Manning, running with the unconscious David McCarter scooped up in his arms like a child, felt the skin on his neck and face tighten with stinging intensity at the sudden rush of heat. Behind him Calvin James ran with the helicopter med kit backpack in one hand, their Armenian prisoner clutched in his other hand.

Behind him Encizo tried to cover their retreat, spraying his weapon wildly as the team ran for the marginal shelter of the building. Machine-gun and assault rifle rounds burned through the air around the fleeing Phoenix Force veterans, snapping next to their ears and kicking up gouts of dirt from the ground. The gunfire was relentless.

Operating in a state of combat reflexes, Encizo twisted and pitched a fragmentation grenade underhand behind him. As it bounced away he lifted his machine pistol and directed a burst at an enemy fire team using a narrow alleyway as an approach to the engagement. His rounds slowed their advance long enough for the grenade to explode and funnel a wave of shrapnel down the narrow enclosure.

A heavy-caliber slug struck the ceramic plate in the back pouch of his Kevlar vest. The plate shattered under the impact inside its bullet-resistant weave, stopping the round from penetrating. The blunt force of the bullet hit the Cuban combat swimmer and flung him forward, whipping his head back and sending him spinning.

Encizo picked himself up as Hawkins and Grimaldi made the door to the building. His weapon had spun away, and as he pushed himself up off his hands and knees he tried desperately to find it. He spotted it just as a line of rounds cut across the dirt, slammed into the receiver and buttstock, busting them apart into useless fragments.

Carrying McCarter, Gary Manning plunged through the door kicked open by Hawkins and ducked inside the building. A searing-hot lance cut across Encizo's deltoid, plucking up his fatigue shirt and splashing him with his own blood as he spun around from the impact of the round.

Digging in his heels, Encizo sprang forward, sprinting hard for the building as several streams of gunfire poured out of the street behind him. He ran hard, lungs screaming and heart pounding as he cut for the open doorway. Beside the wooden frame a burst of fire pockmarked the wall with crater wounds. Putting his head down, Encizo sprang forward and dived through the opening.

He landed on one shoulder and rolled over, coming up inside the room to see Jack Grimaldi sprawled on the floor, bleeding steadily, his pistol in hand. T. J. Hawkins stood above him, wrestling with an AKM-armed insurgent.

Hawkins twisted the rifle up and slammed an uppercut elbow strike into the rebel's face, knocking his head back.

The Texan drove his knee into the man's midsection and doubled him over while pulling the Kalashnikov free. The terrorist fell backward, empty hands flailing as Hawkins spun his captured rifle around.

Calvin James fired past the poised Hawkins and drilled out the man's throat and jaw with a tight 3-round burst. The corpse spun farther back as it fell, spinning like a top and spraying blood out in a fat arc that splashed into Hawkins like a child's water balloon.

Encizo came up and snatched the AKM Hawkins had initially been using off the ground. He shuffled forward and took up a position by the open door even as more and more fire began to impact around the entrance. Almost immediately he was forced to duck his head back around the corner.

"The burning chopper is keeping them back for now," he shouted toward his teammates. "But we can't stay here. Not for long."

"We may not have a choice," James yelled back. The team medic moved up to inspect the still unconscious McCarter. "The Brits have backed out. We're not looking at the cavalry coming anytime soon."

Manning took up a defensive position at an open window and looked back. "What's that mean for David?" The strain was clear even over the noise of incoming gunfire.

"Nothing good. We need help!" James snapped.

At the door Encizo cursed so loud the shout cut through the racket, causing James to snap his head in the direction of the door.

The Cuban had leaped to his feet and was firing the machine pistol from a Weaver stance, unusual for the situation. Past the burly shoulder of the combat swimmer James saw a rushing figure, torso laden with canvas pouches he knew had to be filled with some form of plastic explosives.

Encizo fired a third burst into the man, and James felt his heart lurch with hope as the crazed suicide bomber began to fall. Then the man disappeared and the shock wave of the IED vest detonation rocked the battle. Smoke rolled forward and Encizo's body was catapulted backward and bounced off the floor. James hunched his shoulder and threw himself over the inert body of David McCarter as rubble and dust rained down and scattered across the men in the basement.

Manning was thrown against the wall and turned as he pushed himself clear. He swept up his stolen AKM and raced toward the door. At the edge of the now shattered doorjamb he threw the weapon up and began firing out the door and into the smoke.

His weapon suddenly cut short and he snarled in frustration, slapping on the magazine to try to seat the round in the breech. Encizo, still crawling on all fours, came up beside him, his pistol in one hand and a grenade in another.

As Encizo lobbed the bomb, Manning snapped the bolt on his assault rifle back and cleared the jam. Snapping the stock into his shoulder, the Canadian special operations soldier began firing even as enemy rounds continued to strike around the opening.

"McCarter's stable but he won't last!" James shouted from where he hunched over the unconscious Briton.

Gary Manning turned to answer just as a machine gun blast knocked him backward into the room.

# CHAPTER TWENTY-ONE

*Managua, Nicaragua*

Able Team picked themselves up and leaped to their feet.

Their weapons came up as the last echo of the shaped charge rattled through the room. Rubble and mortar and bits of rebar lay scattered everywhere in mounds and piles, and a man-size breach had appeared in the basement wall.

"Go!" Blancanales shouted.

The former Green Beret brought his MP-5 around and triggered 3-round bursts as harassing fire while the rest of his team hauled the prisoner up and shoved him forward. Schwarz leaped through the hole into the Managua subway tunnel and Lyons shoved Bao through the breach after him. Lyons saw a black-clad commando lurch to his feet next to a building support pillar and shot him through the head. The man's Kevlar helmet jerked to the side and the body spun away as Lyons turned and dived through the opening.

Scooting backward on his taped ankle, Blancanales fired burst after burst with the H&K submachine gun until he was close enough to spin around and dive through the breach himself. He landed on the other side and came up immediately, his muzzle tracking back toward the hole Schwarz had constructed to cover the egress point.

Behind him Lyons and Schwarz quickly surveyed the area. They were in a molded concrete tube flattened on the bottom to accommodate train tracks. They looked in both directions of the tunnel, unsure of their exact location in regard to the memorized schematics.

"There!" Schwarz shouted, and pointed.

Lyons looked and saw the dim outline of the silent subway train standing dark about thirty yards away. He hooked his arm underneath Bao's, applying leverage and putting the Chinese spy up on his toes. "Let's go."

Schwarz took the lead, letting his submachine gun drop to the end of its cross-body sling and rest against his body armor. He reached back and pulled up his PDA. He thumbed through the options until he had what he wanted, then he tucked it under his belt for quick access and hurried forward.

Lyons followed close behind using his intimidating physicality to cow the prisoner and keep him moving forward, his free hand wrapped around the pistol grip of his H&K MP-5. Behind them Blancanales pulled rear security, shuffling backward despite his injured ankle and keeping his weapon trained on the hole leading back into the commercial tower basement.

Just as Schwarz reached the first in a line of subway passenger cars Blancanales saw a black canister arc through the hole in the wall and immediately recognized a flash-bang grenade.

"Grenade!" Blancanales shouted, partly to warn his team and partly to equalize the pressure he knew was coming. Mouth still stretched open, he spun and dropped an eyelid in a quick blink before the flash and explosion.

Beyond him in the subway tube Carl Lyons shoved Bao to the ground and fell on him even as Schwarz cursed loudly and ducked up against the shielding bulk of the subway car.

The tunnel filled with light like a bolt of lightning followed by a hard, sharp bang that battered into the three

Americans. The effect was negated by both the distance from the blast epicenter and the fact that each member of Able Team had trained with such frequency against just such devices that they were responding to the threat immediately.

Knowing the flash-bang was intended to facilitate the Nicaraguans' pursuit, Blancanales swung over onto his belly and held the trigger down on his submachine gun, washing the blast hole down in 9 mm Parabellum rounds. His weapon kicked and bucked in a staccato pattern and shell casings arced out of his ejection port and tumbled to the tracks beneath him.

He saw a dark silhouette in the breach stagger as the bullets struck him and then he fell back. Behind him another man was dropped but a third SWAT trooper dived forward, shouldering his way into the tube beyond the blast hole. The commando swung up an M-4 carbine and triggered a blast. Blancanales was forced into a reorientation of his fire from the breach toward the trooper. Already centered, his rounds struck the man from twenty-five yards and pummeled into him with merciless accuracy. The time it took for Blancanales to kill the Nicaraguan allowed two more of the SWAT commandos to gain a position in the breach.

Their 5.56 mm rounds burned down the tube, forcing Blancanales more tightly onto his stomach. He lifted his own weapon at an awkward angle and returned fire, spraying the area. Behind him Lyons risked rising to his knees despite the flying rounds and burned off bursts over Blancanales's body, laying out a horizontal wall of lead and throwing back at the attackers.

The big ex-cop pushed Bao forward until the bound Chinese agent bounced off the rear platform of the subway car. Still firing, Lyons shouldered in behind the man and shoved him upward. Rounds pinged and ricocheted off the superstructure, spiderwebbing the reinforced glass of the windows and showering them with sparks.

Inside the subway car Schwarz sprang into his predetermined course of action knowing that the survival of Able Team now rested in his ability to operate like the electronics genius he was.

He spoke into his throat mike as he charged down the central aisle of the car, his voice strained from his exertion but remaining calm enough to replay the situational realities.

"Stony, this is Able," he said.

"Go for Stony," Price's calm voice responded.

"We are in the tunnel and I'm preparing to initiate takeover of the transit unit."

"Understood," Price acknowledged. "I'm giving you Hunt."

"Gadgets, I'm here," Wethers said.

His voice was warm and well-modulated and Hermann Schwarz knew he spoke with all the power of that IBM Bladerunner and Cray supercomputer combination behind him. The effect to the embattled Schwarz was every bit as calming as an infantry soldier learning air support was en route.

At each car Schwarz was forced to use his fighting knife to pry open the doors, sliding the blade tip between the black rubber seal then levering them back until the automatic hydraulic switch was engaged.

Sweat dripped from Schwarz's face and collected in pools at his belly, armpits and crotch, staining the fabric dark. He was in peak physical shape but the strain of sustained adrenaline bursts had left him winded and gasping for air. The air in the shut-down subway car was stale and tasted artificial, contributing to his feelings of claustrophobia. The weapon hanging from its sling off his front had been so frequently and continuously fired that it radiated heat like a camp stove and the barrel glowed hot in his NVD monogoggle lens.

He moved through four empty and dark subway cars after establishing his link with Wethers and arrived at the cockpit at the front of the lead car. The doors here were of the same hydraulic dividers as the passenger cars with the addition of an electronic key card security access system.

Behind him down the train he heard the sound of gunfire and heard Lyons roaring curses. Concentrating intently, Schwarz tried to block all external stimulus from his mind, focusing sharply on the task at hand and the sat link communication connection he had to Stony Man tech wizard Hunt Wethers.

For springing the simple civilian commercial security system Schwarz would not be called upon to utilize the power of Stony Man's supercomputers. For this task his NSA-upgraded PDA was more than equal to the challenge. Working quickly, he used a generic key card imprint connected to the PDA by its earphone jack, allowing both the receiving and transmitting of information.

Using his thumb the Able Team electronics specialist called up the appropriate program on his device, then initiated it. His screen winked into a green graph pattern and a bold line appeared at the top of the display. It blinked three times and began to slowly descend the screen. Each graph was filled with a number like a Sudoku puzzle. Each of the numbers began reducing or multiplying in rapid eyeblinks as the solid bar graph traveled downward over them before winking out, one after another.

When the bar line reached the bottom of the screen it blinked an additional three times and the electronically controlled door unsealed and slid open, allowing Schwarz to step inside the cockpit.

Behind him he could hear Blancanales and Lyons shouting over the bursts of gunfire. This was going to be tight, he realized.

"I'm inside," he said to Wethers.

"Copy, Gadgets," Wethers replied in his academically dry voice. "I am now shutting down the electrical grid for the subway system diagnostic program. They will not be able to track the process of your train. Set up the sat link and I'll initiate the hack-and-slash protocol with our Cray and Bladerunner."

"Understood," Schwarz replied. "Give me fifteen seconds to hook the system."

"Copy," Wethers said. "We're standing by."

The interior of the subway was modern and ultra-high-tech. A panel system of gauges, displays and controls was arrayed in front of deep leather pilot seats and slanted view screens. Schwarz dropped into the engineer's seat and began powering the unit up.

He shut the doors behind him and locked them down to prevent any stray or purposeful rounds from sabotaging his efforts. Humming a song softly to himself, he connected his PDA to the engineer's CPU and then uploaded the signal to his sat link relay system.

"Stony, we're good to go," he informed Wethers.

"Copy," Wethers replied. "Initiating knock program." After a pause he announced, "The train is yours."

Schwarz heard the unmistakable sound of the hydraulic brake system releasing and then the hum of the powerful electric engine flood online in one smooth moment.

"I'm directing our airlift asset to your extraction zone," Wethers said. "Good luck."

"Able out," Schwarz replied. He reached up and clicked

his enhanced Bluetooth accessory over. "All aboard who's coming aboard. We're rolling hot."

THOUSANDS OF MILES AWAY in the Stony Man Computer Room Carmen Delahunt and Huntington Wethers began initiating the complex attack on the Managua infrastructure that would keep power flooding toward Able Team's hijacked train, black out any capability the Nicaraguan authorities would have to track its progress and prevent equally fast subway systems emergency maintenance vehicles from giving chase.

Standing behind them Barbara Price felt an immense weight lift off her shoulders. At least for now one of her teams appeared headed for safety. Now she had to go to Brognola on behalf of Phoenix Force because it was going to take intervention at the highest level to save the unit trapped in Brazzaville.

CARL LYONS DUCKED his head as a hail of 5.56 mm rounds shattered the Plexiglas window next to him. Shards of reinforced glass sprinkled down around him and coated Bao with the plastic slivers.

Crouched just in front of Lyons and the prisoner, Blancanales fired his MP-5 in rapid aim-and-burst patterns that painted the subway tube with tight groupings of 9 mm Parabellum rounds. Nicaraguan commandos, being driven forward by a massive officer in the rear of the unit, stubbornly pushed on. Two burst groupings struck a shotgun-wielding police commando, shattering his ballistic glasses and leaving his eye sockets bloody fissures. The man's skull exploded outward and red spray struck the back of the man's Kevlar helmet and squirted downward to stain his black vest and fatigues.

Blancanales grunted with pain as he forced his injured ankle to support his weight long enough for him to leap back through the subway door. Lyons dropped to a knee and swept his own submachine gun up to his shoulder and triggered four, 3-round bursts as cover fire above the scrambling Blancanales. His rounds struck walls and ricocheted like buzz saws through the circular tunnel. There was a sound like a baseball bat on naked flesh and a commando screamed as gouts of muscle were torn from his thigh and he collapsed in agony.

Ortega was behind his men screaming updates on the Americans' movements. His angry gaze snaked out across the distance and found Lyons's cold eyes for a single instant. The subway train suddenly kicked into life and began rolling down the track.

Furious, Ortega screamed his outrage and started forward, driving his men ahead of him like a cowboy starting a stampede. The police commandos came up, all caution gone, and charged forward, firing their weapons wildly, hurtling a fence of lead down the tube to rattle and spark as bullets struck the supercarriage of the train.

Lyons threw himself flat and rolled to the side out of the way of the barrage even as Blancanales tumbled over in the opposite direction. Unable to contain his enthusiasm Schwarz, seated comfortably up front, hit the enter button on his secondary keyboard and laughed out loud as a train whistle sounded, echoing down the tube to taunt the frustrated Nicaraguan commandos.

Ortega stopped running as the train pulled away. His personal cell phone came out of an equipment pouch on his web gear and he quickly dialed a number from memory. In his role as leader of his nation's premier direct-action unit he had found myriad ways to pad his paycheck.

It was time to pull a positive out of this disaster. "Tell Xi-Nan his man has been taken by the Americans."

# CHAPTER TWENTY-TWO

*Brazzaville, Republic of the Congo*

Manning raced up the interior steps and kicked open a door. Behind him Hawkins and Encizo formed the other part of his fire team. Before they made the roof the ground floor had to be cleared well enough to transport the unconscious McCarter.

Behind them Grimaldi and James held the ruined stairwell, guarding against the assault militia fighters and watching over McCarter. If a pathway was going to be punched through the interior defenses toward freedom it would have to happen quickly to be of any use to the ex-SAS trooper.

Inside the room an irregular prepping a Claymore mine turned and reached for his weapon. There was a loud crack in the narrow hall and cordite filled the air like a flower bouquet. The militiaman's eyes crossed as they tried to see the sudden hole in his flat, low forehead, then he tumbled to the ground.

"Rafe, set the room on fire and let's sweep toward the front," Manning said.

Rafael Encizo produced a lighter and ignited the cardboard boxes stacked against the wall. Once he had a fire the three soldiers began to move farther down the hall, Hawkins covering their rear security while Manning led from the front.

He kicked open a door. Encizo covered his motion in one direction while Hawkins secured the hall in the opposite sector. Manning saw an empty office. He let the door close. From the end of the hallway he heard men shouting. A door opened and Manning sank to one knee on the floor, bringing his stolen AKM up to his shoulder.

Three irregulars armed with AKM assault rifles charged into the hall. Instantly, Manning and Encizo opened up on them. Their tight, figure-8-patterned bursts scythed into the knot of gunmen and ripped them apart. They tumbled over each other and fell in a pile on the ground, where blood flowed from them in a red flood across the linoleum flooring underneath the fluorescent light.

"Let's go!" Manning said.

The fire team moved quickly down the length of the hall, weapons up until they got to the door the men had charged out of. The outflung arm of a dead militiaman held the door open several inches.

Manning stepped over the mangled corpse and snap kicked the door open before moving inside. Encizo moved into the room behind him, weapon up and tracking as Hawkins took up a defensive overwatch to prevent a surprise attack.

Manning shuffled into the room covering his vectors with tight motions of his weapon. He paused in the middle of the room and slowly lowered his weapon, taking in the scene. Behind him Encizo cleared behind the door and the ceiling before lowering his own weapon and whispering a curse in Spanish.

The man hung from chains bolted into the wall. Inside the handcuffs attached to the chains the man's fingers stuck out at odd, painful angles and he had only raw, bloody patches where his fingernails should have been. His mouth had collapsed inward like that of an old man, his cheeks hollow and his lips stained with blood. Most of his teeth had been yanked from his mouth.

A blindfold had been used to cover his eyes and a ball-gag shoved in his mouth. His head hung limply between his outstretched arms. On a tray set on rollers a butane torch, a pair of pliers and some bloodstained garden shears rested. Forgotten on the floor where the man rested on his knees was a three-foot length of black garden hose.

On a rickety card table set against the wall Manning saw an unzipped bowling ball bag. Even from his angle Manning could see it was filled with stacks of U.S. dollars. Next to it on the table was a blood-splattered, blue Congolese police uniform tunic and a Beretta 92-F automatic pistol. Scattered on the table like bloodstained dice, the long root-nerves still attached, were the man's pulled teeth.

"They were videotaping it," Encizo whispered. "Look."

Manning looked up. He saw the little video recorder set up on a silver-legged tripod. "Take it. They might have been torturing him for information. Whatever they're interested in, Stony Man is interested in."

Encizo collected and secured the recorder while Manning moved closer to the man. He leaned in, ignoring the stench as he looked for signs of life. Manning reached out and put two fingers against the man's neck at the carotid artery, searching for a pulse.

He could find none.

"Let's go," he told Encizo.

The two warriors headed for the room door as gunfire broke out again in the hallway.

Manning looked out the door of the room and saw Hawkins prone on the ground. The ex-Ranger fired his Kalashnikov in cool bursts, using the dead bodies of the torturers as a hasty fighting position. The Phoenix Force commando was positioned so that his fire was directed down the hallway in the direction they had first penetrated the building.

Manning threw himself against the right side of the door and angled his weapon outward to add his fire to that of Hawkins. Encizo crouched on the left-hand side and swung the barrel of his stolen AKM around the corner. He began triggering long blasts of fully automatic fire as the Stony Man task force fought hard to shift the momentum of the battle away from the attackers.

"I can't see them!" Manning shouted above the roar of the weapons. "How many are there?"

"Four!" Hawkins shouted back. "They must have come in off the stairwell opposite ours. There must be a coordinating officer outside the building directing them."

"Rafe," Manning said. "Check T.J.'s six."

Encizo stopped firing and repositioned his weapon so that it was aimed in the opposite direction. The Phoenix Force combat swimmer threw himself belly-down on the floor and peeked his head around the doorjamb to try to cover Hawkins's back.

Manning leaned out of the door and sprayed down the hall. He saw two of the enemy irregulars firing the hall from positions behind the open doors leading out toward the stairwell. The fighters aggressively answered the Americans burst for burst.

Hawkins suddenly lifted his Kalashnikov up at an angle, turning the weapon sideways. Manning heard the *bloop* as the commando triggered the Russian 30 mm grenade launcher slung under the barrel. The rifle recoiled smoothly into his shoulder and there was a flash of smoke as the round arced down the hallway.

Manning instinctively turned away as the HE round rammed into the wall at the end of the hallway and detonated with a thunderous explosion and flash of light. The crack was sharp and followed by screams. The hallway acted like a chimney, filling with dark smoke from the detonation.

Manning seized the initiative hard on the heels of the grenade explosion. He leaped over the rifle barrels of both Encizo and Hawkins, slid across the hall, bounced a shoulder off the wall and centered his weapon down the hall. He shuffled forward firing his weapon in tight bursts toward the positions he had witnessed before the explosion.

Behind him Hawkins rose to his feet and began to move down the hallway, as well, firing in tandem. Behind them Encizo rolled into position and covered their rear security with his drum-magazine-mounted AKM.

Manning caught a silhouette in the smoke and raked it with a Z-pattern burst. Beside him Hawkins matched him step for step, his weapon firing. Manning's target spilled out onto floor, his chest and throat looking as if an animal had clawed it out.

"Magazine!" Manning warned.

Manning hit the magazine release with his finger and dropped his almost empty magazine. His other hand came up with a fresh banana-clip magazine and slapped it into place. Manning's thumb tapped the release and the bolt slid forward with a snap as a round was chambered.

Manning brought his weapon up, scanning quickly for a target. The smoke from the grenade blast hung in the air, reducing vision. Hawkins put a man down then finished him off with a 3-round burst to the back of the head. Manning risked a look over his shoulder to quickly check on Encizo's status.

Just as Manning turned he saw Encizo come up out of a crouch. The man lunged toward the open door where he and Manning had found the tortured man.

"Grenade!" Encizo screamed.

Manning saw Encizo stretched out vertical as he dived, five feet up in the air, his weapon trailing behind him as he lunged forward and his other hand out ahead of him as if he were doing the crawl stroke while he swam.

Directly under the leaping man's boot Manning saw the black metal egg bounce once then get caught on a sprawled leg of a dead militia fighter. There was a flash of light and suddenly Manning was slapped down.

His world spun and he hit the floor hard enough to see stars. His vision went black for a heartbeat then returned. Once again he had been struck deaf. He lay still for a moment, stunned by the force of the blast. He blinked and the ceiling came into focus.

He saw a dark shape move beside him and turned his head in that direction. The hallway lit up as the muzzle-flash from Hawkins's weapon flared like a Roman candle. The ex-Ranger fired in one direction. Manning saw his face twisting as he screamed his outrage but he heard no sound.

Manning blinked. When he opened his eyes again he saw Hawkins roll onto his back and fire the Kalashnikov down the hallway between his sprawled-open legs. With a rush, sensibility rammed into Manning and snapped him back into the present.

He sat up and his hearing returned instantaneously. He looked down and saw that he still held his Russian weapon. Down the hall he saw starbursts of yellow light through the fog of smoke as militia fighters charged the position. Manning leaned against the wall before lifting his Kalashnikov and returning fire. He squinted and saw Encizo lying motionless, his legs trailing out from the doorway of the room.

The torn and headless torso of one of the torturers lay on top of the Cuban's body. Another one of the bodies that had been caught up in the blast had had its clothes lit on fire.

Manning sprayed down the hallway. He saw his green tracer fire arc into the debris and dust and smoke, and saw other green tracers arc back at him. Suddenly he saw a muzzle-flash to the right of the hallway and closer than before. He twisted at the hip and fired in response.

A man folded at the waist out of the fog and pitched forward. As he tumbled to the ground Manning put another burst of 7.62 mm slugs into his body. Beside him Hawkins rose up off the ground, keeping the barrel of his weapon trained down the hallway.

Manning held his fire for a moment and forced himself to stand. No enemy fire came from the hallway. Manning took a look behind him, counted the three dead men he and Hawkins had shot. The Phoenix Force commando had stated there were four when the ambush had begun.

Manning took a step down the hallway, weapon ready. He saw the crater where Hawkins's 30 mm round had impacted and the black scorch patterns spreading out from the center. He saw a severed arm lying in the hall in a puddle of blood and he turned back down the hallway.

Hawkins jogged forward, weapon up. Manning followed him, his weapon on his shoulder. Hawkins reached the still Rafael Encizo and reached down to pull the torso off his teammate's body. Manning drew even with him as Hawkins knelt beside the wounded Phoenix Force commando.

"Rafe," Hawkins said, "can you hear me, brother?"

Manning passed the room without looking, his eyes searching for targets. As he passed a downed militia fighter he heard a moan and saw the man move. Manning whirled like a whip snapping and triggered a burst into the man, who shuddered and then lay still.

Manning snapped his weapon back around. At the end

of the hallway, through the smoke and haze of dust he saw a door. He moved quickly to it and pulled it open. He sank to a knee and risked a look around the corner. A long hallway floored with mosaic tile and painted a creamy brown stretched nearly thirty or forty yards toward the front of the building.

A bearded face peeked around a corner at the end of the hallway and Manning instinctively fired a burst. The head ducked back to safety around the corner. Manning pulled himself back around his own corner.

"How is he?" he shouted at Hawkins.

"Out," Hawkins answered.

His voice was flat, lacking inflection. Manning felt a chill pass through him. Not another brother, he thought. He pulled his tactical radio from off his web gear H-harness fitted over his now filthy and blood-soaked black fatigues. He keyed the mike.

"How's your sitrep?" he asked without preamble.

"Still in close contact but no more suicide charges for now," James answered from the stairwell.

"Encizo took a hard one. He's unconscious, but I think that's it. I'm sending him back to you with Hawkins before I finish this hallway."

"Time is a factor," James said. From out of the mike Manning could clearly hear the sound of gunfire.

"Understood," the big Canadian said.

Manning tucked his radio away and fired a blind burst down the hall. He turned back and saw Hawkins frantically working on the inert Encizo.

"We have to go," he said. "Get Rafe back to Cal."

Before Hawkins could answer, Manning heard a loud thump strike the door next to them. He didn't think, but simply reacted. Manning rolled up onto one hand, his leg curled beneath him, and leaped forward. He landed on top of the startled Hawkins and forced the Phoenix Force operator down over the unconscious and bleeding Rafael Encizo.

Behind Manning the hand grenade went off like a peal of thunder and blew the door off its hinges to send it flying into the hallway, followed by a billow of smoke. Manning lifted himself off Hawkins and Encizo as debris and dust rained down on the men. Manning swooned and shoved hard against the doorjamb, forcing himself upright.

He felt as if he'd just downed a bottle of tequila and taken a ride on a Tilt-A-Whirl. He gritted his teeth, snarling against the pain and disorientation. He scooped up his weapon and thrust the barrel around the edge of the door and pulled the trigger.

The weapon kicked and bucked in his hand as empty shell casings arced out and spilled across the bloody floor. He burned off half a magazine. Immediately machine-gun fire answered his burst and a maelstrom of heavy-caliber bullets sizzled through the blown-open door and hammered the wall behind Manning.

"Take him and go!" Manning shouted. "Get to the stairwell—get to Cal. I'll hold them off!"

Hawkins didn't argue. Letting his Kalashnikov dangle from its strap, he bent and pulled Encizo into a sitting position. The Cuban's head rolled loose on his neck and underneath a shroud of his own blood the man's skin was deathly white and starting to tinge with blue.

Hawkins squatted, tucking his butt underneath his shoulders and securing his grip on Encizo's shredded and smoking clothes. He grunted and lifted straight up, driving with the powerful muscles of his buttocks and thighs. Encizo rose as Hawkins did and at the top of the arch Hawkins ducked under the limp soldier, shouldering his weight easily.

Manning sprayed the hallway through the door without looking. Again his burst was answered with sustained heavy-caliber fire. Hawkins turned and looked toward Manning.

"Go!" Manning shouted. "Go. I'm coming."

Hawkins nodded once and turned, running toward the back door by which the Stony Man task force had first accessed the building. He slid in the blood splashed across the linoleum but did not go down, and Manning directed his attention toward the door.

Whatever else happened he had to give the Phoenix Force commandos time to get to the stairwell. He would hold off the militia fighters located in the front of the building as long as he could, then make his own break.

A burst of machine-gun fire tore down the long hall, then trailed off, and Manning heard the familiar thumping bounce of a hand grenade coming his way. He looked at the threshold of the doorway and saw the black metal sphere roll into the hall beside him.

He swung his left arm down like a handball player and slapped the grenade back along the hall. He didn't look to see how far it traveled but instead tucked his head between his arms and rolled away from the open door. He felt the shock waves traveling out of the hall slam into his back.

He pushed himself up off his belly and swung back toward the door. He thrust the muzzle of his weapon around the corner and fired until he burned off the last bit of his magazine.

He turned and began to sprint down the hall away from the position held by the rest of Phoenix Force. He dropped the spent magazine as he ran and fumbled for another in his web gear. His combat boot came down on a blue-gray loop of intestine and he fell hard, landing awkwardly on one knee. Pain lanced out from the hinge joint and he gasped in surprise at the intensity of it after all he'd already suffered.

He forced himself up and kept running, his Kalashnikov carbine at his side. He reached an open door leading into the hallway and ducked into the empty room. Manning paused, his appropriated AKM held at the ready as he stood by the door. His feeling of disquiet had not subsided. He couldn't place his unease, and that made it all the more bothersome. He stalked forward, pausing before heading out into the hall.

He stopped, sensed nothing, moved forward.

All hell broke loose.

# CHAPTER TWENTY-THREE

Manning was not a superstitious man but when he stepped through the door and entered the hall, the soldier felt as if he had moved into a field of static electricity. The hair on his arms and the back of his neck lifted straight up as cold squirts of adrenaline surged into his body. The night fighter reacted instantly, without conscious thought. He dropped to one knee and leaned back in the doorway, sweeping the barrel of his AKM up and triggering a blast.

The unmistakable pneumatic cough of a sound-suppressed weapon firing on full automatic assaulted Manning's ears across the short distance. Shell casings clattered onto the linoleum floor, mixing with the sound of a weapon bolt leveraging back and forth rapidly. Manning felt the angry whine of bullets fill the space where his head and chest had been only a heartbeat before.

Manning targeted diagonally across and down the office hall, firing his Russian assault rifle with practiced, instinctive ease. He let the recoil of the carbine shuttering in his strong grip carry him back through the doorway behind him in a tight roll. From his belly Manning thrust his muzzle around the doorjamb and arced the weapon back and forth as he laid down quick suppressive blasts.

The 7.62 mm rounds were deafening in the confined space and his ears rang from the noise. Manning reached up and jerked his monogoggle night-vision device down so that it dangled from the rubber strap around his neck.

He heard the bullets from his assailant's answering burst smack into the Sheetrock of the outer wall.

From the impacts, Manning determined the shooter was using a submachine gun and not an assault rifle, though he was hard-pressed to identify caliber with the suppressor in use. Manning scrambled backward and rested his rifle barrel across the still warm corpse of a dead militia fighter. If there was more than one irregular in that specific position, and they were determined to get him, they would either fire and maneuver to breach the room door, or possibly use more grenades to clear him out.

There was silence for a long moment. Manning's head raced through strategies and options. If the terrorist's intent had merely been escape, then why had he bothered to stay behind or try to take Manning out? If the unknown assailant was armed for a quiet kill, then that would indicate that he was probably not carrying ordnance much heavier than the silenced SMG being used now.

The main thing, Manning's experience told him, was regaining momentum. He quickly stripped an extra rifle from the dead bodyguard and hooked the sling over his shoulder. Conscious of his vulnerability, Manning high-crawled back toward the door. He maneuvered the barrel of his AKM out the entrance and triggered an exploratory blast, conducting a recon by fire. Precious seconds ticked away.

Immediately, Manning's aggressive burst was answered with a tightly controlled one. Bullets tore into the wooden doorjamb and broke up the floor in front of his weapon. Manning ducked back; he had seen what he needed. He had found a way to exploit his heavier armament.

The gunman had taken a position across and two doors down the hall from the room where Manning was now trapped. From that location the gunman controlled the fields of fire up and down the hall, preventing Manning from leaving the room without exposing himself to withering short-range fire.

Again Manning triggered a long, ragged blast. He tore apart the door of the room directly opposite him, then ran his larger caliber rounds down the hall to pour a flurry of lead through the sniper's door. Tracer fire lit up the hallway with surrealistic strips of light like laser blasts in some low-budget science fiction movie. Manning could smell his own sweat and the hot oil of his AKM. The heavy dust hanging in the air, kicked up by the automatic weapons fire, choked him. His ears rang and, over everything else, even the fever pitch of excitement, was the smell of burning cordite.

Manning ducked back around as the gunman triggered an answering burst from his SMG. Manning heard the smaller caliber rounds strike the wall outside his door, saw how they failed to penetrate the building materials. It confirmed his suspicions that he was facing a light-caliber weapon.

Manning snarled, gathering himself, and thrust his weapon out the office door a final time. He triggered the AKM and the assault rifle bucked in his hands. Manning sprinted through the doorway hard behind his covering fire. His rounds fell like sledgehammers around the door to the room of his ambusher. Hot gases warmed his wrists as the bolt of his weapon snapped open and shut, open and shut, as he carried his burst out to improbable length even as he raced forward.

Two steps from the room door Manning's magazine ran dry and the bolt locked open. Without hesitation Manning flung the empty weapon down and dived forward. The big man's hard shoulder struck the door. Already riddled with bullets, the flimsy construction was no match for Manning's heavy frame and he burst through it into the room.

Manning went down with his forward momentum, landing on the shoulder he had used as a battering ram and somersaulting over it smoothly. He came up on one knee and swung his second AKM carbine off his shoulder, leveling it at the wall separating his position from the gunman's. Manning triggered his weapon from the waist, raking the weapon back and forth in a tight, low Z-pattern. The battlefield rounds chewed through plywood, Sheetrock and insulation with ease, bursting out the other side.

Still firing, Manning smoothly uncoiled out of his combat crouch, keeping his weapon angled downward to better catch an enemy likely pinned against the floor. His intentions were merciless. Momentum and an attacker's aggression were with Manning now. Coming to his feet, he shifted the AKM pistol grip from his right to his left hand. His magazine came up dry as he shifted his weight back toward the shattered door to the room.

Manning reached for his Beretta 92-F with his free hand as he fired the last rounds through the looted AKM. He was moving, lethally graceful, back out the door to the room. His feet pirouetted through a complicated series of choreographed steps as he moved in a tight Weaver stance. Out in the hall, smoke from weapons fire and dust billowed in the already gloomy hall.

Manning stepped out long and lunged forward, sinking to one knee as he came to the edge of his ambusher's door. He made no attempt to slow his momentum but instead let it carry him to the floor. He reached the edge of the enemy door, letting the barrel of the pistol lead the way. He caught the image of a dark-clad form sprawled out on the floor of the room.

The 9 mm pistol coughed in a double tap, catching the downed figure in the shoulder and head. Blood splashed up and the figure's skull mushroomed out, snapping rudely to the side on a slack neck. A chunk of cottage-cheeselike material splattered out and struck a section of bullet-riddled wall.

Manning popped up, returning to his feet. He moved into the room, weapon poised, ready to react to even the slightest motion or perceived movement. After the frenzied action and brutal cacophony of the gun battle, the sudden return of silence still felt deafening, almost oppressive. Approaching the dead man, Manning narrowed his eyes, trying to quickly take in details. Muzzle-flash had ruined his night vision.

Frustrated, Manning snugged his NVD back into position and turned the IR penlight on. The room returned to view in the familiar monochromatic greenish tint. Manning looked over at the dead gunman's weapon. From its unique silhouette Manning instantly recognized the subgun as a PP-19 Bizon. Built on a shortened AKS-74 receiver, it had the signature cylindrical high-capacity magazine attached under the foregrip and the AKS folding buttstock. The weapon was usually associated with Russian federal police or army troops, but international arms merchants had been peddling them more and more as the Russian economy went through its series of crises.

"I'm clear on this end," Manning said into his radio. His voice was hoarse from strain.

"Just in time," James answered. "Encizo has a bump on the head but he's up and about. With that hall clear, I say let's get out of here."

"I'm rolling to your twenty now," Manning answered.

As he ran through the building the sound of gunfire echoed louder and louder until it drowned out everything else.

*Managua, Nicaragua*

CARL LYONS HELD the sat phone to his ear. "That's it," he said. "I just turned Bao over to the boys in black. He's on a one-way ticket to a black site for interrogation. Once we clear up this matter we can start rolling north."

"I think you should reconsider hitting Bao's arm's dealers," Price said. "Let a CAG or ISA team do it. You've just been through the ringer."

"We want to finish this up ourselves—we're good. Besides, we have Charlie Mott right here with a Little Bird. We can hit 'n' git in five minutes. In and out, no loose ends. We wait for JSOC to scramble a team the Chinese might get word of Bao's snatch and go to ground. We go now or we might never get 'em." Lyons paused. "Besides, Charlie's got that present basket for us from Kissinger. I can't stand to let good ordnance go to waste."

"No, I suppose *you* can't," Price replied, voice droll.

"This is why people love me, Barb."

"What people? Where?"

"Well, just humanity in general."

"Ten minutes, Carl," Price instructed, voice serious.

"Ten minutes, boss lady," Lyons acknowledged, and signed off.

Putting the sat phone away, he ducked into the team vehicle behind the steering wheel.

"They're on the fifth floor," Schwarz said. "Room 519. There's at least three of them in there but I think more like twice that."

"Building materials?" Blancanales asked.

"Reinforced concrete for load-bearing structural, but only Sheetrock covered by wood between rooms. The doors have a lock, single dead bolt and chain."

"Windows?"

"Commercial variety. Set in the wall with no balcony. They open inward with a metal-clasp locking mechanism. Set into four even quadrants of windowpane around molding and wood frame. High quality but not security."

"Wall penetration will be a problem with our weapons," Lyons said.

"C-2 breaching charges on the door and shotguns with buckshot or breach-shot for the takedown?" Blancanales suggested.

"What's security like in the hotel?"

"They have a single Managua uniformed police out front armed with pistol and submachine gun. They liaison with hotel private security, who have a heavy presence in the lobby and restaurant area. They have hourly passes through the room halls. They have 9 mm side arms," Schwarz answered. "I think we could get in and do the takedown. It's getting out without slugging it out with security forces I'm doubtful of."

"Position to snipe on the window?" Blancanales asked.

"Negative. There is a large mall across the street—45,000 square feet. No defilade and no angle other than up trajectory. Lousy for shooting."

"That kind of exposure rules out rappelling down the outside, even if we could get to the roof." Lyons rubbed at his chin, thoughtful. It was going to come down to Charlie Mott.

"Bait and switch followed by a bum rush?" Schwarz suggested.

"How do we get out?" Blancanales countered.

"I think I SPIE a way." Lyons smiled. "Schwarz, I'll

need you to find us a good covert LZ on the edge of Managua, toward the east and pinpoint the GPS reading."

"That'll work. Depends on how fast Mott can get us his bird. This'll have to be fast with the city alive with cops and military. And did I mention fast? Very goddamn fast," Blancanales said.

"Has Charlie ever let us down yet?" Lyons answered.

SCHWARZ WALKED OUT of the hotel and dodged traffic as he crossed the busy street. Blancanales pulled out from the curb and met him as he crossed the median. Schwarz opened the passenger-side door and slid into the seat.

"It's a go," he said.

"Good," Lyons replied from the backseat. "Let's do it."

Driving quickly, the Stony Man task force circumnavigated the luxury hotel and pulled into the parking lot of the mall, quickly losing themselves among the acres of parking for up to 1,500 vehicles. A State Department courier with no association with the mission would pick up the vehicle five minutes after Able Team left the area.

Over the horizon, in the hot Nicaraguan night, Charlie Mott was already inbound in a AH-6J Little Bird attack helicopter from a Navy ship offshore. The clock had started running on a tightly scheduled and overtly aggressive Lyons operation. Dressed in their casual clothes the men moved fast toward their objective.

The hotel loomed above them as they crossed the street. Lyons felt his rising consternation at the broken jigsaw of the international web woven around the Chinese intelligence agent. Phoenix Force hunting targets in Congo, his own prisoner snatch followed within minutes by this search-and-destroy operation, all of it leading to…what? Not knowing filled the Able Team leader with a terrible frustration that could only be expressed through focused anger.

Now Lyons had an opportunity to do what he did best: go blood simple. He intended to seize the chance to vent his frustrations in righteous wrath against violent international criminals. It was a relief, a short-lived blessing.

Walking fast, Able Team moved onto the Managua sidewalk. They sweated freely in the early air, dressed in black body armor under their civilian clothes with various weapons and tools attached for instant use once the dynamic entry began. The ornate wall ringing the hospitality structure was broken by a gate opening upon the loading dock where deliveries were made.

Managua was a security-conscious city in a volatile region. Yet its problems were minor compared to other neighboring narco-states, and the well-developed sense of paranoia evident in some other Central and South American countries was largely missing despite sporadic narco-terrorist attacks. As such its security was as capable of being exploited as those in other, more violent nations.

They reached the back gate, hands sliding into black driving gloves of kid leather. As one, the three men reached up and swept their long coats to one side. The tan or black coats tumbled forgotten to the ground. Under the blue jeans and tan cargo pants, black leather and canvas combat boots trampled the coats as they sprang into action.

Black balaclavas were pulled into place, obscuring the Stony Man commandos' faces from internal CCTV cameras. Schwarz pulled a pair of short-handled bolt cutters from under his vest as Rosario Blancanales grabbed the chain and padlock looped around the chain-link fence gate and held it up.

Schwarz cut through the chain in one easy motion. Blancanales pushed the fence gate open as Schwarz dropped the bolt cutters next to the forgotten raincoats on the ground. The Stony Man task force rushed through the opening, Schwarz taking the lead.

As they ran, the three commandos swung out their implements and firearms so that by the time they reached the fire door Schwarz had scouted earlier they moved in only their body armor and rappel harnesses, weapons out and at the ready.

Each man carried the Viper JAWS 9 mm at either shoulder or hip, and all three wielded Saiga 12K Russian .12-gauge assault shotguns with folding stocks and shortened barrels. The 8-round box magazines went into a weapon designed on the AK-74M paratrooper carbine. Loaded with #1 buckshot, the rounds were considered the most effective man-stoppers, even over #00 and #000 buckshot loads. They were also considered generally more efficient at causing blunt trauma through protective vests or even in general when compared to the fléchette round loads.

The first two shells in Schwarz's Saiga 12K were breaching rounds designed to penetrate the civilian locks on interior doors. The outer fire door was made of metal, reducing the effectiveness of the rounds and potentially signaling the team's presence before they had fully exploited their surprise advantage.

As they reached the fire door Blancanales allowed his combat shotgun to hang from its strap across his torso. He pulled a two-foot-long titanium crowbar fitted with rubber grips at the end from a carabiner holster on his rappel harness. While Lyons and Schwarz covered him, shotguns at port arms, the ex-Special Forces member went to work.

Without preamble Blancanales wedged the comma-shaped end of the cut-down tool under the overlapping lip of the steel fire door. Throwing one big boot up on the other door, he grabbed the crowbar in both of his gloved hands and yanked back sharply.

There was a screech of metal and then a loud pop as the door snapped open. A fire alarm began to wail. Blancanales dropped the crowbar and grabbed the door with one hand as he scooped up the pistol grip of his Saiga with the other. Lyons went through the door, shotgun high, followed hard by Schwarz.

# CHAPTER TWENTY-FOUR

Once the other two were inside the hotel Blancanales stepped through, letting the fire door swing closed. The Able Team operatives took the stairs in a rapid leapfrog pattern. The stairs themselves were metal and set into the wall with a three-rail guard running along the outside edge. The staircase ran up in a squared spiral with a flat landing at each level where the doors opened off on the guest hallways. The cacophony of the midnight fire alarm was deafening.

Lyons bounded by to the second floor, then covered the area as Schwarz and Blancanales raced past him, the pounding of their boots echoing up and down the vertical shaft. At the third floor Schwarz provided rearguard action as Blancanales and Lyons charged past him.

The skills of the commando or the paramilitary operative existed in a form like an inverted pyramid, with each layer of skills resting on the small, more fundamental level below it. Communications, medical, explosives, computer and other specialties like scuba, free-fall parachuting or piloting were all dependent on certain core abilities.

At the heart of these abilities were physical fitness and personal weapon marksmanship. Conditioning to the level of a professional athlete was the entry-level trait necessary for inclusion in the fraternity of special operations troops, which also included the ability to put bullets downrange at a superior level of accuracy.

The Stony Man commandos were no different, and their fitness routines were exacting. Loaded down by implements and equipment while carrying weapons, the three elite operators raced up the steep stairs with all the cardiovascular endurance of triathletes or Nordic Olympians.

Blancanales covered the landing on the fourth floor and Lyons followed Schwarz past the balaclava-covered ex-Green Beret. At the fifth floor Lyons stepped onto the landing and off to the left as Schwarz rushed forward. The Able Team operator snatched open the public access door leading onto the guest floor hallway.

Lyons rushed through, weapon up and in place at his shoulder, his teammates hard on his heels. A few hotel guests, eyes sleepy and hair mussed, had opened their doors and stuck their heads outside in response to the fire alarm. At the sight of the night-suited and balaclava-masked intruders they screamed or shouted in terror and slammed their doors shut tight.

Lyons knew that security, already alerted by the fire alarm, would now have guest reports to guide their response protocols. He began to race faster down the hall. Speed, aggression, violence of action, superior firepower remained the mantra of conducting raids.

The hotel decor was dark wood and thick carpeting with soft lighting and gilt-worked mirrors. The place paled in comparison to Salvatrucha's suites but was still four star.

The occupants of room 519 hadn't opened their door in response to the alarm. Lyons streaked past their door, ducking under the spy hole set at eye level in the muted wood tones of the door. He spun around and put his back to the wall on the handle side of the door, weapon up. Schwarz ran up and halted in the middle of the hall at a sharp angle to the door as Blancanales slid into position against the wall on the side of the door opposite from Lyons.

Schwarz's shotgun immediately roared. The breaching shot slammed into the door just behind the handle. A saucer-size crater was punched in the solid building material. Schwarz shifted the semiautomatic combat shotgun's muzzle and fired his weapon again, blowing out the dead bolt.

The door shivered under the twin impacts of the special shotgun rounds. The booming of the assault gun echoed sharply in the narrow hallway over the wailing fire alarm. The door shook open, trailing splinters of wood and pieces of stamped metal. Schwarz stepped forward and kicked the door wide before peeling back.

Blancanales leaned in and pumped two loads of #1 buckshot high around the corner for covering fire as Lyons squatted and let his flash-bang device roll over the threshold. The canister-shaped grenade bounced into the room as Lyons swung back and propelled himself up out of his crouch.

A flash of light like a star going nova followed the deafening concussion of the grenade's bang with a brilliant flash. Lyons swung through the door, Saiga shotgun held at his hip and ready. Rosario Blancanales followed hard behind him as Schwarz brought up the rear.

Lyons saw an opening to his left and covered it with his shotgun. It was a door to the hotel room's bathroom and he caught a glimpse of a shoeless man in trousers and a white cotton T-shirt staggering against the sink. A Skorpion machine pistol lay on the tile by the European-style toilet.

Lyons's hail of lead punched the MS-13 Nicaraguan mercenary in the chest and cracked his sternum. The man was knocked across the bathroom counter, and blood splattered the dressing-room-style mirror and sizzled on the lightbulbs.

The suite was a luxury suite with two big bedrooms

opening up on a common living area and bar. Blancanales, second in line, raced past the engaged Lyons and peeled off to the left, followed hard by Schwarz, who stepped to the right.

A wet bar and service sink took up the front part of suite, while toward the far wall three couches and a massive ottoman had been set up like a capital E around a large-screen television. When Salvatrucha had footed the bill for the Nicaraguan cell's logistical support he hadn't skimped. Three men in various stages of undress were in the room, attempting to scramble back up to their feet and recover various submachine guns.

Rosario Blancanales took the man on the left. He wore a huge gold hoop in his ear and his long hair was swept back in a ponytail. He wore silk boxers and a stunned expression on his face as he looked up into the gaping muzzle of Blancanales's combat shotgun. Blancanales pulled the trigger and the man no longer possessed a face to wear any kind of expression on at all.

Still firing from the hip, Blancanales swiveled as a second man rose, fumbling to bring around an H&K MP-5. A trickle of blood flowed from the broken drum of the gunman's right ear and splashed the bare skin of his shoulder. Blancanales's point-blank shot knocked him to the carpet and tossed his jaw into the television screen behind him.

The third Central American in the room lifted his Skorpion and turned it toward the balaclava-covered killer who had just gunned down his fellow gang members. Schwarz's #1 buckshot hit the man with sledgehammer force in the neck and left shoulder, and the mercenary folded at the knees and flopped like a fish to the floor.

The muzzle of a second MP-5 was thrust around the door of the left bedroom. Schwarz fired a blast from the hip, tearing through the wood frame and wainscoting around the door. Lyons stepped between Blancanales and Schwarz, firing a blast of harassing fire as he charged the bedroom. Blancanales moved to cover him as Lyons entered the room. The Saiga bucked hard in Lyons's hands as he stood in the doorway finishing the killer off.

Schwarz moved quickly to the door of the second bedroom. He kicked the door open and entered the room. He fired a blast through the closet and then checked under the bed, finding nothing.

"Clear!" he shouted, using Spanish to mislead any potential witnesses and reduce any sense of an American footprint on the operation.

"Clear!" Lyons answered from the other side of the suite.

The Stony Man hit team folded back into the room. A haze of gun smoke hung in the air and trailed from the barrels of their shotguns. Cordite stink was a bitter perfume and the metallic sent of blood was pungent.

"Let's shake it down," Lyons said. "Gadgets—" he indicated Schwarz "—cover the door."

Schwarz was already in motion as Blancanales and Lyons began looking for paperwork, cell phones and laptops to loot. They had discovered nothing other than three unattended cell phones when Schwarz alerted them from the room door.

"Company, security," he said. "Time to roll."

"Which side?" Lyons demanded.

Schwarz dropped his box magazine from the Saiga. "Elevators," he replied. "Two, with pistols and radios." He slammed a fresh 8-magazine into the shotgun, this one with a short strip of green tape on one side.

"We go out to the right. Let's roll," Lyons ordered as both he and Blancanales replaced the magazines in their assault shotguns with the same green-tape-marked ammunition clips.

Schwarz thrust his Saiga 12K around the corner of the door and unleashed three blasts of specialty ammunition. Hard-packed, nonlethal beanbags spread out down the hall and knocked the startled security officers to the carpet like wild haymakers.

Schwarz rolled back around the door and Blancanales stepped around him, tossing a concussion grenade. The bang as it went off rang even the Stony Man commandos' ears inside the room. Schwarz turned the corner and entered the hallway. Lyons and Blancanales spilled out of the room, turning to their right as they raced for the staircase.

Lyons sprinted hard down the hallway, Blancanales hard on his heels. Behind him he heard Schwarz fire his shotgun twice more and he was able to pick out the brutal smack of the riot-load beanbags as they struck flesh even over the hotel's blaring fire alarm.

Lyons kicked open the door and held it against the wall as Blancanales went through. Schwarz caught up and all three of team members raced up the staircase. Three stories up Lyons heard angry voices shout out from beneath them. He leaned over the railing and triggered a double blast of his shotgun, hoping the thunderous sound would spook anyone following them.

Schwarz yanked the pin on a flash-bang grenade and let it drop down the spiral well. It fell three floors and detonated, the echo chamber effect of the stairwell redoubling its effect on the security forces below Able Team.

They reached the top floor forty-five seconds later, breathing hard but not disabled. Lyons pulled a road flare from a cargo pocket as Schwarz dropped his shotgun's magazine for a second time. It clattered as it landed on the concrete landing before the roof access door.

Rosario Blancanales covered the stairwell as Schwarz triggered his shotgun, firing a breaching shot into the door. The team, moving with well-oiled precision, rushed through the door and out onto the roof of the hotel.

The lights of early-morning Managua blazed around them and they could hear the cars and horns of the commuters from below. The lights of the city shone like beacons in the distance. Police sirens rushed closer, sharper and more staccato than the blaring fire alarm wailing below them. Lyons popped his flare and tossed it through the air ahead of him.

It fell on the roof, burning brightly. Rosario Blancanales pulled a spring-loaded door wedge from a pocket and dropped it down in front of the blown door. He kicked it into place and triggered the spring. Instantly a V-shaped wedge of hard rubber locked into place, jamming the door shut.

From overhead they heard the *whump-whump-whump-whump* of a helicopter sweeping in toward them. They looked up as the Little Bird flared hard and settled down over them. A long, thick rope uncoiled and hit the ground. Loops of canvas had been sewn into the rope and the three commandos moved forward and hooked on at two points with their D-ring carabiners.

The technique was called SPIE, or Special Patrol Infiltration/Extraction, and was common among recon troops and special operations forces. Lyons gave the signal once Schwarz and Blancanales showed him thumbs-up and the Little Bird shot straight up out of its hover. The three men went into the arms-spread position to avoid spinning.

The helicopter pilot swung the nose of the Little Bird around and pointed it toward the northeast. The tail rotor elevated above the main blades it sped off toward the LZ whose GPS coordinates had been programmed by Schwarz earlier. A vehicle and clothes awaited them there.

The raid had lasted seven minutes from the time they had cut the padlock on the fence to the time the Little Bird had pulled their SPIE rope off the hotel roof.

*Brazzaville, Republic of the Congo*

WITH THE PATHWAY to the staircase cleared, Phoenix Force raced for the roof of the building.

Hawkins kicked open the door to the building's staircase and swept up his rifle. The stairs ran up four stories to a door perched atop a set of scaffolding stairs and leading to a roof. Quickly scanning for movement, Hawkins sprang forward and began sprinting up the stairs. Behind him Calvin James grunted along, carrying McCarter.

The ex-SEAL was afraid to carry the big Briton in a fireman's carry over one shoulder because of McCarter's injuries, and the close contact with the militia fighters made a two-man improvised stretcher carry a virtual impossibility. Phoenix Force needed every gun swinging if they were going to make it to the roof.

Because of this James cradled the Briton like a baby in his arms. The weight was debilitating, causing his biceps and low back to scream in protest. Each step felt as if his thigh muscles were going to rip clear of the bone at the knee. His lungs worked like bellows and sweat soaked him, sliding down his face in rivulets of stinging salt. His will and discipline were all that kept him moving. In his arms McCarter lay unconscious, a single jostle away from death.

Behind him Rafael Encizo and Gary Manning were firing continuously to keep the rushing militiamen from gaining a foothold on the stairs. Twice Encizo dropped HE grenades to destroy the staircase and make it impassible, but each time the screaming zealots below them managed to scramble past. Jack Grimaldi, reduced to his sidearm, fired his magazine empty, dropped it out of the well and slapped another one home in the pistol butt.

Rafik Bagdasarian stumbled up the stairs, his hands still bound behind his back. The Armenian ran, willing to escape the hell storm of fire pouring through the building around him. The intelligence operative realized that it was not trained commandos with precision strike capability who were attacking the foreign strike force now, but tribal militia, uncoordinated, poorly trained—loose canons who would cut him to ribbons with their grenades and wild automatic fire. Perversely, he knew his only chance at survival lay now in running with his captors.

Pistol and submachine-gun fire hammered up the angled causeway, ripping through Sheetrock and twice striking the already pummeled Encizo in his flak vest. The Cuban and big Canadian's aim was telling and below them blood flowed in rivers down the smoldering stairs as more rebel irregulars paid the ultimate price.

Hawkins sensed motion from a door in the third-floor stairwell. He spun, swinging his rifle up, but the militia gunner was already through the doorway, a Czech Skorpion vz-83 in his hands and chattering out 9 mm Markarov rounds in a near point-blank hailstorm.

Four rounds struck the spinning Hawkins, clawing through his outer flak vest and slamming into the Kevlar weave of his NATO body armor. The Texan grunted under the impact and rocked back on his heels. His finger was on the trigger of his looted rifle as he fell backward and struck the concrete wall.

He triggered a blast from the hip and the round caught

the submachine gunner under the chin, hacking out the flesh of his neck and coring out his spinal cord. The man plunged backward through the open door and, still gasping from the bruising impact, Hawkins sent an 8-round burst through the opening after him.

Manning, climbing up the staircase backward, fired a long burst over Encizo's head. His finger found his throat mike. "Stony, how's our ride coming? A little update might raise our morale!"

# CHAPTER TWENTY-FIVE

Barbara Price responded immediately. "Official channels have closed off. You need to gain the roof and hold out. We have contracted a private military contractor with airlift assets. Their rotors are spinning at the Brazzaville International Airport right now. As soon as they verify the funds transfer to their bank, they'll roll. At that time you'll need to pop smoke. I'll provide a commo link between you and the pilot."

Manning risked a glance up the stairs and saw James struggling with the slack weight of McCarter. The fox-faced British commando's head lolled on the end of a loose neck and his skin was ashen from blood loss and shock. Jack Grimaldi, gasping for breath, held his pistol in a two-fisted grip and pulled the trigger three times.

"They have to have level-one trauma assets. James needs the gear," Manning shouted into his throat mike. "Can they swing that?"

"They do close protection and route security for British diplomatic assets so they have a full combat medic contingent and a Mi-17 medium-heavy lift helicopter." Price paused then continued, voice dry. "Frankly, it's a better deal than we could have gotten from the government there."

"Copy!" Manning shouted over the firing of weapons. "We are en route to roof."

Three steps below him Encizo hurled two more HE grenades into the stairwell. The black metal spheres bounced off the concrete wall and rebounded down the stairs with sharp, metallic clunks. The explosion rocked the building's foundations and black smoke poured up the stairs, enveloping the team as Hawkins managed to finally reach the roof access door.

Hard morning sunlight slammed into the ex-Ranger's eyes, blinding him momentarily as he stumbled forward. Behind him James staggered through the door and eased the limp McCarter down onto the roof, his mouth hanging open as he gasped for breath. Black smoke roiled out through the doorway as first Manning and then Encizo gained the roof.

Manning reached out and shoved the Armenian, Bagdasarian, down to the roof with a single hard push. The intelligence operative and terror paymaster struck the roof hard enough to split his lip and draw blood. Terrified and helpless the man went down and stayed down, his eyes closed and his mouth repeating a mantra of childhood prayers.

Behind the Armenian, Encizo dropped to his belly and burned off the rest of his magazine into the smoke of the down-slanting stairwell. Manning shuffled forward and pulled an OD canister from his web gear, popping the spring on a green smoke grenade before rolling it away from the group toward the corner of the building roof.

Grimaldi went to a knee just outside the door, keeping the muzzle of his pistol orientated toward the prisoner even as his eyes scanned the adjoining rooftops, hunting for threats.

Hawkins immediately took a knee and swept his sniper rifle, scoping the rooftop topography surrounding the trapped team, hunting for targets and scanning for threats. For one long impossible moment there was silence. The morning sunlight rising out behind the silhouettes of the city turned the scene a pleasant, mellow gray.

Then from below them a voice screamed in fury and a barrage of weapons fire poured up toward them from the street. Around them the cinder-block facade parapet circling the roof began to disintegrate. Mortar chips flew out like shrapnel in jagged shards as rifle and machine-gun rounds tore into it. Automatic weapons fire poured over the edge and marksmen began firing on the group from elevated positions in nearby buildings, accompanied by the unmistakable sound of rocket-propelled grenades striking the building sides below the team's position.

Hawkins turned in tight circles, stroking his trigger with calm detachment and repeating the pattern in a seemingly endless loop: transition, acquire, engage, transition. Militia snipers armed with SVD Dragunov Soviet sniper rifles fell, two-man machine-gun teams deploying RPK automatic weapons, and RPG crews all fell in a harrowing forty-five-second stretch as the Texan put heavy-caliber round after heavy-caliber round through a succession of faces and skulls appearing on rooftops and in windows across from the building.

Even as Calvin James worked feverishly to stop a fresh round of bleeding from the comatose McCarter—his fatigues splashed with blood like the apron of a butcher at the stockyards of his home city of Chicago—Encizo and Manning took up positions behind industrial conduit vents on the roof. Using stolen Kalashnikovs they burned the barrels soft with continuous fire to suppress the moving teams. Grimaldi huddled belly down, one eye never leaving the terrified prisoner.

A random round arced out of nowhere and struck James between the shoulder blades, shattering the ceramic plate held there in a pouch on his Kevlar vest. He tumbled forward and his face was pushed deep into McCarter's bloody bandages, turning his face into a crimson mask. He pushed himself up, gasping for breath at the shock, the muscles of his back spasming in protest at the blunt-force trauma.

He threw himself prone over McCarter's body as more rounds began to chew up the gravel-and-tar roof. "Jesus Christ!" he snarled, looking up.

He saw Hawkins jerk back as a sniper round burned past his shoulder, ripping fabric and gouging a crease through his deltoid that splashed blood like syrup onto the roof. Hawkins recovered, cursing, then reorientated his weapon and squeezed off a round.

"I got an RPG-29 team!" Hawkins suddenly shouted. "RPG-29!"

Manning felt himself grow cold at the words, and both he and Encizo threw themselves flat, almost instinctively. The RPG-29 was larger version of the more common RPG-7 Soviet-era weapon. Produced in 1989, it packed a considerably larger warhead and was more accurate than its low-tech little brother.

The heavy RPG warhead streaked low over the roof, leaving a contrail of brown smoke like a linear fog just inches above the team's sprawled bodies. Encizo started swearing in rapid-fire Spanish as he rolled over and began spraying the building housing the RPG team. Using the distinctive smoke line left by the rocket, each member of Phoenix brought all of their firepower to bear on the fifth floor of a Brazzaville tenement in frantic hope of suppressing the next round from the high-explosive grenade launcher.

"Phoenix, this is Stony Man," Price broke in. "Your team is rotors up over Brazzaville International. ETA under two mikes. Repeat, ETA under two mikes. Pop smoke! Pop smoke."

"Copy!" Manning replied. "Smoke is good, smoke is good."

Suddenly an RPG-29 round erupted from a rooftop. Hawkins swiveled in his shooter's crouch and killed the gunner but the round was already shrieking toward them, eight metallic fins popping out like switchblades to stabilize flight. It slid over the top of the parapet facade and pushed across the roof, just missing a line of dirty white PVC pipes to explode against the cinder blocks of the parapet on the far side.

The antipersonnel TBG-29V thermobaric round spread flame out, pushed hard by the concussive force of the 105 mm warhead. The parapet burst outward, spraying chunks of masonry into the street below. On the roof the members of Phoenix Force were pushed hard into the gravel-and-tar roof, their bodies bruised under the explosion. James used his body to shelter the helpless McCarter as Hawkins was jerked off his knees and slammed into the low wall around the roof.

Encizo lifted his head, his vision blurry and his ears ringing from the blast. He felt half a dozen stinging wounds from shrapnel on his scalp, arm and exposed leg. He saw Jack Grimaldi sprawled out like a rag doll. The Stony Man pilot lifted his head, and his face was awash with fresh blood. Encizo's own blood coated him in a sticky mess. He blinked hard against the effects of the blast and forced his vision to focus. He saw Rafik Bagdasarian.

The Armenian had been between him and the RPG-29 warhead and had taken the brunt of the blast. The left side of his body looked like ground hamburger. The broken corpse lay in a pool of blood and the entire purpose of their mission was missing half his skull.

"Rafik is dead, goddammit!" Encizo snarled, pushing himself up.

"Christ!" Manning echoed from only a few feet away. A long gash had been opened in the Canadian's forehead and he was bleeding freely.

"Screw it!" James shouted from across the roof. "There's the chopper!"

Encizo and Manning turned to look and saw a fat, powerful Chinook CH-47D rolling toward them over the rooftops of the Brazzaville slum. M-61 Vulcan cannons opened up from each side of the warbird and burped out 6,600 rounds a minute of 20 mm ammunition. Around Phoenix Force the city block began to disintegrate.

Dinner-bowl-size craters exploded from the buildings around them, the ballistic gouges coming one right on top of the other almost faster than the eye could follow, collapsing structural supports inside the buildings and causing floors to sag and crash downward. On the streets, knots of fighters and vehicles were ripped apart by relentless strafing from the Vulcan autocannons as the big helicopter swooped in.

Gary Manning dropped his stolen AKM and grabbed the mutilated corpse of Bagdasarian. With a grunt the big Canadian picked up the dead Armenian and rushed him toward the edge of the building. He snarled and heaved the body over the edge of the building to let it tumble down to the street below.

The message was as clear as it was simple.

The Chinook hovered into place next to the building and Manning saw a bearded door gunner in OD flight suit and nondescript helmet smile at him from behind mirrored aviator glasses, a burning cigarette dangling from his mouth.

Manning turned and ran toward James as the medic

struggled to lift the unconscious McCarter up. The far side Vulcan continued to fire but even with that cover enemy fire still burned across the roof. The rotor wash battered them like hurricane winds and the roar of the engines was deafening.

Manning reached down and lifted in unison with James, bringing McCarter up as Encizo rushed past them, half dragging a disorientated and bloody Hawkins. The Canadian and the ex-SEAL turned and jogged toward the Chinook. Through the open cargo bay James could see the Vulcan firing in a virtual sheet of flame.

They made the edge of the building and saw Encizo on the helicopter reaching out for the inert McCarter between two civilian dressed men, one white, the other Asian. The private contractors helped yank McCarter into the safety of the helicopter and immediately James scrambled in afterward as the medic team began setting up IVs and cutting his bloody clothes clear. A second later the blood-smeared Grimaldi had made his way into the helicopter.

The door gunner nearest them spit his burning cigarette out and cut loose with the Vulcan as Manning got into the helicopter. On the building four militia gunmen had gained the roof access door and were racing forward, Kalashnikovs up and firing. Rounds arced through the open door and pinged off the armored superstructure of the Chinook. A stray round struck some interior hosing and pressurized fluid began to spray outward.

The pilot gunned the engine and lifted the Chinook upward as the door gunner used the 20 mm rounds to blow the militia fighters into bloody chunks. Manning looked over and saw James working feverishly alongside two medics in a state-of-the-art medic station.

He felt the powerful helicopter surging upward and he looked out through the open door, his adrenaline bleed-off leaving him numb and exhausted. He saw buildings torn to rubble or riddled like sieves. Bodies and parts of bodies were splattered across the street in the hard light of morning. Vehicles and buildings smoked like chimneys as flames ripped through them.

It was a hollow feeling that filled him as he watched the rebel slum fall away. Phoenix Force had failed, he realized. His mouth tasted like blood and ashes. He turned to find the British mercenary grinning at him from behind the Vulcan autocannon.

"You're bloody lucky your check cleared in time, mate." The man laughed.

# CHAPTER TWENTY-SIX

The Chinese warlord Illustrious studied his fingernails. He sat perched in a metal folding chair on a concrete floor in the middle of an airplane hangar. Hooded members of his elite protection corps stood sentry around him, submachine guns dangling from weapon straps.

On the floor in front of him sat a stainless-steel drain stained scarlet by the dripping blood trickling down the body of the hanging man and splashing into the floor. The man was naked and his body was covered in livid bruises and abrasions. He hung by the wrists from a length of chain attached to the blade of an industrial forklift, his arms stretched so far above and behind his head that his shoulders had popped out of their sockets. The muscles of his abdomen worked to help his lungs feed his body oxygen. His left eye had completely swollen shut and his right eye had been reduced to a slit. His cheeks looked hollow and sunken because over the course of a week every tooth in his mouth had been knocked out of his head.

Illustrious opened a file folder in front of him and began leafing casually through the contents. His eyes flickered across neat rows of information and over several photographs of varying quality.

"You are Michael Connor," Illustrious said. "United States State Department, six years. You are assigned to the Organized Crime Unit of the CIA's Investigation and Analysis Unit."

Illustrious looked up from his file. He cocked his head and studied the tortured man hanging in front of him. He lifted his right hand and used the thumb and first finger to smooth the lay of his fastidiously trimmed mustache.

"You were, roughly speaking," Illustrious continued, "discovered six miles from your embassy. Talking to a known drug dealer, human trafficker and triad member."

Bloody drool spilled out of the agent's mouth as he tried to make his mutilated lips and broken jaw into a smile. "I told you before," he said in perfect Farsi, "I got lost in a rush-hour traffic jam. I was asking for directions."

"So you said," Illustrious conceded. He turned and nodded once to the hooded, shirtless man standing behind the prisoner.

The Water Dragon Triad protection corps soldier stepped forward and raised a ham-size right hand. The fingers of the Chinese's fist were covered with a pair of stainless-steel brass knuckles. The interrogator dropped into a boxer's crouch and fired a hard hook into the helpless American's kidney with a sound like a baseball bat striking a side of hanging beef in a slaughterhouse.

Connor moaned in shock and swung wildly on the end of his chain. He lost control of his bladder and rust-tinged urine splashed down the front of his legs to mix with his blood on the floor by the drain. He made a sound like an animal low in his chest.

"Honorable Illustrious!" a voice called from the hangar door. "Most honorable Illustrious, I have a message!"

The Chinese spymaster turned away from the American. His personal assistant hurried into the hangar carrying a briefcase Illustrious knew contained a secured laptop capable of a satellite uplink. As the slim man in tan business attire crossed the fifty yards of open concrete toward the scene of the interrogation, Illustrious removed a silver clasp case and extracted a Turkish cigarette. He used a gold lighter to light it and exhaled a cloud of blue-gray smoke.

"What is it?" he snapped in Mandarin as the man came close.

The assistant eyed the American, then the hooded figures standing in a loose circle around the grisly scene. "It's…delicate," he said finally.

"Fine, give me the rundown," Illustrious answered, speaking now in French. It was a second language he shared with the assistant and one the two men had used many times before to discuss sensitive subjects in the presence of underlings, lower ranking organization members and, at times, members of their family.

"Our representative at Credit Suisse contacted us."

Instantly, Illustrious was on alert. The second largest Swiss bank was the primary holder of money used as operational funds for the triad and the more clandestine projects of his protection corps. Illustrious managed these funds, and several of an even more covert and personal nature, beyond the oversight of the People's Revolutionary Council. Instantly he was keyed into what his aide-de-camp was saying.

"There is a problem?" Illustrious demanded.

"Certain inquiries have been made through back channels at the SIS about specific numbered accounts," the aide said, referring to the Swiss Intelligence Service. "Our representative at Credit Suisse suggests we may want to alter some of our procedures. New international antiterrorism laws have hampered banking privacy."

Illustrious frowned. "Which accounts—primary or secondary?" Primary accounts were those large accounts containing funds used by the Special Revolutionary People's Committee. Secondary accounts held the "black" funds used by the triad to conduct operations beyond China's borders.

The aide paused, clearly reluctant to admit something he knew his volatile boss was going to be unhappy to hear. His eyes shifted away from Illustrious's intense gaze and the pink tip of his tongue darted out to lick at his dry lips.

"The account numbers were those comprising the tertiary interests," the aide whispered.

Illustrious sat back in his chair as if he had been slapped across his face. The color drained from his face and his stomach cramped into knots as cold squirts of adrenaline flooded his system. The banking representatives had been so convincing in their promises of anonymity. Their assurances had been ironclad, his guarantee of secrecy absolute…

Illustrious lifted his cigarette to his lips and dragged deeply. The end flared brightly as he inhaled the strong tobacco smoke. His eyes blinked steadily as his thoughts raced.

"The tertiary?"

The aide merely nodded.

Illustrious suddenly leaped from his seat and flicked his burning cigarette to the ground. It landed in a pool of Michael Connor's blood and urine, and extinguished with an audible hiss.

"I am tired of this!" Illustrious snapped in Mandarin. He jerked his manicured finger at the hooded guards. "Get this garbage out of my sight!"

Instantly the triad grunts sprang to obey, lowering the forklift until the American was allowed to crumple onto the bloodstained concrete floor where they began to unhook the prisoner from his chains.

Illustrious stalked back and forth, pacing relentlessly. As custodian of billions of dollars in operational and covert funds utilized for purchasing power beyond China's border, he had very quickly discovered that opportunities abounded for him to personally enrich himself. He had approached such opportunities with vigor and used the resulting funds to acquire even greater influence and power. But such actions were treason to the Revolutionary Council, and if found out, his personal wealth was his own personal death order, most likely from the General Secretary himself.

Damn those bankers! he thought furiously to himself. They had promised and now everything was in jeopardy... He stopped. It had to be the Americans. Perhaps the Taiwanese, but even then only as agents to the Americans. He choked on his fear and rage as the triad guards lifted Connor.

Illustrious snapped. With a strangled cry of anger the warlord rushed forward and yanked a 9 mm pistol from the belt of one of his thugs. Cursing wildly, Illustrious racked the slide and shoved the barrel against Connor's head.

The exhausted CIA agent looked at the warlord with his single eye. He pulled back his swollen and split lips in a ghastly, bloody semblance of a smile. "Fuck you," he whispered.

The pistol shot echoed off the hangar walls.

The guards dropped Connor's corpse and backed away as the furious Illustrious emptied his pistol into the broken body of the American. The Chinese intelligence manager screamed with each shot, cursing furiously and venting his anger. The gun went empty in his hand, and he pumped the trigger several more times, producing nothing more than a dry *click-click-click*.

Illustrious threw the pistol aside in disgust and turned on the triad troops. "Get out!" he screamed. "Get out now!"

Instantly the squad turned on their heels and hurried toward the door of the hangar, leaving the bloody body behind them. As the last hooded commando exited the vast, open building, Illustrious turned toward his aide, still breathing heavily. He lifted a shaking finger and pointed toward the laptop the man was carrying.

"We must hide those funds," Illustrious said. "Do it. Do it now."

Fifteen minutes later he got word that his top man in Managua was missing and his personal representative in Brazzaville dead. Illustrious picked up the phone and dialed. The Americans had struck and it was time to return the favor.

*Washington, D.C., Capitol Building*

HAL BROGNOLA WAS NOT having a good day.

He sat in front of a Senate subcommittee on antiterrorism cursing furiously to himself. The Farm's teams had just returned and there were after-action briefings to perform, reports to read and important decisions to make. Instead of doing that he was sitting behind closed doors begging for his money. It made him disgusted.

He had just answered a question about presidential authority obtained for a recent mission in Russian Georgia. He had had to tell the curious senators that the operation was sealed by executive order and that their clearances were not high enough for him to disclose details to them.

Such a revelation had gone over like a loud fart in a quiet church, and when he had subsequently submitted his special access program paperwork as evidence in the hearing, the situation had just grown more tense.

"Mr. Brognola." Donald Hascomb, the senator from Virginia, spoke up. "I just have a few more questions."

"Of course, Senator," Brognola acknowledged.

The big Fed kept his face perfectly neutral. Hascomb was no friend to direct-action special operations. He performed a watchdog role to help dampen what he saw as Administration excesses in counterterrorism and covert actions. If they knew the half of it, Brognola thought wryly to himself.

"My briefing indicates you work for Justice. Is this correct, Mr. Brognola?"

Brognola leaned forward and spoke into the microphone. He sat at a hardwood desk covered with his papers. The senators on the subcommittee sat at elevated positions arrayed in a half-moon in front of him.

"That is correct, Senator."

"What is your position?"

"As I said in my introduction, I am the head of the Sensitive Operations Group."

Hascomb made a show of reading a paper in front of him over the edges of his bifocals. He frowned, obviously displeased with what he was seeing. He lifted his eyes and regarded Brognola.

"I do not see Sensitive Operations Group listed along with any of the standard divisions, agencies or offices falling under the departmental organizational umbrella. Does the designator 'group' mean you are a subdivision?"

Here it comes, Brognola thought. Anytime politicians or lawyers started asking questions to which they already knew the answers, a setup was coming.

"Yes and no," Brognola said.

"Yes and no?" Hascomb repeated.

"SOG was intended and organized as an extrachannel formation. We existed apart from other Justice Department divisions, agencies and offices. I remain subordinate only to the head of the Executive Branch," Brognola paused. "That's the President," he added helpfully.

"Yes," Hascomb replied, voice loaded with dryness. "I realize the President is the head of the Executive Branch. Thank you, Mr. Brognola."

"You're welcome, Senator."

"You make yourself sound like an autonomous warlord slipping through the cracks of our bureaucracy."

Brognola remained silent. The statement had not been a question and he would not let himself be sucked into giving away easy points. It was clear Hascomb was headhunting now.

"Mr. Brognola are you listening?" Hascomb demanded after a lengthy pause.

Brognola looked up. He really wanted a cigar. Even after all this time the need to smoke was still with him. "Senator, I assure you that I am indeed listening. I'm just attempting to ascertain the direction of your questioning."

"Let me be clear," Hascomb fired back. "We are here to approve your budget and until I get some questions answered I'm not ready to sign off on your pet project."

"Senator, I must be explicit. Most of the information you desire is not mine to give you."

Senator Hascomb looked as if he was on the verge of a stroke. The man took a deep breath, let it out and immediately began attacking again. For the next forty-five minutes Hal Brognola underwent the interrogation, leaving his inquisitors stymied, frustrated and angry.

During the course of his interview he received a text message that changed everything.

# CHAPTER TWENTY-SEVEN

Brognola stood on the steps of the Washington Monument and looked out over the thin crowd of tourists milling around the length of the Reflecting Pool. The sky above him was the color of lead with a low cloud ceiling and the promise of rain on the chilling breeze that whipped up the edges of his tan Burberry coat. He shifted his briefcase to his off hand and dialed a number on his secure cell phone. He could have been a lawyer or a lobbyist or a minor bureaucrat in some anonymous government alphabet-soup agency.

He plugged in the number on his speed dial and slid his phone back into the case on his belt, using the Bluetooth attachment to continue his conversation. While he waited for the connection to go through he let his gaze travel over the groupings looking for his contact.

"How are things going, Hal?" Barbara Price asked.

"Other than Senator Hascomb crawling up my ass with a magnifying glass?" Brognola returned. "Not bad. Of course getting a text message from the Chinese consulate during my subcommittee meeting put me a little off my game."

Instantly, Price was keyed in. "The Chinese? What do *they* want?"

"All it said is that a representative wanted to discuss the fallout from, quote, 'Managua,' end quote."

Price cursed foully. "Chinese involvement might possibly

explain how their bully boys could end up on scene so damn fast."

"It's a possibility," Brognola admitted, still scanning the crowd. "But if they were in bed with them and MS-13, why contact us? For that matter, how did they trace the op to us and not the Agency's Special Activities Division or a Pentagon outfit?"

"I don't know, Hal. Maybe you could ask them when you meet."

"Very funny. Has Wethers got me up on the Keyhole yet?"

"We're locked on to your GPS signal but we're working through the cloud cover. I still think you should have let a team of blacksuits roll backup."

"I'm not in danger. They want something."

"Everybody does."

Suddenly on the edge of the stairs Brognola caught a flash of movement out of the corner of his eye. "Going silent," he murmured.

A tall Chinese man in an immaculate executive business suit beneath a camel-hair coat approached. The man's hands were covered against the damp by black kid-leather gloves and his Italian shoes had been polished to a high shine.

The man walked up to the much taller Brognola and nodded once, not offering to shake hands. Brognola concealed his surprise and realized why no greeting was necessary; he knew this man. He was standing in front of the deputy attaché to the Chinese ambassador—or, as it was understood in intelligence circles, the man responsible for all Chinese espionage efforts inside the United States. Intelligence briefs had put the man outside of the country for the past two months.

"This is a surprise, Xi-Nan," Brognola said.

"I am here to do you a favor," the man said.

"Really?" Brognola was not going to insult the man's intelligence by claiming to be a minor functionary in the Justice Department. This was an extraordinary meeting and the sheer audacity of it made Brognola want to shiver.

"Your team did exceptionally well in Managua."

"It seemed their top unit was onto them from the beginning. Many people would say it was an extraordinary intelligence coup for them."

Xi-Nan snorted and looked away. "The regime is a joke. Propped up by Colombia and not ready for prime time on the world stage. It was our agent who intercepted your communications and triangulated the signal."

"I see," Brognola said. It was surprising that Xi-Nan had so readily admitted Chinese involvement.

"Our advisors in Nicaragua do their job because it is imperative that Beijing counters Russia globally, lest an imbalance of power worldwide threaten our border stability."

Brognola merely nodded. There didn't seem to be anything for him to add and he wasn't going to talk simply to hear the sound of his voice. Whatever Xi-Nan had to say, he would get to soon enough.

"The world is a very complicated place, Mr. Brognola. It is my job to help guide my country through treacherous political waters. I understand well that you and I share similar vocations, which often puts us on different sides of the same issue."

"But not in this case?"

"My superiors do not believe that a continuation of our difficulties would be advantageous to our relationship. A shift toward more conservative political thought by your nation could only serve to strain our national interactions. Especially when we have so heavily invested in your national debt."

Brognola felt a cold chill surge through his body. "You have some knowledge that would be of benefit to us?"

Xi-Nan nodded and reached out his hand. Brognola responded in kind and took an envelope from the Chinese intelligence operative.

"The elements of our triads are furious about Managua and Brazzaville. More volatile elements in the organizations there want action. Everything you need to know is on the flash drive inside that envelope."

Xi-Nan turned his back on the big Fed and began walking away. He paused and looked back over his shoulder. "China has acted in their own best interests just now, not America's. You would do well not to forget that."

Brognola remained silent and watched the Chinese operative disappear into the crowd. He looked down at the envelope in his hand, contemplated it for several seconds, then turned and began to move toward his car at top speed.

*Stony Man Farm, Virginia*

BARBARA PRICE ENTERED the War Room in the basement of the Farmhouse. She found a rumpled-looking Hal Brognola sitting at the conference table reading something off his phone. A cup of coffee sat beside his elbow, untouched, and he needed a shave.

"You look like hell," she said, sitting next to him.

He gave her a wan smile and put his phone away. "Truth in advertising. How's Aaron doing with that flash drive?"

"There was a Trojan virus inside it. Akira caught and killed it."

Brognola snorted. "Figures. But the info?"

"I've already alerted the teams," Price answered. "It

seems our Chinese friend Xi-Nan has alerted an El Salvadorean cell. There's an attack coming. We're running on short notice and two steps behind. The Agency boys down in Camp Xray have given us some info that, when we tie it to the Chinese information, puts them in our crosshairs."

"That's our SOP," Brognola said. "Send Able after the cell. I've just been texting the Man. He wants a message sent. I want you to mobilize Phoenix and get me a plan to bring Illustrious down."

Price smiled. "We're on it. But San Salvador is one thing. What about the rest of that information?"

"Taking down criminal warlords with intelligence ties to the Chinese government is something we've done before," Brognola answered. "And in China."

"Yes, Hal," she agreed. "But never at the behest of the Chinese government."

"Well, to be fair, it's only at the behest of one part of the government. The rest of the government isn't going to look too kindly on what we're doing," he pointed out.

"Which will leave us with one hell of an in with the Chinese intelligence and defense organizations. Maybe the best in the U.S. has ever had."

Brognola nodded. "It's worth the risk."

*San Salvador, El Salvador*

THE BARGE RODE the gentle Pacific waves. Its lights were blacked out, its silhouette low as it held a bearing just off the coast. The five blades of the MH-6J Little Bird began to turn. The engine started to whine as the blades began picking up speed in long, looping rotations that rapidly increased in speed.

Jack Grimaldi watched his rpm climb to a fever pitch then reached over and hit the engine baffle, effectively muting the helicopter's engine noise by more than seventy percent. He took the slack up out of the yoke and felt the landing skids lift off the heavy metal plating of the barge deck.

"Airborne," he announced into the PA system.

Carl Lyons, sitting beside him in the copilot seat, looked out the blackened glass of the Little Bird's door and watched the dark shape of the barge fall away. Behind him the other two members of Able Team adjusted themselves in their 3-point harnesses, primary weapons kept muzzle down between their feet.

As the lights of San Salvador swept closer, Lyons felt the aches and pains and exhaustion of his past combat melt away. He was a hungry predator on the hunt, an animal designed to kill in order to thrive. He was in a race and to the fleet would go the contest.

In this city, the second largest in Central America, a Chinese triad mission controller had launched a terrorist cell north in the United States. Able Team was tasked to take the man out and discover the location of the death squad now operating on American soil.

Grimaldi banked the helicopter hard, running south down the coastline toward the rural outskirts of the sprawling topography. Below them the water was dark and the jungle a black smudge against the shoreline.

The Stony Man pilot looked up, absorbing the readout from his GPS display, then cut in hard toward the mainland. The Little Bird hopped over the canopy of trees and entered a small valley filled with isolated farmhouses and acres of pasture and fields.

"We're rolling close," Grimaldi warned the team over the intercom.

"Copy," Blancanales and Schwarz echoed from the back. Lyons lifted his fist and gave a thumbs-up gesture.

Grimaldi reached out with his left hand and flipped up a red switch cover, revealing a flip-toggle guns systems ignition. He clicked the silver metal switch in the on position and instantly the nose-mounted electronic chain gun hummed to life.

Twin FLIR spotlights clicked on, painting a two-story ranch-style villa into brilliant illumination through the team's night-vision devices. The building was solidly built and adjoined by a barn, animal pens and two large corrals filled with several horses now frightened into frantic movement by the Little Bird's approach.

The Chinese had used Salvatrucha's connection as boss of the Nicaraguan gang MS-13 to move their agents north. The farm belonged to members of the international criminal group that had managed to survive the violent ordeals of their teenage years and invest their drug and extortion profits in real estate.

In exchange for cash and weapons the MS-13 middle management crew had provided the Chinese criminal cell with a safehouse. The safehouse was a crime scene with potential evidence and Able Team intended to secure the property.

The helicopter swooped in low, avoiding power lines as Grimaldi banked the Little Bird and put the skids down on the crushed gravel of the driveway. Immediately, Able Team exited the cargo bay, the bull pup Pancor Jackhammer automatic shotguns up and ready as they charged the house.

Grimaldi instantly powered the chopper up, climbing steeply as the ground team raced forward toward the house. From his superior position, the Stony Man pilot let the Little Bird drift over the sprawling two-story ranch house until his nose gun was covering the side and rear entrances.

A line of dark SUVs were parked in front of the house,

the automobiles in stark contrast to some of the surrounding rural poverty. Cocaine flowed up through San Salvador toward Houston and San Diego from South America, and cash flowed back the other way. The Salvadorean bosses of MS-13 had figured out a way to secure their cut and it showed.

Lyons raced forward, breaking into a sweat in the heat and humidity of the Central American tropical zone. As far as Brognola and the Stony Man crew could ascertain, the El Salvadorean terror cell was already boots down on American soil and when presented with a race for time Carl Lyons always chose head-on confrontation as his preferred fallback play.

Even with the mufflers engaged the Little Bird's engine noise was obvious. Rotor wash beat down on the team in a persistent gale. Their plan for the surprise advantage in this case relied not on stealth but on speed and violence of action.

The Able Team commandos jogged forward in a loose triangular phalanx, cutting through the rows of parked SUVs, their shotguns up and ready to unleash a torrent of .12-gauge lead at the first sign of resistance. Once the scene had been pacified then mercy was an option, until then the Stony Man operatives remained as keyed up as a school of sharks on the verge of a feeding frenzy.

Lyons shifted his gaze back and forth as he jogged toward the front lawn. The house was quiet and dark, a discrepancy to the coke-fueled activity he would have assumed customary to a MS-13 gang haunt. The hairs on the back of his neck stood on end with an almost preternatural suspicion.

He watched the front door separated from the lawn by a low, wide veranda. Curtains obscured dark windows; nowhere was there a sign of motion. Over the house the

Little Bird hovered like a Jurassic insect bathing the structure in IR spotlights visible only through their night-vision devices.

Lyons felt Schwarz and Blancanales drift out toward his flank in unspoken agreement. He took a breath and felt his body ache in response from the battering it had taken. His torso, as well as those of his teammates, was covered with deep, punishing bruises.

Two steps more and he was around the canopy of a Ford F350 on monstrous tires. He slowed and narrowed his eyes against the gloom. He came to a stop, looking down. Schwarz and Blancanales caught his motion and held up themselves.

The body lay sprawled on the ground, the limbs splayed out. The dark-skinned, muscular figure was dressed in a white ribbed cotton tank top perforated with bloody divots. An M-16 A-2 lay a yard off in the dark grass. The man's jaw was slack, his pink tongue lolling out, his eyes bulging until the whites seemed as big as saucers.

"Shit," Lyons whispered.

He lifted his head and looked toward the house. On the low veranda he saw a second corpse, partially obscured by an overturned piece of patio furniture. The top of the corpse's head had been cored out and a Remington 870 pump shotgun lay just out of reach of noodle-slack fingers.

"They've been hit already!" Blancanales swore.

Glass broke as the picture windows on the front of the house exploded outward. Starfish patterns of muzzle-flash winked from the darkness and the metallic crescendo of full automatic weapons fire erupted.

Hermann Schwarz went down instantly, dropping face-first onto the lawn without a word, his weapon unfired. Blancanales had the bull pup Jackhammer up and returning fire even as Lyons unleashed his own combat shotgun. The twin .12-gauge shotguns burped a lead net toward the structure. Bullets whined off the luxury SUVs to either side of Blancanales as the ex-Special Forces commando walked his own fire across the front door and dumped four rounds through the first window. The curtains jumped and danced as his blasts cut through the hanging fabric. He saw a dark form stagger backward, the unmistakable outline of an H&K MP-5 SD-3 in one wild thrown hand.

Blancanales held up his fire long enough to adjust his aim and Lyons triggered his weapon into the lull, shredding the front of the house with his shotgun blasts. A large-caliber rifle on full auto suddenly burped out of the darkness of the house with a sharp staccato of overlapping bangs. The heavy metal slugs ripped through the air in spinning tornados, forcing Lyons to the ground and sending Blancanales spinning off behind a vehicle.

With sledgehammer blows the 7.62 mm rounds smashed into a car behind Lyons and walked up the body of the vehicle. Divots the size of golf balls crumpled the frame and shattered the glass of the windows before a tracer round scorched into the gas tank and ignited the SUV.

It exploded in a ball of yellow flame and black smoke, sending heat and car parts rolling out with lethal force. Lyons, already on the ground, felt the flesh of his exposed skin redden and then tighten instantly as the heat burned him. His face was driven into the gravel of the driveway and he heard Blancanales curse in fury at the sudden assault.

Hermann Schwarz remained unmoving.

Suddenly the Little Bird was overhead, its rotor wash blowing the flames back as Jack Grimaldi swung the helicopter around. The nose gun opened up with relentless, merciless fury and empty shell casings rained down like hail. The machine gun rounds tore into the building, ripping it apart.

The walls and roof were ripped open as if a chain saw had been taken to the structure. Glass shattered into slivers and shards and adobe-style stucco was cracked and battered into craters and chunks the size of plates. Lyons forced himself up, forced himself forward to take advantage of the cover offered by Grimaldi's guns to make his approach.

His body screamed at him in protest even through the adrenaline surge that powered him. The Pancor Jackhammer .12-gauge felt heavy in his hand; the metallic curve of the weapon trigger was slick with his sweat as he made the porch.

Muzzle up, Lyons approached the bullet-riddled remnants of the front door.

# CHAPTER TWENTY-EIGHT

*Stony Man Farm, Virginia*

Hal Brognola surveyed Phoenix Force with a sour eye.

The team looked exhausted, beat to the bone and heavily abused. In the vernacular of his early days with the FBI, they looked rode hard and put away wet. And, he reflected, if wet meant bloody then by God the cliché was appropriate.

Setting down his coffee mug, Brognola eased back into his seat. His eyes flickered to the screen on the far wall above Kurtzman's head. A map of Africa, centered on Congo, was up on the HD screen. A digital readout in the lower left-hand corner showed the current time in the capital.

Just as impressive in his diligence and sense of duty had been the battered Jack Grimaldi. The pilot had upon return simply swallowed a fist full of ibuprofen with a couple of go pills the military prescribed pilots on long missions and had taken off to support Able Team in Central America.

At the huge conference table in the War Room, Calvin James studied his BlackBerry intently, reading updates on McCarter's medical condition, committing the information to memory. Manning was going over Kurtzman's report on Illustrious, page by page, as Encizo and Hawkins discussed the situation quietly with a tired-looking Barbara Price.

Everyone in the room was drinking Kurtzman's coffee

without the usual round of mandatory quips and sarcasm—a sure sign of overwork. But, Brognola noted to himself, overwork was the primary operational zone for Stony Man. He took out his phone and sent a text message of instructions to his secretary back in the Justice Department. He had an 8:15 a.m. meeting with a liaison from Homeland Security he would have to bump to just after lunch.

The door to the War Room opened and every head turned to watch Carmen Delahunt as she rushed into the room. The redhead looked slightly breathless and her hair was mussed from where she'd obviously been wearing her VR helmet.

Unfazed at finding herself the center of attention she turned and addressed Kurtzman where he sat in his chair next to the broad form of Gary Manning. "We pulled it off," she said simply.

Kurtzman's grizzled face split into an evil grin. "You guys managed to hack a Swiss bank?"

"It was the battle of supercomputers." The ex-FBI agent smiled. "That firewall in Berne was better than what the Russians are using. But the contents of Illustrious's personal accounts have been transferred and warning systems sent to update him on the transfer. Akira is inside the Water Dragon Triad system." She paused, then added, "The Swiss could teach that crew something about encryption and ICE measures."

"Did Illustrious take the bait?" Brognola asked.

Delahunt flashed him a vicious, triumphant smile. "Yes, he did, Hal. Once he thought his personal money was in danger he went into overdrive. He's making his excuses now—to close out and transfer an account of that size he'll need to be on-site, in Berne."

Barbara Price leaned forward, eyes glittering and bright

with her excitement. "That means a plane, and that means the Indian Ocean, which means international water and airspace, which means once he is airborne he's ours."

Brognola leaned forward, face grim. "That's just exactly right. The Man could not have been any clearer on this. If the Chinese want a shadow war, then we're going to give them one at every turn. And we're not going to burn ourselves out killing foot soldiers, either."

"Conflict by coup d'état," Manning said with grim satisfaction. Next to him Calvin James and Rafael Encizo both nodded their heads in agreement. At the end of the table T. J. Hawkins looked primed, the left side of his face a massive blue-black bruise.

"Exactly," Brognola agreed.

Barbara Price turned and took in Phoenix with an encompassing, motivated gaze. "You boys ready to take a plane ride?"

THIRTY MINUTES LATER Stony Man auxiliary pilot Charlie Mott ferried the prepped and primed Phoenix Force by a Bell Industries helicopter to the secured-access landing strip of Wright-Patterson Air Force Base. Within spitting distance of the infamous Hangar 18, actually a brick storage building, the team boarded a special-operations-capable version of the B-2 Spirit Stealth bomber.

The bomb bay had been modified into a personnel transport area, and ten minutes after loading their weapons and gear onto the clandestine aircraft they were airborne.

*San Salvador, El Salvador*

MOVING IN A PRECISE DRILL the Stony Man duo headed under fire toward the house. They approached a long series of French doors issuing smoke through the blown-out glass.

They advanced in a bounding overwatch, modified to exploit speed, but basically consisting of one commando holding security while the second leapfrogged forward to the next point of cover.

Twice their path was cut by armed men rushing to help engage the swooping Little Bird. The first time Blancanales took the shirtless man down with a short burst, followed up immediately by Lyons's finishing shot to the head. The second time a shoeless bearded fighter with the profile of a professional bodybuilder sprinted around a tight cluster of native Brazilian walnut trees with a drum-fed AKM in his massive fists.

Both men turned and fired simultaneously from the hip without breaking stride. The crossfire cut the giant of a man into ribbons and knocked him back among the stand of trees.

As Lyons and Blancanales ran they could hear people screaming from around the compound and once they heard a long ragged machine-gun burst answered immediately by Grimaldi's M-134 minigun. Lyons cleared the deck over a column of concrete pillars supporting a low, wide stone rail encircling the patio. The explosive force of hand grenades had cracked and pitted its surface but failed to break the stone railing.

Lyons landed on mosaic tile, waves of heat from the burning building washing over him and casting weird shadows close in around him. He saw a flat stone bench and took up a position behind it, going down to one knee. He began scanning the long line of patio doors with his main weapon while Blancanales bounded forward.

Blancanales passed Lyons's hasty fighting position in a rush and put his back to a narrow strip of wall set between two ruined patio doors. He kept his weapon at port arms and turned his head toward the opening beside him. From inside the dark structure flames danced in a wild riot.

Blancanales nodded sharply and Lyons rose in one swift motion, bringing the buttstock of his M-4 up to his shoulder as he breached the opening. He shuffled past Blancanales, sweeping his weapon in tight, predetermined patterns as he entered the building. Based on what he was seeing, Lyons made the snap decision that this wasn't a rival criminal network raid but was, in fact, an elite commando cleanup crew.

Blancanales folded in behind him, deploying his weapon to cover the areas opposite Lyons's pattern. It felt as if they had rushed headlong into a burning oven. Heavy tapestries, rugs and silk curtains all burned bright and hot. Smoke clung to the ceiling and filled the room to a height of five feet, forcing the men to crouch below the noxious cover.

In a far corner the two men saw a sprawling T-shaped stair of highly polished Mexican woodwork now smoldering in the heat. A wide-open floor plan accentuated groupings of expensive furniture clustered together by theme.

The bombs had rendered much of the floor plan superfluous. Slowly the two men turned so that their backs were to each other, their weapon muzzles tracking through the smoke and uncertain light. Smoke choked their lungs and stung their eyes. They saw the inert shape of several bodies cast about the room among the splinters of shattered furniture. One body lay sprawled on the smoldering staircase, hands outflung and a stream of blood pouring down the steps like water cascading over rocks.

Lyons moved slowly through the burning wreckage, amazed that it had been unobservable from the outside. Approaching twisted bodies, he searched the bruised and bloody faces for traces of recognition.

From the beginning of this campaign Lyons had felt

more like a frontline soldier on this battlefield than on many others in his endless campaigns leading Able Team. His combat had been directed against not a specific, identifiable enemy led by a single powerful or charismatic figure, but rather an army with officers and troops but no single embodiment of the evil he faced. Like an assault force smashing through emplaced defenses to sweep behind enemy lines Lyons had killed the enemy as it appeared in front of him with little information with which to personalize his struggle by. He grasped that this man Illustrious had put everything into motion, but the layers between the Chinese warlord and Lyons seemed huge.

He had not come to know the details of Illustrious's operation in the manner by which Stony Man had pursued so many other enemy leaders, mafia dons, intelligence operatives and terrorist generals. There was nothing specific about the fight; it was total war, killing the enemy as you found him without reservation.

His battle against Illustrious was a battle of attrition fought out in a hard slug from one urban foxhole to the next. Now he had driven his enemy ahead of him, battered him into a final, defensive stand and Lyons risked all to deliver the knockout blow that would destroy the organizational capability of the triad leader's terrorist syndicate. His engagement would not be finished until he had assured that the dragon's head was cut off and cauterized. Any clue that could lead him to the location of the terror cell now operating within the homeland had to be pursued at any cost.

Lyons searched the dead for the faces of his enemy's leadership cadre. Around him the heat grew more intense and the smoke billowed thicker. Blancanales moved with the same quick, methodical efficiency, checking the bodies as they vectored in toward the stairs.

Lyons sensed more than saw the motion from the top of the smoldering staircase. He barked a warning even as he pivoted at the hips and fired from the waist. His shotgun lit up in his hands and his blasts streamed across the room in hailstorms of lead.

Lyons's .12-gauge rounds chewed into the staircase and snapped railings into splinters as he sprayed the second landing. One of his rounds struck the gunman high in the abdomen, just under the xiphoid process in the solar plexus. The deadly lead speared up through the smooth muscles of the diaphragm, ripped open the bottom of the lungs and cored out the left atrium of the gunman's pounding heart. Bright scarlet blood squirted like water from a faucet as the target staggered backward.

The figure, indistinct in the smoke, triggered a burst that hammered into the steps before pitching forward and striking the staircase. The faceless gunman tumbled forward, limbs loose, and his head made a distinct thumping sound as it bounced off each individual step on the way down, leaving black smears of blood on the wood grain as it passed.

Lyons sprang forward, heading fast for the stairs. Blancanales spun in a tight circle to cover their six as he edged out to follow Lyons. He saw silhouettes outside through the blown-out frames of the patio doors and he let loose with a sheet of antipersonnel buckshot.

One shadow fell sprawling across the concrete divider and the rest of the silhouettes scattered in response to Blancanales's fusillade. Blancanales danced sideways, found the bottom of the stairs and started to back up them. Above him he heard Lyons curse, and then the Able Team leader's weapon blazed.

To Blancanales's left a figure reeled back from a window. Another came to take its place, the star-pattern burst illuminating a manically hate-twisted face of strong Asian features. The Phoenix Force commando put a double tap into his head from across the burning room and the man fell away.

"Those were the Chinese," Lyons shouted.

"Clean 'em out and search the bodies—it's all we have," Blancanales answered immediately.

Lyons nodded and let loose with three bursts of harassing fire aimed at the line of French doors facing out to the rear patios and lawns as Blancanales spun on his heel and pounded up the steps past Lyons. Outside, behind the cover of the concrete-pillared railing, an enemy combatant popped back up from his crouch, the distinctive outline of an RPG-7 perched on his shoulder.

Down on one knee, Lyons fired an instinctive blast but the shoulder-mounted tube spit flame in a plume from the rear of the weapon and the rocket shot out and into the already devastated house. Lyons turned and dived up the stairs as the rocket crossed the big room below him and struck the staircase.

The warhead detonated on impact and Lyons shuddered under the force and heat. Luckily the angle of the RPG had been off and the construction of the staircase itself channeled most of the blast force downward and away from where Lyons lay sprawled. Enough force surged upward to send Lyons reeling even as he huddled against the blast. He tucked into a protective ball and absorbed the blunt waves.

He lifted his head and saw Blancanales standing above him, feet widespread for support and firing in a single blast of savage, accurate fire. Lyons lifted his Pancor and the assault shotgun came apart in his hands. He flung the broken pieces away from him in disgust and felt his wrist burn and his hand go slick with spilling blood as the stitches from his Managua wound came apart under the abuse.

He ignored the hot, sticky feeling of the blood and cleared his .357 Magnum Colt Python from its underarm sling. He pushed himself up and turned over as Blancanales began to engage more targets. As he twisted he saw something move from the hallway just past the open landing behind his fellow Stony Man operator.

Lyons extended his arm with sharp reflexes and stroked the trigger on the big pistol. A single .357 Magnum round found the creeping enemy high in the chest, just below the throat.

The killer's breastbone cracked under the pressure and the neck muscles were hacked loose from the collarbone. The back of the target's neck burst outward in a spray of crimson and pink as the massive round burrowed its way clear.

"Go!" Blancanales shouted.

The Puerto Rican Green Beret bent to snatch up a fallen M-4, then swung it back and forth in covering fire as Lyons scrambled past him to claim the high ground. Lyons pushed himself off the stairs and onto the second floor. Stepping over the bloody corpse of his target, he turned and began to aim and fire the .357 Magnum in tight blasts.

Under his covering fire Blancanales wheeled on his heel and bounded up the stairs past Lyons. At the top of the landing he threw himself down and took aim through the staircase railing to engage targets below him in the open great room.

From superior position the two Able Team warriors rained death down on their enemies.

"Hold the stairs!" Lyons growled, rising to his feet. "I'll check the site, then we'll un-ass the AO."

"Get 'er done," Blancanales acknowledged as he coolly worked the trigger on his stolen M-4.

Lyons moved quickly along the hallway. Smoke burned his throat and irritated his eyes, obscuring his vision as he hunted. He worked quickly, checking behind doors as he moved down the hall. Flames kept the corridor oven-hot and the hair and clothes on broken bodies smoldered as Lyons hunted to verify the dead.

Behind him Lyons heard Blancanales's smooth trigger work keeping the animals at bay. He refused to waste energy on being angry but deep inside of him he was frustrated at his own intelligence failure that had missed such a huge number of combatants in the compound. He couldn't afford to let it cloud his attention now.

He came upon a body and picked up the head by the hair. The face looked like it had been taken apart by a tire iron and was puffy, bruised and covered in blood but Lyons was still able to identify the man as an MS-13 street soldier.

He turned the corner in the L-shaped hallway and saw the corridor blocked. An avalanche of ceiling beams, flooring, ruined furniture and body parts completely obstructed the hall. Flames licked out, spreading heat and destruction with rapid ferocity. The Chinese attackers had been liberal in their use of thermite and HE grenades, and Lyons realized the primary assault on the compound could have only been finished mere moments before his own untimely arrival.

A bit of debris caught Lyons's attention. His eyes widened as he stepped forward to get a better look. In the corridor was a mahogany-colored Savali Pristine briefcase made from dyed crocodile hide. The prized status symbol in EU boardrooms was just the sort of thing a man like Mara Salvatrucha would have given out to his couriers.

"Well, look at that," Lyons murmured.

Lyons reached down to pull the crocodile-hide case out from under the debris that pinned it. There was a brief moment of resistance, then the case came loose in his hand so suddenly he was overbalanced and went stumbling back. His heel caught on a length of wood and he almost fell. He backpedaled like a pass receiver, then cut to the side and came up against the wall.

Lyons clutched the Savali briefcase under one arm as he used the back of his web harness to secure the potential find, then continued on.

He backed down the corridor and pulled a grenade from his web gear suspenders. The AN-M14 TH3 incendiary hand grenade weighed as much as two cans of beer and had a lethal radius of over twenty meters that spread its burning damage out to thirty-six meters; in the hallway its destruction would be concentrated, spreading fire and contributing greatly to the overall structural instability of the building.

Lyons yanked the pin on the hand grenade and let the arming spoon fly. He lobbed the compact canister underhand and let it bounce down the short stretch of hall before ducking around the corner to safety. The delay fuse was four seconds, which gave him plenty of time to achieve safety.

Both he and Blancanales carried the incendiary grenades. They were heavier than some other, more modern hand grenades, but their power was undisputed and they made a nice compromise to more powerful but larger satchel charges.

Lyons moved in a fast crouch toward the once ornate landing where Blancanales fired down from his defensive vantage point to cover Lyons's search-and-destroy mission.

Lyons spoke into his throat mike. "Able to Stony. I have a structural blockage—our operation is finished. Site destruction verified to acceptable factor of certainty. Over."

# CHAPTER TWENTY-NINE

*Stony Man Farm, Virginia*

Brognola looked up at Barbara Price.

"What do you think?"

The honey-blond Stony Man mission controller sat on the edge of the War Room's massive conference table, a cup of coffee in her hand. She cut her eyes away from Brognola toward Aaron Kurtzman. From his wheelchair Kurtzman deftly worked at his keyboard.

"I think, Hal, that you handed me a complete operation tied up with a pretty pink bow." The former NSA manager began ticking points off on her slender fingers. "Initial intelligence. Field reconnaissance. Logistical support to include transportation. Safehouse with arms, explosives, equipment and fresh changes of underwear."

Brognola, seeing her starting to really warm up, gently interrupted. "Your point, Barb?"

"My point is that it's one thing working with Agency, or Homeland or even Pentagon. It's what, in part, we were designed to do from the beginning."

"But?"

"But." Kurtzman spoke up. "That's not exactly what's happening here."

Price nodded. "This is a Chinese operation gig from scratch to burn. You're just plugging the boys in as interchangeable with Chinese spies or commandos." She paused and shrugged. "Or the triads, for all that goes."

"You start doing this, in this fashion," Kurtzman added, "then where does it end?"

"It ends with General Xi-Nan in our pocket," Brognola pointed out. "Look, this isn't an attempt to set up our crews. It's our specialty—last minute, high degree of difficulty, direct action. This isn't an attempt by the Pentagon to claim our turf—it's a professional favor that'll create a back door into China. It's an unprecedented chance."

"China initiated this directly," Kurtzman argued. "It wasn't a request or system of briefings channeled through Homeland or the Executive Office. They've thrown an end run, broken the cone of silence and come to us face-to-face. Something's changed."

"How do we know he's not working to finish us off?"

"Look, I ran Xi-Nan through the Agency once I read the code paroles he'd built into the flash drive. He's been a deep-cover mole for the Agency for decades. Now, we've got him. That's an awesome coup for Stony Man. The President has already signed off. Let's not keep going over this, people."

Price pursed her lips then folded her arms. "I'll alert the boys."

THE WAR ROOM WAS crowded.

The five members of Phoenix Force and three of Able Team were arrayed along the conference table like company officers at a corporate board meeting. The mood was upbeat and a current of emotional energy hummed in the room, just below everyone's awareness. The chance for action had revealed itself again, and the men of Stony Man were ready to take it up.

Barbara Price eyed both Hermann Schwarz and David

McCarter. She couldn't believe their recuperative power after only a week. But she'd seen it so often she was no longer amazed.

"The Water Dragon Triad is running a safehouse on the outskirts of Beijing. It consists of six rooms, the entire seventh floor of a residential building, about half a block away from a local police precinct," Barbara Price began.

From his wheelchair Kurtzman worked his keyboard. On the large screen recessed into the wall a digitized satellite map of the world appeared. Latitude and longitude readings scrolled down as the head of the cyberteam dialed up first Asia, then China, then Beijing. On the screen high-definition optics revealed buildings and streets.

"That building is your target," Price said.

On the screen the image split to provide a text scroll listing building materials, window pane thickness, door construction, plumbing and electrical diagrams and a schematic drawing of the industrial blueprint.

Manning and Schwarz, the explosives specialist on each of their respective teams, began taking notes.

Rosario Blancanales, turned toward his unit commander, Carl Lyons. "We can put a sniper position on that building at the intersection across from the target. We'd have exposure on two sides to the building plus elevation on its roof. Also we can cover the major avenues of approach."

"Not perfect," Lyons agreed. "But just about all we can do."

"We are going to ensure police response is down during the time frame," Kurtzman said. "I have Akira and Hunt working on it now. We'll simply crunch through their phone lines and shut everything down. We aren't going there to leave Beijing cops dead in the street."

"What about any response from Chinese assets?" Calvin James asked. The ex-SEAL reached up and stroked his close-cropped mustache with a hand the color of burnished onyx.

"The genesis of this operation is our problems with Chinese boys getting U.S. boys dead. Most especially the triad branch," Price said. "I've seen the information the General Xi-Nan gave Hal and it's smoking-gun, slam-dunk stuff. The men holed up in that apartment building are ruthless killers. They're either just coming from some terror mission or they're going to some terror mission. If the triad wants to protect them, then they're exactly the kind of targets within Chinese intelligence we want to cull."

"Bang-bang," Hawkins said.

"Numbers?" McCarter asked. The ex-SAS commando was the leader of Phoenix Force. As such he would be the first one into the building when the time came.

"Anywhere from a squad to a platoon," Price answered. "Armed with light weapons, grenades, standard stuff."

"That's a little ambiguous," McCarter pointed out.

"As far as it goes all you're really, really concerned with is *this* man," Kurtzman said.

He tapped a key and a picture of a middle-aged Asian man filled the screen. He was handsome and well groomed in traditional dress. Each member of the Stony Man teams scrutinized the picture closely, committing each detail to memory as closely as they had the target building's industrial specifications.

"Who's this bastard?" Hawkins asked.

"Illustrious, triad warlord and Communist intelligence agent," Price replied. "And for the next twelve hours he is your raison d'être."

"Did you say triad and intelligence?" Rafael Encizo interrupted.

"Yes," Price answered. "Ever since reacquiring Hong

Kong, mainland China has been utilizing criminal syndicates as espionage networks."

Encizo leaned his stocky build back into his chair and whistled. He carefully scrutinized the picture of the triad kingpin up on the screen.

Silence greeted Price's proclamation.

Then David McCarter let out a long, slow whistle as James shook his head in disbelief.

"This explains why the Xi-Nan handed this off to us," Manning muttered.

Brognola spoke up. "Our man in Beijing, Xi-Nan, is terrified of Illustrious. He can't get him using his own resources. My contact hoped to pull a bureaucratic riposte by coming to us."

"Who cares what's holding up the pinheads. I've always liked killing triad agents who were secretly Communist spies," Lyons said.

Calvin James arced a questioning eyebrow at Blancanales. The other man just shrugged his shoulders.

"Then I suggest we get cracking," Price replied. "We only have a narrow window to make this work."

# CHAPTER THIRTY

*Beijing, China*

Carl Lyons regarded the target building through his night-vision scope.

He ran the next-generation Starlite model attached to his baffled SVD sniper rifle along the exposed windows, putting each dark square in his crosshairs before smoothly scanning onward. He looked for fixed points to use as quick landmarks once the shooting started as he played the optic across the building's roof.

"Able Actual in position. All clear on roof," he murmured into his throat mike.

Across the street on the second leg of their L-shaped overwatch positions Rosario Blancanales nestled in closer to the recoil pad on the buttstock of his own silenced SVD. "Able Beta in position. All clear on primary and secondary approach routes," he replied.

Lyons shifted his scope, running it along the length of a fire escape leading to the dark alley that would serve as Phoenix Force's primary insertion point. "Able Epsilon, status please?"

In the back of the blacked-out 1970s model delivery van Hermann Schwarz eased back the charging handle on his RPK machine gun. The muzzle of the weapon was set just back from the access panel covertly placed in the rear door of the vehicle.

"Six o'clock clear," Schwarz conceded.

From his rooftop position Lyons touched a finger to his earjack. "You copy that, Stony?"

"Copy," Barbara Price's cool voice responded on the other end of the satellite bounce. "Phoenix Actual, you are clear on approach."

"Phoenix Actual copy," David McCarter responded. "En route."

Carl Lyons pulled his face away from his scope and quickly did a security check of his area. It was very early in the morning and the residential block was like a ghost town. Despite this, the leader of Able Team felt naked and exposed.

Because the Farm's teams were operating black inside China, local coordination and cover had been impossible. Able Team had taken their positions only minutes prior to the strike, dressed as Beijing riot police to disguise their Western features and delay any alert to the authorities. They were still exposed to a confused, frightened and potentially hostile indigenous population should their positions be discovered.

Speed and aggression of action on the part of Phoenix Force was their best hope at this point.

Across the street from Carl Lyons, Rosario Blancanales shifted his scope and took in the alley running next to the target building. A blacked-out delivery van with a side sliding-panel door identical to the one occupied by Hermann Schwarz suddenly swerved into the alley.

Instantly, Blancanales shifted his aim and began scanning his overwatch sectors to provide Phoenix Force with security.

In the alley Phoenix Force exited the vehicle, leaving the engine running. The dome and cargo lights had been disabled so that the five-man team looked like black shadows leaking from a dark box as they approached the building's side entrance.

T. J. Hawkins produced a claw-toothed crowbar and the countdown began.

ON THE SIXTH FLOOR of the target building, Illustrious put his cup of strong coffee down and dragged heavily on his cigarette. His eyes squinted against the harsh smoke as he surveyed the room.

Three hollow-eyed men in Western business suits with Skorpion machine pistols were spread across the room while a fourth man, their boss, spoke with quiet tones into a satellite phone.

Two men, explosives experts from the smuggling cell under the Chinese triad, carefully rigged the package with powerful Semtex plastic explosive. Arms dealing was a lucrative branch of triad operations.

It was a warm night in Beijing, but all the doors and windows to the apartment were tightly closed for security reasons. Illustrious had stripped off his expensive robes and was wearing only a ribbed white cotton T-shirt. His olive skin was damp with sweat.

The Chinese man carefully lined up packets of Japanese yen on the table. The currency coming to a total that was the equivalent of five thousand U.S. dollars. It was the sum to be paid to the smuggler's family upon completion of the task.

Illustrious thought how nice and cool the vice dens of Hong Kong would be, or his palace in Xiang Province. But he grew so bored there. He loved being out on the edge of the operations—not too close, but close enough to feel the vicarious thrill of murder plotted and murder committed.

He placed the last stack of money on the table, made

eye contact with the smuggler, nodded, then began putting the money into a manila envelope. Once he was done he stubbed out his cigarette and immediately lit another. He smoothed down each side of his thin mustache where it ran into the sparse hair of his goatee.

He inhaled deeply, filling his lungs with smoke. Across the room the leader of the triad unit abruptly clicked his phone off. He turned toward the kitchen table and his suit coat swung open, revealing his own machine pistol in a shoulder holster.

"Ki-jang," the triad street leader said, and smiled. "My brother, we are ready. You go to riches!"

The teenage smuggler looked down as one of the triad explosives engineers placed the backup detonator in his hand. Another triad operative stepped forward and began to use black electrician's tape to secure the ignition device to the smuggler's hand.

Neither Illustrious nor the triad officer bothered to tell the smuggler in the chair that there was a ignition fail-safe built around a Nokia cell phone constructed directly into the bomb. If he was caught smuggling the package into Taiwan then one push of the Chinese intelligence agent's speed dial would counter any hesitation the teenager might feel.

Illustrious could feel a sense of euphoria, a giddiness at what was about to happen, surge through him. The illicit thrills of Hong Kong paled in comparison.

HAWKINS LEVERED the crowbar into place beside the dead bolt and wrenched it open. The metal-and-mesh outer security door popped open and swung wide. Sidestepping it like a dancing partner, Hawkins moved forward and reinserted the crowbar into the doorjamb.

The Texan's shoulders flexed hard against the resistance

and in an instant the dead bolt was ripped out of its mooring. He stepped to the side and threw the crowbar down. Rafael Encizo, AKS-74U Kalashnikov carbine held at port arms, ran forward and kicked the door out of the way.

He darted into the building, sweeping his muzzle down. Calvin James followed in close behind him, his own AKS carbine covering a complementary zone vector. Directly behind them Manning and McCarter folded into the assault line, weapons up in mirror positions.

Freeing a Russian AK-47 RAK .12-gauge automatic shotgun, Hawkins stepped into position and began covering the team's rear security as they penetrated the building.

Across the street from his elevated vantage point Lyons spoke into his throat mike, "Phoenix is hot inside."

A second later Barbara Price acknowledged him. "Copy."

Both Blancanales and Lyons made additional sweeps of their zones. The streets remained deserted, buildings dark and silent. Inside the target building Phoenix Force rushed down starkly illuminated hallways and up dim staircases.

From the outside Lyons played the scope of his 7.62 mm SVD along the windows of the assault floor. As he swept the crosshairs past a window it suddenly exploded with light as heavy drapes were thrust aside by a swarthy-looking man in a cotton T-shirt.

Lyons instantly reoriented his weapon. His focus narrowed and the man's face leaped into sight with superb clarity. Lyons felt the corners of his mouth tug upward in a grin. Oh, most wise Illustrious, Lyons thought to himself. Merry Christmas to me.

He initiated radio contact. "Be advised," he warned. "I have eyes on Primary. Primary confirmation."

"Phoenix copy," McCarter responded. "We are at the door now."

"Understood," Lyons replied. He tightened the focus on his sniper scope.

Lighting a cigarette, Illustrious moved out of the way, revealing an angle into the room. Lyons's optic reticule filled with the image of a second man, seated at a kitchen chair. The ex-LAPD detective felt his eyes widen in the sudden shock of recognition. Suddenly a balaclava-clad man in a business suit appeared in the window and snapped the curtains shut.

Lyons held back on his shot, trying desperately to work his com link in time. "Phoenix!"

On the other end of the com link McCarter was giving Hawkins a nod. The ex-Ranger stepped forward, swung up the RAK 12 and put the big, vented muzzle of the shotgun next to the doorknob and lock housing. The .12-gauge roared as the breaching round tore through the mechanism like a fastball burning past a stupefied batter.

Hawkins folded back as the massive shape of Gary Manning stepped forward, sweeping up a massive leg into a tight curl. He exploded outward in a heel-driven front snap kick that burst the already damaged door inward.

Rafael Encizo shot through the opening and peeled left, AKS-74U up and tracking as Calvin James peeled off to the right. As McCarter followed by Hawkins and Manning sprinted into the room, Encizo killed a man armed with a Skorpion submachine gun. Men started cursing.

"Phoenix! Phoenix, explosives—" Lyons warned.

The warning came too late to stop the assault force's forward momentum. McCarter swung around, searching for the threat. He saw Illustrious throwing himself through the air, leaping away from a terrified-looking teenager strapped down with a tan suitcase festooned with blocks of Semtex and bundles of wires.

"Bomb!" McCarter screamed.

# CHAPTER THIRTY-ONE

Bullets burned across the room as the situation descended into chaos. Manning struck Calvin James with a brutal shoulder block, knocking the ex-SEAL back into McCarter and toward the door.

Skorpion-wielding men in business suits spun and began trying to track targets. McCarter was driven backward as his eyes found the smuggler's. The kid's gaze had glazed over, his mouth hanging slack. From out of his peripheral vision he saw the other members of Phoenix Force crowding in as he fell through the door.

Over their shoulders he saw the teenager squeeze his hand into a desperate fist, thumb hunting for the ignition. We're not going to make it, he thought.

Outside the building a wave of fire suddenly erupted outward into the night, filling the optics of both Lyons and Blancanales.

"Phoenix! Phoenix!" Lyons shouted into his throat mike.

There was no answer.

Black smoke roiled up into the air as orange flames licked at the inside of the building. Lyons popped up, breaking down the SVD sniper rifle with quick motions. He quickly slung the carryall over his shoulder and stepped to the edge of the building where he snapped his rappel rope into the D-ring carabiners of his slide harness.

He went over the edge and dropped six stories to the

street. Lights were coming on in buildings up and down the street. Lyons came out and saw Blancanales already on the ground and sprinting for the van where Hermann Schwarz was at the wheel.

Suddenly, David McCarter's voice broke the still.

"Be advised," McCarter growled. "We are up and we are bloody leaving. Illustrious escaped but we are in pursuit."

The relief in Barbara Price's voice was obvious even over the sat link. "Good copy, Phoenix."

Sliding into the van's passenger seat, Lyons turned toward Schwarz as Blancanales jumped into the back. "Let's make sure all five of our birdies make it into their rig and then make a rapid strategic advance to the rear."

"Are we calling this a success?" Schwarz asked.

"Not until we get Illustrious," Lyons replied grimly.

INSIDE THE BUILDING Phoenix Force picked themselves up off the floor in the hallway. Their ears rang from the sharp crack of the explosion and dark smoke obscured the interior ceiling above their heads.

"Let's go, people," McCarter said. "Find Illustrious."

Hawkins looked around. The door to the target apartment had been blown off by the blast and he could see that the outside wall on that side of the building had been blown outward, leaving a sagging ceiling and a gaping hole exposing empty space out over the street below. Fire burned in lively pockets.

"Jesus," Encizo suddenly cursed. "The stairs we came up hugged that wall—there's like a fifteen foot gap here!"

Around them in the building Phoenix Force could hear people stirring, calling out in panic and milling in confusion. The building was rife with triad foot soldiers. McCarter instantly went on alert, his weapon up.

"Gary," he ordered, "check the staircase down the hall."

"I'm on it," Manning answered, moving out. He ran down the hall, bent low to avoid the thickest part of the smoke and kicked open a door at the opposite end of the corridor. "It's good!"

"You heard him," Calvin James shouted. "Let's move, people."

McCarter spun and covered the hall as his men ran down the passage and entered the stairwell. "Go!" he barked. "I've got security!"

The other four members of Phoenix Force rushed through the doorway just as the first of the enemy combatants exploded into the hall. The man, bald and dressed only in pants with an automatic pistol in his fist, shouted an angry warning and lifted his weapon.

McCarter killed him, but there was a chorus of answering shouts and a volley of fire erupted outside the hall initiating a storm of lead that tore into the hall. More glass from the few unbroken windows shattered, falling inward, and the wood paneling was shredded. After his initial burst McCarter threw himself to the floor, directing his momentum over a shoulder and rolled clear of the hall, keeping below the hail of gunfire.

McCarter spotted a big man armed with a black machine pistol appear from the door of a room directly across the hall from the suicide smuggler. The giant shouted an order and peeled back from the doorway. A second man ran forward, Kalashnikov assault rifle slung over his shoulder and across his back.

McCarter swore. The man went to one knee and leveled an RPG-7 at the end of the hall. Rising, McCarter turned and sprinted. The 84 mm warhead could penetrate twelve inches of steel armor; it would blow through even a reinforced door with ease. McCarter scrambled across the floor and leaped into the air.

McCarter struck the floor and slid across as a fireball blew through where the door had been and rolled into the already devastated room like a freight train.

Shrapnel and jagged chunks of wood lanced through the air. His ears still rang from the explosive concussion and his face bled from a dozen minor lacerations, but his hand was steady on the trigger as Chinese gunmen rushed through the front door.

The first shooter breached the door, AKM assault rifle up and at the ready. McCarter put him down with a triple-hammer burst from his submachine gun. The combatant hit the burning floor like a bag of wet cement. The man running in behind him looked down as the point man hit the floor. He looked back up, searching for a target, and McCarter blew off the left side of the man's face.

The third man in the line tripped on the second man's falling corpse. McCarter used a burst to scythe the man to the ground and then put a single shot into the top of his skull. Through the swirling smoke and angry screams McCarter saw a round black metal canister arc into the room.

McCarter cataloged the threat instantly: RG-42 anti-personnel hand grenade. Length: 121 mm. Weight: 436 grams. Blast radius: 22.9 m.

He popped up off his belly onto his hands and knees as the grenade hit the floor inside the hall and bounced toward him. Leaving the AKS where it lay, McCarter dived forward, scooping up the bouncing hand grenade. His hands wrapped around the black cylindrical body.

He hit the floor hard from his short hop, absorbing the impact with his elbows. He rolled over onto one shoulder and thrust his arm out, sending the grenade shooting away from him. It cleared the corpses in the entranceway and bounced up and out the hall doorway on the far side. Mc-Carter heard a sudden outburst of curses and he buried his head in his arms. The grenade went off.

Another cloud of smoke billowed in through the doorway on the heels of the concussive force. McCarter came to his feet, scooping up the AKS submachine gun. He shuffled backward and crouched next to the wall, heading for the door to the staircase down to the street level. McCarter caught a flash of movement and spun toward the blown-out doors of two apartments across from their original target.

"David!" Encizo's voice blared in McCarter's earjack. "We're coming."

"Negative!" McCarter shouted back.

He saw two men in khaki jackets rush up to the shattered doors, holding AKM rifles. McCarter dropped to one knee beside the wall and brought up the AKS. He beat the men to the trigger and his submachine gun spit flame. It recoiled steadily in his hands and shell casings arced out to spill across the floor.

"The stair is too narrow! I'm coming to you!"

McCarter put two rounds into the face of the first man. Bloody holes the size of dimes appeared, slapping the man's head back. Blood sprayed in a mist behind his head and he slumped to the ground, his weapon clattering at his feet.

McCarter shifted smoothly toward the second gunman. They fired simultaneously. The muzzle-flash of the man's weapon burst into a flaming star pattern. The sound of the heavier caliber assault rifle firing was thunderous compared to the more subdued sound of McCarter's 9 mm subgun.

The 7.62 mm rounds tore into the molding of the wall

just to McCarter's right. The rounds tore through the building material, gouging fist-size chunks from the wall and door frame, spilling white plumes of chalky plaster dust into the air.

McCarter's burst hit the man in a tight pattern. The bullets drilled into the receiver of the AKM, tearing it from the stunned commando's hands. Two more rounds punched into his chest three inches above the first, staggering him backward.

McCarter came up to his feet, the AKS held up and ready. He triggered two rounds into the stunned gunman and took him down, blowing out the back of his neck. McCarter danced to the side and, still facing the front of the hall, held the AKS up and ready in one hand. He stepped back into the stairway door.

A gunman came around the corner of one of the rooms, chattering Kalashnikov in his fists. McCarter put a burst into his knee and thigh, knocking the screaming man to the floor. He put a double tap through the top of his head. Brain matter and bits of skull splattered outward.

McCarter moved in a backward shuffle toward the stair, realizing that what had been billed as a safehouse by intelligence had actually been more along the lines of barracks—a significant and unsubtle difference. He took fire from the open door and swiveled to meet the threat as another pair of gunmen rounded the corner from the front hall. McCarter threw himself belly down, his legs trailing out behind him down the stair, angling his body so he was out of sight from the shooters in the hall.

McCarter swept his submachine gun in a wide arc, spraying bullets at the gunman firing through the shattered hall. One of the men's weapons suddenly swung up toward the ceiling, and McCarter caught a glimpse of him staggering backward into the dark though he never saw his own rounds impact.

He lay on the stairs, only his arms and shoulders emerging from the door to the stairwell. He rotated up onto his right shoulder to get an angle of fire on the entranceway. He saw one of the triad gunmen rushing forward and shot the man's ankles, bringing him to the floor. McCarter fired another burst into the prone man, finishing him off, only to have his bolt lock open as his magazine ran dry.

McCarter let the AKS dangle across his chest as a second commando leaped over the body of the first and charged forward. The skeletal folding stock of his AKS-74U pressed tight into his shoulder and he fired the weapon as he bounded toward the Phoenix Force veteran.

McCarter put his hands against the floor and snapped up, clearing the edge of the doorway. Bullets tore into the floor where his head had just been. He twisted on the stair and jumped downward. He landed at the bottom, his legs bending to absorb the impact, just as he had been taught during paratrooper training. He took the recoil, felt it surge back up through his heels and rolled off to the side. He turned in the direction of the side door to the lower level on the building. He got up and ran to the ground floor, men screaming above him.

A burst of gunfire echoed in the stairwell and 5.45 mm rounds tore into the floor where McCarter had landed. He went up against the wall at his back and pulled a 9 mm Glock-17 from its holster. He heard boots thundering on the stairwell and he bent, swiveled and thrust his gun arm around the corner. He triggered four shots without exposing himself.

There was a satisfying thump as the gunman pitched forward and bounced down the stairs. He spilled out at the bottom of the stairs, sprawling in front of McCarter, and his weapon skidded out from his hands. The ex-SAS trooper triggered a round into the back of the man's head and snatched up his fallen weapon.

Another figure appeared at the top of the stairs and took a shot at him. McCarter leaped back out of view of the stairwell, grabbing the AKS-74U up by its shoulder sling. Bullets struck the corpse of the dead Chinese triad gunner. McCarter caught a motion from his right side in time to see a man in a white T-shirt charge through an interior door. McCarter did a double take; the mustache and goatee were unmistakable. It was Illustrious attempting to flee.

McCarter fumbled to bring the AKS to bear but didn't have time. He let it dangle from the strap and brought his 9 mm pistol up as he dropped to one knee. Instead of firing from the hip Illustrious paused to bring his AKS up to his shoulder for a more accurate shot. The triad leader's hesitation was fatal.

McCarter's shot took him in the throat. From the door to the alley outside Hawkins fired a second burst, targeting the triad master criminal and blowing off the back of his skull. Immediately, McCarter spun in a tight crouch and fired blindly up the stairwell for the second time. There was an answering burst of automatic gunfire, but no sounds of bodies hitting the floor.

McCarter holstered his pistol and took up the AKS. He quickly ducked his head into the stairwell before thrusting his carbine around the corner to trigger a burst. Using the covering fire to keep the enemy back, McCarter snagged the dead man at the bottom of the stairs over to him by his belt.

"Can we go, boss?" Hawkins shouted. "Engines running!"

"You bet!" McCarter confirmed. "We nailed Illustrious."

McCarter pulled a Soviet-era RGD-5 antipersonnel hand grenade from the dead thug's belt. Like the RG-42, it had a blast radius a little more than seventy-five feet. He held his AKS up by the pistol grip and stuck his thumb out. He used his free hand to help hook the pin around his extended thumb. He made a tight fist around the pistol grip of the AKS and pulled with his other hand, releasing the spring on the grenade.

McCarter let the spoon fly. He turned and put a warning burst up the staircase to buy time. He counted down three seconds and then chucked the grenade around the corner and up the stairs. He turned away from the opening as the blast was funneled by the walls up and down the staircase, spraying shrapnel in twin columns.

Ears ringing, McCarter made for the door to the building down the short entrance hall. He came up to it, AKS held at the ready. The door hung open, broken. From outside he heard gunfire as the Phoenix Force commandos engaged targets firing from the windows above them. A figure darted past the open door as he came up to it and McCarter gunned him down while Hawkins backed toward the running vehicle, burning rounds off at targets above him.

A triad soldier jumped into the hall and flopped onto his belly, throwing a bipod-mounted RPK 7.62 mm machine gun down in front of him. McCarter jerked back outside the doorway as the machine gunner opened up with the weapon's 660 rpm rate of fire, sending a virtual firestorm in McCarter's direction.

McCarter's heart pounded as he moved, beating wildly in his chest. McCarter's perception of time seemed to slow as adrenaline speeded up his senses to preternatural levels of awareness. His mind clicked through options like a supercomputer running algorithms. His head swiveled like a gun turret, the muzzle of his weapon tracking in perfect synchronicity.

He saw no movement other than his team down the alley. Inside the hallway he saw wood chips fly off in great, ragged splinters from the withering machine-gun fire. He heard the staccato beat of the weapon discharging. He sensed something and twisted toward the staircase. A khaki-clad man with a beard rushed off the stairs.

McCarter had the drop on him and gunned him down. The AKS bucked hard in the big Briton's hands and he stitched a line of slugs across the Chinese gunman's chest. Geysers of blood erupted from the man's torso and throat as the kinetic energy from McCarter's rounds drove him backward. The man's heel caught on the out flung arm of his compatriot and he tumbled over, dead before he struck the ground.

McCarter scrambled back out the door. He saw a flash from the stairs and felt the air split as rounds blew by his face. McCarter fired wildly behind him for cover as he rolled up and across the alley. He swung back around and covered the staircase and the side door, prepared to send a volley in either direction. His finger tensed on the smooth metal curve of the trigger.

There was a lull in the firing for a moment and McCarter heard Manning screaming instructions. A haze of smoke hung in the hall and the stench of cordite was an opiate to McCarter's hyperstimulated senses. A burst of fire broke out from behind him.

"Let's go!" James shouted.

McCarter stood, weapon up, and made to turn toward the vehicle. A final, crazed triad gangster burst out the door as more weapons fire burned down from above. The Briton's 5-round burst tore out the man's throat as the van pulled up next to him. Hawkins leaped in the back and spun, spraying fire wildly.

McCarter turned, pumped his legs and dived in the back. He landed hard on the vehicle floor and heard the sound of squealing rubber over the din of weapons fire. He tried to get to a knee but Manning jerked the wheel hard as they took the corner and he was thrown into James.

"Are we calling this win?" the ex-SEAL asked, voice dry.

"Let's call it a win-win," McCarter replied. "After all, the Chinese wanted him neutralized just as much as we did."

As relieved as he was to complete the Beijing component of their overall mission, the Phoenix Force leader couldn't help but think of the innocent lives lost in the battles in Africa and Central America. Nevertheless, Stony Man had prevailed and he and his teammates would savor the satisfaction of a job well done—until the next summons came.

\* \* \* \* \*

# TAKE 'EM FREE
## 2 action-packed novels
## plus a mystery bonus

## NO RISK
## NO OBLIGATION
## TO BUY